Mulligan

J.S. EDWARDS

Printed by CreateSpace, an Amazon.com company
Available from Amazon.com and other retail outlets.

ISBN: 0692499105
ISBN-13: 978-0692499108

Cover design by Holly McIntyre Hartigan
Dandelion photo by Gary McIntyre
Sad child photo by © Yarruta | Dreamstime.com

To my husband, Eddie:

Without you I would never have been able to follow my dreams and make them become reality. You are the best side of me, my happiness, my laughter, and always my love.

ACKNOWLEDGMENTS

I would like to thank: My editor and publisher, Kelly Zientek-Baker: Your unwavering support and commitment made this journey a positive experience. You are the best, and it is a privilege to work with you in every aspect.

Holly McIntyre Hartigan, my illustrator: You took my thoughts and captured them perfectly. Your talent is exceptional.

And our daughters, Samantha Raye Kauffman: Your commitment and assistance is and will always be priceless; Jessica Rae Comstock: The constant strength you show in your own life inspires others to never give up.

Mulligan:
A shot that, against the rules, allows an opponent to take a second chance, a do over.

PROLOGUE

We all grow up with our own degrees of damage. We have our own ability to live with moments and events in our lives that we would prefer to erase, change, or forget completely no matter what age we are. We are the innocent ones that others consider expendable. We spend our lives trying to shake the dark memories that seek refuge in our minds and try to own us. They attempt to keep us hostage like a common criminal that takes over our lives without permission. We are expected by those who tried to break us as children to grow into shattered, dismissed, and fragile adults. We can't allow ourselves to be defined as the tiny human fractures that they intended to discard and leave behind. Let us prove to ourselves that we are resilient and refuse to break. We are a world of humans with imperfections. There's no room for hatred of those that we will never understand. Only after we decide to leave the past behind can we move forward. Only then, can we embrace life. We will live and breathe the air of the free and untainted. We the children, the underdogs, and the misfits of the world, will break the chain for the next generation.

We — those that so desperately seek a second chance— are the mulligans of the world.

CHAPTER ONE

My childhood began as somewhat of a human science project. It was more of a "let's see how much I can screw up a kid and see if she is still standing at the end" kind of thing. However, once I was old enough to get my hands on storybooks, those were what kept me from erupting like a science fair volcano. I would fantasize about living in a castle with my mom. She would be the queen and I would be the princess. Those books opened a whole new world for me and made me realize that anything seemed better than where we were.

"Normal" was a word that described someone or something, but it definitely wasn't me, my mom, or our life. I wanted her to get the roaches off the walls and talk to me for more than five minutes. I wanted a pair of clothes that fit, weren't filthy, didn't smell like urine, and had only belonged to me. I wanted nothing more than to feel like a regular kid just for a little while. I didn't think my wants were selfish, although I was the only one of us that thought that.

Our relationship was simple. We were a team, close and inseparable, allowing no room for anyone else. She protected me, but I protected her as well. The question of what or whom we were protecting each other from was the real mystery. My mom was my world.

She was a beautiful lady, tall and slender with long blonde hair that was usually pulled back in a thick ponytail. I loved her eyes and the way they looked like shiny blue marbles. She had tiny features that sat perfectly on her flawless skin. I would often watch her without her noticing. She reminded me of a puzzle that was thrown into the air with all the pieces scattering to the floor. She would walk in circles around the apartment smoking cigarettes one after another. Her mouth would move as if she was speaking, but words would never escape her lips. She didn't know I was there. I was invisible on these days when she was in another place far from where we were. It was all right, though. Sometimes I wasn't sure I existed either.

With my mom, it was like trying to take that puzzle and put it back together again. The border of a puzzle is always the easiest. It framed whatever picture was in the process of being put together. The challenging part began when you tried to figure out the inside. All the pieces looked the same, but if just one piece was missing, you knew that it would never be completely put together. Somehow I knew that my mom was missing a piece or more, and her puzzle was never going to be quite right.

We lived in an apartment in Upstate New York above a butcher shop, above the sounds of meat and cheese slicers, people yelling out orders, and the smell of blood. A few times a day sirens would race by the front of our apartment and all the sounds would fill my head at the same time. It felt as though they were drilling into my teeth, while sharp shards of glass filled my ears, causing me tremendous pain. Often I would find myself sitting with my hands over my ears, rocking back and forth trying to block them out. They seemed to be coming from everywhere. Once I asked Mom what the sirens were. She explained what ambulances, fire trucks, and police cars did. How they each helped in their own ways. How they had their own sirens and used them for different reasons.

The small living space we called home was one large room where my mom's mattress laid, a kitchen, and a small bathroom. The bathroom had a crumbling shower. We had to place a towel on the floor so the loose and broken tiles wouldn't cut our feet, and the water pressure was so weak it took forever to wash our long hair. The small sink wasn't big enough to place both our hands inside. The toilet looked as though it may have been white at one time. It was gross, dirty, and smelled constantly of rotten eggs. Our kitchen had a small sink with a rotted out bottom and was connected to the wall in the corner. We had to place a bucket on the floor to catch the drips that leaked from the holes in the bottom. There wasn't a refrigerator or stove, and the counters had long been ripped from the walls, leaving ugly traces of where they once were.

My room was the coat closet in the corner of the apartment. It was pretty small, but so was I. It really wasn't as uncomfortable as it might sound. It was cozy with its door that locked from the inside and my old, red flannel sleeping bag. I had a pillow and a huge pair of thick, black-cushioned headphones that my mom asked me to wear every night due to the airplanes that roared overhead that might wake me. There were coloring book pages that I had made myself taped to the walls, and as far as I was concerned, I had a pretty nice room. Our apartment was dingy, dirty, and the cockroaches ran wild as if they were our pets. I shivered at the thought that one would land on me or crawl up my arms or legs.

On rare occasions my mom and I would snuggle. I loved those special times. However, they were few and far between, and maybe that's why they were so special to me. Even though the sheets were covered in stains and they smelled of bad breath and body odor, the time I spent lying close to her was worth it. Sometimes she would read my favorite book, *The Velveteen Rabbit*, over and over without complaint. On other days when I didn't feel like having her read to me, I would ask her a million questions. If I caught her on the right day and in a patient mood, she would answer them. Regardless of whether or not her answers were true, they were answered. "How old am I?" And "When is my birthday?" were just a few of the questions I would ask her.

"You are eight years old now, and we will celebrate your birthday as soon as someone very special arrives, but until then my love, I'm sorry, but your birthday will have to wait," she would answer.

"Who is the special person, Mommy?" I asked.

She looked at me as if she were seeing someone else. Her eyes became glassy as if she were about to cry and she reached up, gently touching my face.

"You have the most beautiful dark skin and green eyes, my love," she said softly.

"Why is my skin so much darker than yours, Mommy? I forgot what you called it... spinach?" I asked.

"Olive," she said smiling, which made her eyes shine brighter and lighter than they really were. "You're very special, my love, and the angels kissed you to prove it," and as she spoke she held up my left hand as she had done several times in the past.

No matter how many times she told it, I always loved the story she was about to tell me. She traced the mark on my hand between my thumb and pointer finger that looked like a pair of tiny closed lips.

"You see, my love, even before you were born the angels knew you would be someone very special, and they decided that they would leave a special sign to remind you of that. So right before you came into the world, they kissed your hand so you would never forget," she said kissing my angel's kiss.

"I love that the angels left their mark with me, Mommy, it makes me feel like they're always watching over me," I told her, nestling up even closer.

"They are, my love. They always are."

It made me warm inside every time she told me the story of the angels kiss. However, some questions weren't as easy as others because she either didn't answer or would only answer half the question, leaving it to linger like a riddle. I had asked several times – hoping that her story would change – about my real name. Surely it wasn't 'my love.'

She always gave the exact same answer, never wavering, no matter what mood she was in.

"When you're ready you can pick your own name," she would tell me, shrugging her right shoulder as if having a name wasn't a big deal.

"What about when I want to make a friend someday, Mommy?" I would ask. "I can't say, 'Hi, my name is 'my love.' They would think I was weird," I said, following her as she circled the apartment.

I never really knew what she was doing or why, but I was hoping she would give up and just name me.

"I don't have the right to tell you who you should be," she said, stopping quickly without warning, making me run directly into her backside.

I needed to ask as many questions as I could possibly think of when these windows of opportunity opened for conversation.

"Who has the right then?" I asked. "Maybe I'll ask the garbage man or the lady at the pizza place. Maybe they have the right," I said, throwing my hands in the air, knowing she would never give in.

"You are 'my love,' and that is what I will call you until you no longer want me to," she would say again.

She would never answer that question, no matter how many times I would ask. It was greeted with either complete silence or cold dismissal.

"Well do you have a name?" I asked, watching her eyelids grow lazy and knowing her window of conversation was closing.

"Yes, you gave me one," she replied.

"What is it?" I asked.

"My name is Mommy."

She walked away, and I knew that the window had closed completely. I would have to wait until next time for my questions to be unanswered.

She woke me most mornings by presenting me with a warm

juice box and Pop Tart. We would sit on the dirty shag carpet the color of the grease that floats on the top of a pizza. Every few days we would get on our hands and knees to try to get the pieces of dirt and other scraps off the rug. After we ate and cleaned the rug as best as we could, we would go over spelling words. When I got to the point where I was spelling better than she could, she started to stop at the drug store and buy more storybooks for me to read that had bigger words. I read them faster than she could buy them. I cherished each one and read them over and over until I got another one.

I knew my mom and I were far from being a queen or a princess like in my books, but it was fun to imagine. Looking up from the pages and seeing her face in the sunlight that shined through the window onto her hair made it look as if it were made from gold. The way it framed her small face made her look as though she fit the part. I thought she looked way too young to be a queen. She was definitely a princess.

After spelling, we would switch to math. Adding and subtracting came naturally to me. Numbers just made sense, how they all were connected in some way was a game for me to figure out, and I usually didn't take long to do it. Religion was next, and I was never quite sure where she stood on the subject. I know she believed in God, but I don't think she was too sure if God was a man or a woman. It all depended on what mood she was in. Since mom didn't seem to be a fan of either women or men, it was a daily crapshoot as to what her opinion would be. Regardless, what I did know is that God, whatever sex, was a loving, caring, and forgiving God that watched over us from above.

After religion came her favorite subject: politics. Most of it seemed to be her opinion and not actual facts. I didn't know a thing about the government, but I did know her ideas sounded a little odd. I had a hard time believing that "the world was run by people that had their hands tied behind their backs and their voices silenced." You couldn't get much work done in that position, and not being able to speak was even harder than that – that much I knew for sure. Mom never answered my questions on politics. If I tried to ask, which I often did, I was ignored. It was creepy at times and made the hair on my arms stand up when she would look as though she were giving lessons to people behind me. It was so convincing that I would turn around in case I was missing someone that may have snuck in. What she thought was of extreme importance wasn't enough to fill a thimble, but I tried to ease her mind by pretending to believe every word she said. This method of keeping her in a good mood made my day go by smoother.

When learning time was over, so was her urge to talk. So then we would throw a towel over the floor of the shower and bathe, which was difficult and took forever because rain was stronger than our water pressure. Then came lunch, and we stayed in and had our peanut butter and jelly sandwiches. Mom would buy small containers of milk and a bag of ice and place them in our rusted sink. Then, we would head out the door for our daily walk. No matter what the weather was we never missed our walk.

We always went the same way every time. We lived in a typical small town in a suburban neighborhood. The houses, small stores, and take-out restaurants (which we ordered from every night) were all perfectly painted with their shutters snug against the windows, making them look like colorful graham crackers. People were constantly sweeping, trimming, or raking something in their yards or on the sidewalks in front of their homes. Sometimes through their front windows, I could see a family gathered around a real table filled with food, and the faces I could see looked happy. I knew that when I grew up, I wanted to buy one of these houses for my mom. We could eat at a table and sit in one of the white rocking chairs on the porch watching people go by, waving and knowing that we no longer lived in the only ugly apartment in the whole neighborhood. At least it was hidden from the street.

The town square was in the opposite direction of where our walk took us. We went there once a year. It was Mom's special gift to me at Christmas time. The festivities started the day after something they called Thanksgiving. My mom was against that day.

"People should be grateful every day, not just one day a year," she would say.

The store windows were always lit with tiny beautiful lights twinkling in every color. There were green Christmas trees, and even blue, silver, and sometimes, pink ones, but the white ones were my favorite.

"I think those are the ones you see in heaven, Mommy. Do you think maybe this year we could get a small one?" I would ask.

Mom wouldn't reply, but I already knew the answer. We went through the same thing every year, but I didn't care. I still loved it because it was the only time of the year when the air felt like there was something special in it, something magical, and the people seemed to be in better moods, at least for a little while. Santa was there, different Christmas scenes sat in all the store windows, and people that sang songs dressed in costumes and danced around. Just thinking about it made me get all excited. But for Mom, Christmas was another day on her list of dislikes.

"I won't pay a dime for any of this nonsense, my love. It's just another way to take money from hard-working people, and I won't be a part of it. I come here because I know it gives you joy," she would say.

Her 'dislike' list was enormous, and I didn't think she had a 'like' list.

Every day was a mirror image of the day before, over and over again, unless someone put up new decorations or someone else painted their home a new color. That was just about as exciting as it got. We sat on the edge of the marble fountain, with its huge mermaid head spouting water over all the shiny coins that lay on the bottom of the pool. I watched people both young and old toss a coin, close their eyes, and smile as the coin spun its way down to the bottom.

"Why are they throwing coins away Mommy?" I asked.

Why would someone give away to a fountain – a *thing* – money that could add up to warm boots for me someday?

"They're making silly, worthless wishes, my love. They think their coins will make them come true, but they're wrong and wasteful."

Mom sat like a statue and would stare across the street at the old hardware store as if any second it would disappear. While she sat there, rarely blinking, I walked around the small patch of grass that was closest to my mom and blew on every fluffy wish flower I could find. I wasn't allowed to wish out loud, but I made three silent wishes over and over.

I wished for my mom to talk more, for the roaches to find a new home, and for Mom to stop staring at the hardware store every day. I made those wishes every day until I ran out of wish flowers. Mom called them dandelions, but I liked my name for them better. There were always more wish flowers waiting for me after a day or two. Like Mom and I, they always returned to the same spot. I did wonder what I would wish for if I had a coin, if my mom was wrong. It would be pretty cool to toss one and watch as my wish spun its way slowly to the bottom with me waiting with excitement for my wish to happen. I wasn't sure what it would be. It's something I thought about often, but to ever have a coin to begin with was a pretty big wish on its own. Mom allowed me to bring my storybooks with me to the fountain to keep me occupied. I don't know what I would have done day after day without them with so many hours to fill. We stayed until the old man left the store. My mom would watch him closely until he pulled his car away. Afterwards we walked to whichever take-out place we decided to eat from that night: pizza, Chinese, chicken wings, or submarine sandwiches.

"Mommy, why do you sit there and stare at the hardware store every single day?" I asked her one day while we were eating chicken wings.

"It's something I need to do, but it won't be for much longer," she replied.

"Why do you need to do it though?" I asked again. "I don't care how much longer you need to do it. I just need to know why you do something so strange every single day when we could be doing other things."

I tried to show her I was losing patience by slapping both my hands on the sides of my legs and stomping one foot hard on the ground. This was something I had never done before, but I saw a little kid do it in the book aisle of the store and it seemed to get his mom's attention, so I figured I'd give it a shot. She stared at the single chicken wing she had been eating for the last 15 minutes.

"Why do they have to put so much sauce on these? It ruins the flavor," she said in a low, distant voice as if she was half asleep.

She looked to the wall as if it were going to answer her. She had already gone into her own world, and my question went with her, never to be seen or heard again. She always began to dissolve at night, as if she were on a timer. After dinner, I brushed my teeth and went to my room and put my earphones on. I always locked my door until she would come get me the next morning. That night, as I lay there, I was upset at myself. My performance that afternoon was outstanding, and much better than the kid at the store, but it didn't get me any attention or audience. What a horrible waste of talent.

Mom was always watching the stupid hardware store. I always imagined the inside of her head as a huge windstorm with items being thrown around in all different directions. My questions were probably stuck to the sides of her brain like garbage to the side of the curb. I don't know why I felt so upset or surprised by the events today. They weren't different than any other day.

I closed my eyes, ready for the same agenda the next morning.

CHAPTER TWO

One afternoon while taking our walk, a pair of dirty pink panties fell out of the leg of the jeans I was wearing. Mom had just given the jeans to me that morning. I don't even know where she had gotten them. Clothing just appeared in our apartment from time to time with no explanation. A hat, a single glove, sometimes a scarf or a disgusting coat... I wondered at times if she was making wishes somehow from the fountain when I wasn't looking. But then, who would wish for ugly, dirty clothes that didn't fit? I looked down at the panties. They weren't mine! I thought I was going to throw up all over the sidewalk, and I started crying. People walking by turned to look at me, and my cheeks reddened in embarrassment.

"Mommy!" I cried. "Why would you give these to me without washing them or at least checking them? I feel so dirty and gross!"

Tears streamed down my face.

"The nearest Laundromat is five miles from here," she said, sounding annoyed. "Would you like me to drive us there in our invisible car? And where do you suppose I could wash them, my love?"

Her teeth closed together and her voice lowered to a slither. I stopped crying. I had pushed her too far.

"Should I do it in the rusted kitchen sink? In the shower that is barely a trickle?" She swung her arms and her eyes looked wild, "Perhaps in our imaginary washing machine?"

She grabbed my hand tighter than she ever had, squeezing my fingers together. We walked quicker than I'd known my legs were capable of moving, and my fingers burned under her grasp. I was afraid of my mom, with her being as angry as she was with me at that moment, with her slithering voice and tight grip. I wasn't sure what she going to do. I tried thinking of ways I could calm her back down, but I still couldn't understand how she didn't see how horrible I felt about the dirty panties, and how it made me feel like scrubbing my skin with soap for hours.

We were headed to the huge fountain, which was always on the end of our daily walk, except we were going to arrive a lot sooner than usual. It was surrounded with moms with their kids in strollers and people sitting on the edge of it eating their lunches. Once we reached it, Mom threw me in, sneakers and all.

"There's the only washer I have, my love! Spin around until you feel your clothes are clean enough and worthy of yourself. Let me know when you're finished!"

She couldn't care less about the eyes staring and fingers pointing at her. They were all invisible to her. I was devastated and embarrassed, not to mention absolutely freezing. A group of kids laughed at me as I got out quickly. I was trying to get my mom to make eye contact with me to see how hurt I was and then to acknowledge what she had just done to me.

"Mommy how could you do that to me?" I asked her while trying hard to catch up to her. "Mommy, I'm talking to you!"

My voice cracked, and I tried not to cry again. I was trying so desperately to hold back my tears. My teeth chattered.

"How could you throw me in the fountain in front of all those people? It was so cold!"

She was always ten strides ahead of me and the fountain

incident, at least in her head, was already a thing of the past. She turned slightly and asked over her shoulder if Chinese was a good choice for dinner. She could erase things in her head so quickly it was frightening.

I was the one who was still wondering why she did what she did. I was the one who was freezing and who smelled like a sewer from the fountain where I had seen old men pee when they thought no one was looking, where spit and cigarettes were tossed in as if it were an ashtray. I flicked a cigarette butt off the front of my shirt. My mom was never like this. She never did this kind of thing to me.

I watched her walk ahead, and my eyes began watering and a new feeling of invisibility formed around me. I was used to her not seeing me, but not caring what she did to me? This was different, and it hurt me in ways that made my heart feel funny. She was walking ahead of me, and I was wondering if she even remembered I was behind her.

I dropped slowly to my knees, and as they hit the hard ground, I cried. I no longer cared about the panties, the fountain, or the cold water that was making my bones hurt, but I couldn't hold back the feeling of sadness that was consuming me. How could she be my sweet, gentle mom, and then turn into a mean, slithering-voiced person that throws me away and then doesn't even acknowledge me?

"Mommy," I whispered. "What's happening to you?"

I could feel the dampness from last night's rain seep through the ground making my knees colder, and I began to shiver all over. I looked down and saw a wish flower staring back at me. I made a fist and pounded it into the wet earth. While my teeth were chattering so badly I thought they might break, I did know that if I didn't stand up and eventually catch up to her, I wasn't absolutely sure she would ever know I was missing. It was getting darker outside, and just like my mom, I knew that daylight was quickly fading away for the night.

After that, Mom started knocking on my bedroom door to give me the okay to come out later and later every morning. I would get up on my own, which was against one of Mom's many rules. Why? I had no idea, and I never asked. Life just seemed easier to listen sometimes and agree because I knew I wouldn't get an answer anyways. I broke the "don't get up until I get you" rule because I had to use the bathroom and couldn't hold it any longer. When I did, I would find her lying over the toilet like a wet towel. I would hold her long, blonde hair back while she threw up. I would stand over her and gently rub her back telling her she was going to be okay, just like she did when I wasn't feeling well.

She was sick a lot lately, which was starting to make me worry. I was thinking that maybe we should change take-out places. Maybe that's what was making her sick. I ate the same things though, and I wasn't sick. The thing was she didn't really eat anything. I wet a cloth that was lying in the sink and placed it on her forehead.

"It's all right, Mommy," I told her. "You just have a little bug. You're going to be just fine."

"Thank you. I'm sorry, my love," she said. "Mommy will be in to get you in just a bit. Now please go back and lock your door, and we'll start our day in just a little bit, alright?"

"I'll be waiting for you, Mommy," I said and kissed the back of her head.

I peed in the shower only because I had no other choice, and I left the bathroom. I was relieved that my gentle, sweet mommy was back and the other one was gone for now.

A little while later, we started our day just as she said we would. We began our walk like we did every day. Some days, people we passed would give me a sad face and then look at my mom as if she were the devil on earth. It really bothered me, but my mom didn't care what they thought or the looks they gave us. Today made me especially angry because they didn't know that she was feeling sick.

"My love," she said. "I don't see them. They aren't worthy of my time. Time is precious, and I refuse to give them a second of it."

Deep down I was jealous and proud of her for being able to block what other people thought of her. That was something I hadn't inherited, but wished I had because I always saw them. I heard them laugh and call my mom names like 'skank' and 'rag.' I didn't know what those names meant, but I knew they were mean by the faces they made when they said it that was often matched with a loud or angry voice. One time I heard someone yell that my mom smelled up the town and that she should leave. My mom didn't smell. We showered every day, and I thought she smelled pretty. No one ever got close enough to ever smell us anyways except for the one time a lady yelled, "You pathetic trash! Leave the poor child with me so at least she has a chance at life, you selfish gutter rat!"

Mom stopped that day and looked at the woman, took a step towards her, and made a face that made my legs get gooey. I knew my mom could make angry faces, but I never knew she was capable of looking evil. Her eyes looked crazy as if they changed color and were suddenly darker and wider as if they might jump from her head any second and land on the sidewalk. I was sure that someone else was in my mom's body for a minute, and she showed only a few of her teeth like a dog while her nostrils flared. The lady looked scared and walked off quickly. That was the only time anyone had any effect on her. It scared the bees out of me and I was so grateful I wasn't on the other end of that look. I said a silent prayer that I never had to see it again.

Fall was finally on its way, warning us with its little wisps of cold air that would make you shiver, and it started slowly changing our town little by little with its magic paintbrush. It was the prettiest season here; the leaves would change from green to beautiful golds and vibrant reds. They seemed to glow as if the fall made each leaf and tree a piece of art. Our walks in the fall were always my favorite. Everyone had different decorations in their yards or in their windows, like funny looking ghosts that were tied to trees and would swing and twist in the breeze. Scary witches on broomsticks and big pumpkins with faces made into them would sit on display as the dried leaves dropped from the trees and danced in circles around them. On our way home from the fountain it would be getting dark and the pumpkins were lit up. I couldn't wait to see what people made with their own hands and imagination. Mom usually looked around nervously. I didn't think she liked the dark. It made her seem afraid of something that I couldn't see. She acted as if she were looking for something that she had lost, but wasn't sure if she wanted to find it. It reminded me of the cat that lived in the alley by our apartment. It would walk slowly towards us, but run away before it could find out what we had.

Not only were the leaves on the trees starting to turn and change, but so was my mom. Her once slender body was now skin and bones, and her teeth were slowly changing color from bright white to a light brown color. More days than not I was holding my mom's hair back while she threw up. The long blonde ponytail was now thinner, and her cheeks were sunken into her face. She was beginning to look older. I was scared that my mom had more than a little bug. I was thinking it might be a gigantic bug, like maybe it had been a caterpillar, and it was now a huge butterfly that wanted to get out.

One time I got so worried about her I asked if we could walk to the doctor or nurse people so they could give her a checkup.

"They can't help me, my love," was her reply, along with a closed-lip smile.

This confused me. Doctors and nurses were supposed to help sick people.

"Why are you so different, Mommy? Why can't they help you?" I asked.

She didn't reply. I tried again.

"You would rather get weaker and sicker than even try to see if they can help you? You would rather just give up? What do you think will happen to me if something happens to you?" My voice rose. "It's just you and me! Without you I'm all by myself!"

I put my head on her lap and let the tears roll down my face in silence. She started to fade, and I knew my window to talk to her was gone. I had this feeling I couldn't get rid of, like I knew someone was going to sneak up behind me and pop a balloon, but I didn't know when or where.

No matter how sick she was, she got herself together and we walked. However, one day, our routine changed. I planned on looking for wish flowers, but instead of stopping at the fountain, we walked across the street and into the hardware store. She actually started a conversation with a stranger that didn't include ordering food.

"I was wondering if you have any camping equipment?" she asked.

The old man smiled at my mom and then down at me.

"Well, I do have a few items... an old tent, a few sleeping bags, a blow-up mattress and maybe a canteen or two. Would you like to see them?"

She nodded. "That would be nice, thank you."

We walked to the back of the store. There was an old tent and by the amount of dust that sat on top of it, it had been there for quite some time. The old man unzipped it and we went inside. There was a green sleeping bag lying over a blue mattress that had been blown up like a balloon, and it looked more comfortable than my mom's bed. Next to it stood a small table that had a canteen sitting on it. The old man said campers use them to put their water in. It was set up as if it were already in the woods.

"It's pretty dark in here. Can you see anything inside from the outside?" My mom asked as if she were a real camper.

"Nope, when you're camping you wouldn't want anyone to see straight into your tent, now would you?" He replied with a chuckle.

"No, definitely not," my mom said, smiling.

My eyes opened wide and my mouth hung open in shock.

"Do you mind if we use your restroom? My little girl needs to use it," asked my mom.

"No, of course not," the old man said, "It's right this way."

As we closed the bathroom door behind us, I just stared at my mom.

"I don't have to go to the bathroom," I said.

"I know, my love. Just please don't speak until we leave. Can you do that for me?"

"Yes, Mommy," I said. I hesitated, and then I continued, "But you're talking to a stranger. It's so weird! And please don't make us go camping, Mommy. I hate bugs! You know that!"

She got her crazy look back and started to walk towards me. I knew she wasn't herself again and in no mood for questions, so I closed my mouth as instructed, but my eyes never stopped asking, "What the heck is happening to you? What did you do with my mommy?"

She inspected everything: the toilet, the trashcan, the paper towel roll, even the ceiling. Then, we left the bathroom. With the old man nowhere in sight, my mom looked around the building in every direction as if she would have to take a memory test after we left. She looked at the ceiling, walls, windows, and the main door. After what felt like hours had passed, the man finally reappeared. My mom shook his hand, thanked him for his time, and let him know she would consider the items we were shown and to have a good night.

"It's nice to have a new customer," the old man said, smiling at us. "How did you hear about my little place, if you don't mind me asking? I'd like to thank them next time they're in."

"Oh I saw a flyer on the edge of the fountain. I thought I would see for myself. You have a lovely store, sir. Thank you again," my mom said, and just like that, we left.

We started to walk across the street and back towards home without a word. I thought my head was going to explode, so I just let it all out.

"Mommy, are we moving? Are we really going camping? You know how much I hate bugs."

She didn't say anything, so I kept going.

"I've read a lot about the woods in my storybooks. Did you know there's a wolf that can blow a house down? Can you imagine what it could do to a tent? There's a lady that lives there and her house looks like it's made of cookies, Mommy, but you know what? It's a trick! She eats you. She puts you in a huge pot and she eats you. So do you really want to go there?"

Mom kept walking. She never even looked at me. I was feeling desperate. What did she have planned for us? I raised my voice.

"We would die in the woods! And I can't go potty outside. I just can't. I know I will get bit by a bug on my privates. I just know it. I haven't even mentioned the other animals, yet, Mommy. There's more! I don't want to scare you, but the animals? Whoa!"

I put both my hands on my head as if it was about to pop right off of my neck at the thought, and to add drama to what I was saying to her.

At last she said, "You'll see, my love. When the time is right, I will explain everything to you."

Another wonderful performance once again unnoticed and unapplauded.

A few days passed and I woke, again needing to let myself out of my room. There she was, again slouched over the toilet. I had to use the shower, again. I walked over to her as soon as I was done. She was heaving into the toilet.

"Mommy, we need to get you to the hospital place so they can help you."

I held her hair again, but this time it seemed even thinner than the last time.

"Mommy, you're so thin," I said in a confused tone.

"I'm so sorry, my love," she said after catching her breath. "I need you to quickly go back to bed and lock the door. Don't come out until I get you in just a little while. Promise me that you'll try to never come out until I get you, okay?"

"Mommy, sometimes I can't wait that long. I have to go so bad, and sometimes I can't hold it anymore," I explained.

"I understand, my love. Mommy's sorry. I will come to get you soon, okay?"

I walked back and lay down in my room, read one of my storybooks, and waited patiently for her. I decided I was taking her to the hospital if I had to drag her there myself and that was that. I was getting mentally prepared for battle, thinking about every reason she would come up with. I knew I had to stand my ground and tell her it was the best thing for both of us.

Suddenly I heard her voice. Who was she talking to? If she was walking in circles, at least words were coming out this time. Then she screamed. I jumped and opened my bedroom door as fast as I could.

I never expected what I saw next. There was a man with his hands around my mom's fragile neck and he had her off the ground so her feet weren't even touching the floor. She was just dangling there. The man hadn't seen me, but my mom's eyes were looking at me and then at the closet, telling me to go back in. He was yelling something that I couldn't understand. It was almost a loud mumble and he was banging her head against the wall.

Then I remembered it, the bat.

Mommy kept a bat at the end of her bed in case a bad person ever broke in. There was no doubt he was a bad person. I quietly grabbed the bat, snuck up behind him, and with all my might I swung it at the back of the man's head. He instantly let go on my mom and she dropped like a rock to the floor. He took both hands and grabbed his own head where I had made contact. His hands had blood all over them from where I had hit him.

Then he saw me.

I saw the anger, the horribly frightening anger that was coming towards me. His eyes were blood shot and they were wide like a cat's when someone has stepped on its tail. With one swipe of his hand, I flew off my feet and hit the wall. I tried to stand up, but I could hardly see straight and my ears were ringing. Just as I could make out my mom grabbing the bat, he lifted me up off the ground, and hit me again. I went flying in the direction of the kitchen this time. The last thing I heard was something that sounded like a tree branch snapping.

Everything went black and silent.

CHAPTER THREE

When I woke, my head and face hurt with a pain I could never have imagined. I could feel how swollen my eyes were and my ears were ringing so bad that I could barely make out the words my mom was trying to say to me. My head had a drum beating loudly inside it. Mom had tears in her eyes and kept repeating words to me as she held ice in a towel on my face.

"You're going to be all right," I heard her say. "You're my brave little soldier."

My teeth felt like they were loose and my mouth tasted like blood.

"Mommy?"

When she heard my voice, she gasped and hugged me close.

"Who was that crazy man, and why did he want to hurt us?" I asked.

"He was a very bad man, my love, and he was crazy. But he's gone, and he's never coming back, so don't be afraid," she replied.

"Are you really all right?" I asked again. "He had you by your neck, Mommy."

"I'm fine, a little sore, but I'm fine."

I could see a bunch of bruises forming around her neck, an imprint of where his hands had been.

"I wish you had stayed in your room where you were safe and out of danger though," she added.

"How did he get in here, Mommy?" I asked.

"I don't really know my love," she said, wiping blood from my face.

"I heard a big crack like a tree branch," I told her. "What was that?"

"I don't know that either. I hope it was something breaking on him. I think he deserved more than that after what he did, don't you? I think that maybe I should bring you to the hospital so they can make sure you're all right. He hit you several times very hard," she said, starting to cry.

"Why are you still crying, Mommy? I'm okay, and we're okay, aren't we? I'm still really scared that he's coming back, but we're okay, aren't we?" I asked.

"Yes my love, but I'm still very worried about your head, and when we go to the hospital, I need you to know that I won't be able to go in with you, but I will give you a note to give to the person at the desk for the doctor," she replied.

"Why can't you go with me?" I asked, confused.

"I just can't, but they will take really good care of you and make sure your head gets all better," she explained.

"Why though? Why can't you go with me?"

I knew I wouldn't get an answer, so I just let her know that I wasn't going anywhere without her.

"I'm fine, really Mommy. This ice is helping a lot. Honest! All that hurts are my ears, teeth, head, and my face from his big stupid hands. My neck hurts too, but its okay."

She nodded, but her face was sad.

"Except," I said. "Why do I taste blood?"

She held out her hand and there were two of my teeth in her palm. What happened started to sink in and settle in my brain. I wanted to scream, to beat my fists into the door, and kick holes into the walls. We never hurt anyone. We kept to ourselves and were kind, loving people. How do things like this happen? We never did anything bad. The anger was overtaking me. Mom tried her best to hold me, but she was too weak and decided to lie next to me while I cried out my anger and frustration.

After I calmed down, I asked, "Mommy, how would you ever think I could leave you and go back in my room with a man hurting you? He could have killed you!"

I started crying again, but this time at the thought of losing her, not only my mommy, but my best friend, my protector and my absolute everything.

"Don't cry, my love," Mom said. She shook me gently. "Hey! How about this? We will walk to the hospital. It's right around the corner and you will give the person at the desk my note. They will probably keep you overnight, so don't worry or be afraid. It's okay if they do. I will come back here and wait for you."

I sniffed and brushed some snot away from my nose.

"How does that sound?" Mom said. "If you hear them talk about keeping you longer, and you feel fine, look for a sign that says 'Exit' and follow it until you reach outside. You can walk back and we'll be together again. I'll know the doctors examined you, and that you're all right."

I thought about my mom's plan for a few minutes, and I couldn't find anything wrong with it except that I had never slept away from her before.

As we walked to the hospital with my mom's note clenched tightly in my hand, she reassured me over and over that everything was going to be fine.

"Now if they ask you about me, you need to remember never to tell them about me or where we live," she explained.

"I won't, Mommy. I know the rules," I replied.

"The tent at the hardware store was really nice. I think you would really like it there. It's much bigger than your room now, you know?" she said.

"Yeah, I guess," I said. "But I'm not going camping, Mommy, and I'm not being away from you except to get my exam and that's that."

She promised to lock the door in case there were more crazies out there. I promised if they decided to keep me longer after I felt better, that she would be waiting for me by the dumpster so that I wouldn't have to walk back alone, especially with a crazy man out there somewhere.

"I thought you said he was never coming back?" I asked.

I was starting to feel scared again.

"He's not my love, but if I'm not here I need you to go back inside, okay? I love you so much, my love. You need to know this and never ever forget it," she said holding me close.

"Mommy I'm only going for a head exam. I'll see you right here tomorrow, one day more at the latest. Why would I ever forget that you love me? I love you to the moon, the stars, and back again, silly Willy," I said.

I hugged her, noticing again how thin she had become, wishing she would change her mind and come with me so she could have them check her out too.

"Mommy?" I asked once again. "Why can't you tell me the truth, about why you can't come in with me?"

"My love I'm, I'm not..." she began.

"Hey! What are you doing back there?" a man yelled, scaring me half to death.

When I turned back to my mom so she could finally finish the answer I had been waiting for, she was gone.

I walked into the entrance of the hospital and handed the woman behind the desk my mom's note. As soon as she looked up from the note and saw my face, noticing that I was indeed alone, she was on the phone immediately. Once she was done, she sat me in a chair with huge wheels, and I was taken into a room with a curtain instead of a door.

A man came in dressed in a white coat and introduced himself as Dr. Pierce. He was very friendly, but I didn't want to be alone with him. I was afraid that he might be crazy like the other guy. I asked the nurse if she could stay.

"I was planning to," she said with a smile.

The doctor was tall with brown hair that had a lot of white going through it. It was hard to tell if he was young because his hair made him look older, or if he was older and his face made him look younger.

"Now what happened to your pretty little face?" he asked.

"A crazy man hit me hard."

As soon as I said it I could feel jumping beans in my stomach. I had already messed up.

"I mean I fell down some stairs. I'm sorry I'm a little confused."

The doctor looked at the note. It was written on the last page of my *Bunny goes to Town* book. He looked up at me again.

"Well, little one, do you know what this note says?" he asked.

"Yes, I do. It says I am eight years old; that I fell down some stairs, and I need to make sure that my head is okay. I might have to stay overnight, but then I should be fine."

I went over the details again in my head. I was sure that I had gotten it right that time.

"No, sweetheart, it says here that someone broke into your home, beat you and your mommy horribly. It says that," he paused. "It says that your mommy died from her injuries. It says that you are aware of this. That we need to take care of you because the person that wrote this barely knew you or your mommy. It says that she is an old woman and can't take care of you."

This had to be a joke or some test for my head.

"No," I said. "No, that's not what she wrote! That's not what my mommy wrote! That's not what she gave me! You're reading it wrong!"

I was panicking. The room started to spin, and the air started to feel extra heavy.

"Calm down, calm down, sweetie," the doctor was saying. "It's going to be all right. Your mommy gave you this note? Where is she? Where do you live?"

I shook my head, and I tried to breathe. The doctor kept talking.

"I'm sure this is just a big misunderstanding, so let's calm down and get you checked out, all right?"

Were they very wrong or did my mom trick me? She would never do that to me. She was acting strange lately, and I never knew what she was going to do or how she was going to act. No, I decided. No, she loved me so much. She would be waiting for me at the dumpster tomorrow or the next day. I wished I had never walked through those doors into this place.

"This was a mistake," I said to the doctor.

His eyebrows went closer together and his forehead crunched up like a wrinkled shirt.

"I'm fine," I said, trying hard to convince him. "My head feels much better, and I think I will just go home now, but thank you both."

I looked at the nurse. She looked from me to the doctor, her lips pressed together.

"Where exactly is home?" the doctor asked. "We can't let you leave here, especially until we have your head checked out since you've definitely been banged up pretty bad," he said.

"Will I be able to leave once you check out my head?" I asked.

"We will do our best to help you in any way we can, little one, but first we have to get you ready for something called an MRI. It's a test that can see right through your little head, and it lets us know that everything is okie dokie. Isn't that the coolest thing ever?" he said in an overly excited voice

"Yes," I said forcing a smile. "Very cool, will you let me see the note please?"

"I will as soon as we make sure your head is fine. If there's something wrong, it's very dangerous to wait. Now what's your name, little one?" he asked.

I stared at him, and after a few seconds, he asked if I minded being called "little one."

"No, that's just fine," I replied.

He looked at the nurse.

"Could you make sure that room CPS is ready for our new little friend here?"

After I lay there for a while waiting for them to come get

me for the test, my thoughts started to go crazy. What if Mom really wrote those things? Why would she write them? She loved me, and I knew that more than I knew anything. What if the crazy guy hit her head so hard that maybe she was the one that wasn't thinking right and she should be here, not me? The curtain swung open and a nurse smiled at me, introducing herself as Jeanie.

"Hello sweetie would you like to be awake for your test?" she said. "It can get pretty loud. Most patients choose to be asleep because they usually have a headache or a lot of ringing in their ears already."

I chose to be asleep, hoping my ears might stop ringing and my brain would stop spinning with all the questions. They gave me a poke with a needle in my right arm, and it felt like a nasty bee sting, but after that I became sleepier than I had ever been.

I woke up in a real bed with bright white sheets and I felt like I was sleeping on a giant cotton ball. I felt like I was dreaming, but I knew I was awake. Either way, this was a feeling I had never had before. I wasn't sure if I liked it or hated it. My head still hurt and my ears were still ringing, but not as bad as before. The doctor appeared again.

"Hello, little one. I'm happy to tell you that your face is only deeply bruised and there are no breaks. You have a concussion though." He paused when he saw the confused look on my face. "That's when your head is terribly bruised on the inside. We can give you something to ease the ringing in your ears and your headache, but only time can heal a concussion."

I nodded and tried to listen, but my eyes felt so heavy.

"We can talk about all that later though because you still look very sleepy," he said. "We're going to keep you for just a little while longer too, okay? Maybe a day or two, all right?"

In a sleepy daze I thought I hadn't been there very long, so I agreed and fell back to sleep on my cotton ball pillow.

"Sweet dreams, little one."

And the doctor left the room.

The next day I woke to a woman holding a pan of

something that looked like some sort of bread.

"Hello! Johnny cake?" she said.

She was a round woman with brown eyes and short white and grey hair. She had a great smile, one that made you want to smile for no reason. I still looked at her as if she had three heads though.

"That's a very strange name you have. Do you know that?" I asked.

"Name? I haven't given you my name yet," she said, slanting her head to the left and looking at me sideways.

"*Johnny Cake,*" I said slowly as if to remind her.

Maybe she was in the hospital for hitting her head, too. She laughed out loud

"No, no, sweetheart! My name is Miss Margaret Kenny. I work for a special place that takes care of children who don't have a place to stay. I make sure they are all safe and happy," she said, looking at me as if I should clap my hands for her.

"Wow, she hit her head hard," I thought.

Then I wondered if the crazy guy got to her too.

Slowly again I said, "It's okay, Johnny. I have a home where I'm very happy and safe. Have they taken you to the CPS room yet to check your head?"

When she didn't answer, I continued, "It doesn't hurt at all! You're asleep the whole time."

She tilted her head the same way the doctor did when I first arrived.

"I'm not a patient here, my child. I work for CPS. It stands for Child Protective Services. I would like to know where you live so I can make sure it is indeed a safe and secure home for you."

In the doorway stood a man in uniform, and alongside of him was a nurse. I wasn't sure if he was a fireman, a policeman, or if he drove an ambulance.

"Hello," I said.

I asked the nurse if she could come closer, which she did. I explained the situation I was having with Johnny. The nurse tried very hard not to laugh while Johnny sat in her chair and smiled at me.

"She's as crazy as the Mad Hatter," I told the nurse. "But her eyes are also gentle like Bambi's so don't let her fool you. She hit her head all right, really hard!"

Johnny said she would stop back later.

"Good luck, Johnny. Have a nice day and I hope you feel better," I replied.

The nurse let out a giggle and left to go after the crazy woman. The man in the uniform walked into the room and introduced himself as Officer Quinn. I'm pretty sure that meant he was a policeman.

"Am I in trouble?" I asked.

"No, of course not! I'm just here to ask you a few questions if you don't mind," he said.

"You're a policeman, aren't you?"

He smiled.

"Yes, I sure am, but I promise that I'm only here to ask you a few very easy questions."

He placed his hand on his chest.

"Does your chest hurt?" I asked.

"No!" He laughed. "It's just a habit I've had since I was a kid. I put my hand over my chest whenever I want someone to know that everything I'm saying is the truth."

"So you lie a lot?" I asked, now confused.

"No, I don't lie...why you would think I lie?" he asked.

"Well, if you have to do something special every time you tell the truth, you must lie more than not," I said, "At least that's how I see it."

"Well how about we change it to every time I put my hand on my chest, it means I promise everything will be okay?" he asked.

I frowned. "No one can promise everything will be okay! No one! Good luck with *that*, Mr. Officer," I said in my meanest voice.

He didn't answer me. Instead, he took his hat off and scratched his head of brown curls. I crossed my arms and scowled. I was not going to be answering *any* questions for this guy. Who did he think he was, anyway? Just then, the doctor walked in, apologizing to the officer for making him wait.

"No worries, Doctor. I know you're a busy man, and I appreciate your time," he replied.

"She likes to go by 'Little One,' Officer, just so you know."

The doctor winked at me, putting me a little more at ease.

"Well, that's a good name! I like it," the officer said.

The two of them shook hands and sat down by each other. The officer started to ask me questions.

"Little One, I have the note here that you brought with you to the hospital. You told the woman at the desk it was from your mommy, yet the note says she passed away. Can you try to explain what happened?" he asked.

"Can I read it again?" I asked.

The officer looked at the doctor, who nodded his head, and I was handed the note.

"Is your mommy alive? If she is, we need to know where she is," the officer said.

The doctor added with his usual happy tone that everything was going to be all right, and that Officer Quinn was the best of the best. He explained that I was a very lucky girl to have him help me.

"Thanks, Doctor," the officer said. "Well, sweetie, do you think you can help us with all our confusion? Once we get this all figured out, we can let you go home – if your mommy is indeed okay and your home is safe."

I read what I knew was my mom's handwriting. It said exactly what the doctor said it did. My insides turned inside out and whether or not my brain was hurt, I was now sure I was going to die from confusion and heartbreak.

I looked up and said with no emotion, "Really? You'll just let me walk out of here, and I can go home if I just tell you what you want?" I asked.

"You can go home once Miss Margaret..." and when I scrunched my nose in confusion, he smiled and added, "The Johnny lady, who isn't crazy by the way..."

I shrugged and let him continue.

"Once the Johnny lady and I go to your home and double check that it's safe for you, that it's clean, and you have food, that's it. No big deal right?"

I thought about the cockroaches all over the walls. There was no food except maybe some leftover pizza in a box on the floor or some Pop Tarts, and the safety was questionable. We had a crazy man beat us both up for no reason. Everyone at the hospital was very nice, but I didn't say anything and decided that I was sticking to my and my mom's plan. She could explain the note to me once we were together again. I'm sure she had a good reason. I had to shake off the belief that she could have ever meant what she wrote and convinced myself that she needed to have her head checked just like I did. I believed that the crazy guy hurt her head really badly and she was confused.

"Everything is all right. It was a mistake," I said, handing them back the note.

The doctor spoke up and reminded me of how I had reacted about what was written on the note the night before and how I had defended my mom, reassuring me once again that everything was going to be okay and the questions were only being asked so they could all help me. I could see the disappointment in the doctor's face when I told them that I had no idea what they were talking about.

Instead I told them that my headache was getting pretty bad. The doctor said he would get the nurse to get me something for the pain, but I told him all I needed was sleep. I didn't want to have anything that made me sleepy. I was getting out of there. The officer smiled at me.

"I will let you rest, but we will see each other soon, okay?"

He reached out his hand to shake mine. When we did, he looked down at my hand and stared at it.

"Angel's kiss," I said.

"Sorry?" He shook his head slightly. "What did you say?"

"It's an angel's kiss," I said. "They gave me one when I was born."

"Who told you that, sweetheart?" he asked.

"I don't remember... somebody a long time ago."

He looked up, but very slowly. "Please tell me who told you that and let me help you. I promise it will be for the best."

He put his hand on his chest again.

"That's a really weird habit you have, Officer," I said, pointing to his chest. "You might want to have the doctor check you out while you're here, but I'm fine. Really! I am. I just look awful."

I pointed to my face and swollen eyes.

"Goodnight Officer," I said, hoping he would leave. I was anxious to make my escape.

"Goodnight, Little One."

CHAPTER FOUR

I waited until I was sure the hospital was quieting down. All the noises that were abundant through the day were now almost completely gone. Outside my window it was beginning to get dark. I stood up to get a better look just as a nurse walked into my room to tuck me in, but instead she found me standing, throwing up all over their clean and shiny floor. It was such a waste of Jell-O. The nurse said it was common to throw up with a concussion, and that's why they didn't give me anything heavy to eat, but in the morning they would step it up and give me something with some substance in my tummy. Everyone here was so nice. I couldn't wait to have my mom meet them.

After she walked me back to bed and tucked me in again, I wanted very much to stay in the warm, clean, soft sheets, but I needed to see my mom more than anything else. So after someone came in and cleaned up my mess, I attempted my escape once again. I got out of bed and stood there for a few seconds to make sure that I wasn't going to get dizzy or throw up again. I was shaking and my head was hurting, but not enough to keep away from my mom. I grabbed my clothes that were neatly folded in the chair by the bathroom and put them on, leaving my blue hospital nightgown on the chair, folded nicely for them like they did for me.

I walked slowly towards the exit sign and followed it until I reached the outside. I was on the same side of the building where I had left my mom. She said not to leave unless she was with me, and I also knew she would be extra upset that it was also dark outside, but I was worried about her and I was pretty sure I knew how to get home from there. As I passed the houses that I had never seen before, I wondered if mom would let us walk this way once she got her checkup. They were really pretty and it would be a nice change. My head started hurting something awful, and I had to throw up on someone's lawn. There was no way to clean it up, and I was ashamed. When I was better, I would tell them I was sorry.

Finally, I saw our apartment door. I was exhausted and the dizziness was close to taking over my head completely, but the excitement of seeing my mom was far more important, and nothing was going to stop me. Tears of joy ran down my face as I walked in expecting to see my mom standing there with open arms. I was ready for the biggest hug ever. When I opened our door, which wasn't locked, as she had promised, she wasn't standing at all. She was lying in bed. She looked so weak. She reminded me of a baby bird that we found after it had fallen out of its nest on one of our walks. It was so tiny and helpless with its eyes looking too big for its face.

"Is your head feeling better? Did they check you out and make sure you're all right, my love?" she asked.

"Yes, I'm fine, but now it's your turn, Mommy."

I told her I was going to go back to the hospital and get a doctor to come get her as soon as I rested for a few minutes. I told her how she would love the people there. I told her about how they were all nice, and they wouldn't give her nasty looks like the people on the street did. She ignored what I was saying as she did most times.

"Come lie down next to me, my love. I need to talk to you about a few things," she said. "I told you I would tell you what I've been up to when the time was right, and it's time."

She patted the space on the bed next to her for me to join her. I crawled into the creaky bed next to her. The springs poked into my side.

"I need to explain why we walked back and forth to the fountain and the hardware store so many times. It was so I knew you would know how to get there by heart and without me if you needed to," she began.

"I'm not going anywhere without you, Mommy," I interrupted. I didn't know why she was acting so strangely. "I went to the hospital, and they said you wrote that you were dead, but I knew you weren't. I knew you would never leave me, and I was right."

I snuggled closer to her, just wanting to rest, knowing she was beside me, but I also knew she wouldn't stop talking. She was like the mermaid head at the fountain, but instead of water she was spouting out words.

"I had to watch the hardware store from a distance to see how the owner ran his business," she continued as if she was suddenly a recording that you couldn't turn off. "I had to see if there were security cameras, bells on the door, or an alarm system. I had to know what time he opened, took his breaks, and what time he left. He is on an exact schedule. He never misses a beat day after day."

My head started to pound. Why was she saying all this?

"The hardware store is a safe place, my love. Remember the tent in the back that we looked at? That's where I need you to go when I tell you to. It has a mattress, a warm sleeping bag, and people won't be able to see you inside of it," she said.

"Mommy, stop it! Why are you talking like that? I went to the hospital alone, and I'm not going anywhere else without you!"

My chest was tight, and I wanted to cry, but I knew that wouldn't help me.

"I was hoping you would stay at the hospital, but I should have known with how stubborn you are that you would be back," she said, waving her hand in the air as if she was swatting a fly.

"Wait, Mommy," I said. My eyes grew so wide they made the bruises throb. "You wanted them to keep me?"

A thought struck me. I sat up in bed and looked down at her.

"You wrote that you died," I said in an extremely soft voice trying desperately to prevent myself from screaming in disbelief at what she had done. "Why would you do that? Do know how confused and scared I was?"

She closed her eyes, but I shook her shoulder. She needed to hear me this time.

"I escaped from the hospital. They didn't want me to go, but I was so worried about you." I was breathing harder and my hands were shaking. "But you left me, knowing you would never see me again if I hadn't come back here on my own?"

I felt like I was going to throw up again and my head was ready to split in two.

"I wanted to make sure there were people around you to take care of you. As you can see I'm not feeling well, and I can't take care of you the way I should."

I knew she was serious by looking into her eyes. Leaving me at the hospital and never looking back was what she thought was a huge favor for me. She never worried about how it would make me feel or what would happen to me after I got better. She really thought she was doing the best for me. I didn't doubt that for a second. I did however think the puzzle pieces were completely gone now. She would never be whole. And that sent a shiver of terror through me.

"You'll get better, Mommy. I'm not mad at you, and I know you were doing the best for me. I love you." I kissed her forehead and I lay back down next to her. "Please, Mommy. Just let me take you to the hospital. They made me feel better. They'll make you feel better, too. Really they —"

I turned and threw up all over the floor. I wiped my mouth and the dampness in my eyes.

"All right, my love, all right," I heard her say. "I'll go as long as you promise to listen to what I'm telling you. Deal?"

I turned back to her and smiled. "Deal, Mommy."

I was relieved that she was finally going to get a checkup. I knew they could help her. As soon as my head hit the pillow, she continued talking about her crazy plan as if I had hit an imaginary start button. She had never talked this much about anything. It was as if she couldn't stop herself, like all the years of not talking were all coming out in this one night.

"You have to remember that the owner leaves at exactly 7 p.m. every night, even on the weekends," she said.

"No I don't, because I won't be there alone, Mommy. I won't need to remember any of this stuff." I rubbed my forehead. "Please, you need to stop. You're making my heart beat funny, and it's getting hard to breathe."

She only continued rambling as if she hadn't heard my plea.

"He opens up at 7 a.m. exactly every day. He takes his breaks in the backroom at 10 a.m. and 3 p.m. for 15 minutes each. His lunch is at noon and lasts for an hour. He locks the door and puts a sign with a clock on the door saying, 'Will Be back at 1:00,'" she continued to explain without stopping.

"That's it!" I said.

I stood up, telling her I was going to the hospital and that I was going to have them come back to get her so she could stop all her crazy talk. But she continued.

"As long as you watch from the fountain and make sure no other customers are inside, you can enter the building and walk to the tent – quietly, very quietly – there are no bells or ringers on the door." Her eyes were steady on mine. "When he closes at 7 p.m., you can listen for his car to go by the building. That's when you're safe to walk into the bathroom and brush your teeth."

I covered my ears, kissed her cheek, told her I loved her, and I that would be right back.

As I walked toward the door she said, "You promised if I agreed to go to the hospital, you would listen to me."

I stopped, turned and walked back to her side.

"I don't want to hear any more about the stupid hardware store," I said softly.

"Don't worry about having to remember all this. I wrote it

all down and put it in your backpack."

What was she even talking about?

"What backpack, Mommy? I don't have a back pack," I said.

"Only go as far as the fountain and never talk to strangers. My love, if anyone ever asks you about me... well you remember the rules, my love, don't you?"

By this point in this bizarre conversation I gave up. She wasn't going to stop. She was planning on leaving me. She had planned on leaving me at the hospital from the very beginning. I began sobbing so hard I couldn't take a full breath. Pain surged and throbbed through my head harder than it had even when it first happened. Everything she was saying began to echo in my ears.

"If I don't send you to a safe place, they will come and take you from me," she explained. "I couldn't bear that!"

"So leaving me with strangers or alone in a hardware store is better? How do you figure that, Mommy? I feel like you're trying to make me go crazy! Are you? Because I'm starting to feel like nothing is making any sense! Nothing!" I yelled.

"You're strong and smart. Just please remember all that I've told you. I will be right by your side as soon as I can be," she said, looking at me with her weak, fading eyes. "Just wait for me, my love, and I will be there as soon as I can."

"Come on, Mommy! Let's get up and get walking! You started to answer me at the hospital, but that guy yelled and you were gone. Why are you so different Mommy? Why are we so different?"

I was talking a little louder, which killed my head, but I wanted to get through to her.

"We don't have a fancy house or nice clothes, but that just makes us poor, not bad..." Her eyes started to flutter and she didn't finish, leaving me waiting for an answer once again.

"Why are we so different, Mommy? Answer me!"

I grabbed her face as gently as I could and tried to shake her awake, but she was out for the night. I couldn't decide if I should run to the hospital or lie next to her and take her in the morning. I felt so awful that I wasn't sure I could make it back to the hospital anyway. So I lay by my mom. I would just rest for a few minutes, and then I would walk to the hospital and bring back some help.

When I woke up, it was morning. I had slept through the whole night in my mom's bed, which I had never been allowed to do before. She wasn't next to me, which I thought was a good sign. She was up and hopefully getting ready for the hospital. I got up and made my way toward the bathroom when she staggered to the bathroom doorway. There was blood everywhere. It was coming from my mom! Her nose and mouth were dripping. I just stared in horror as more blood poured from her arm as if a balloon filled with blood had sprung a small hole. There was a huge rubber band wrapped around her thin arm. My mom looked so scared. I was a statue, afraid to move. She walked over to me and started to push me towards the door of our apartment.

"NO!" I screamed. I tried to push back. "You need my help! Please, Mommy! Let me help you! I can get you some Band-Aids! I can get you to the hospital!" Tears sprang and streaked down my face. This was all my fault. "I'm sorry I fell back asleep, Mommy! I'm so sorry!"

Her blood was spraying all over the place, and then it was all over me. Her face looked grey, her lips were turning a light blue, and the blood had risen to her eyes. Her beautiful blue eyes were now pools of red.

"You have to go, my love, now!" She was struggling to speak, choking on her own blood. "Please go and remember how much I love you! Keep your promises to me."

What was happening to her? I couldn't feel my legs, and before I knew it I was out the door. She ripped off her watch as if it were on fire and placed it in my hand. I looked down at it, and she used that moment to slam the door in my face. I heard the click of the lock.

No!

I tried the handle, but it wouldn't open. I banged on the door, my fists leaving bloody marks on the dingy wood. I banged as hard as I could, and I screamed for her, but I couldn't hear my own voice. My head was now numb. I felt nothing but a constant echo and ringing. I wouldn't leave her. I knew the nice people at the hospital could help her.

Then I remembered the key she hid under the plastic turtle next to the door. I grabbed it, opened the door again, and I saw my mom. She was walking towards me again, but this time she stumbled and fell and landed on top of me, knocking us both out of the door onto the landing of the steps. I sat up and cradled her head in my lap. I held my mom and told her everything was going to be all right, that I was going to take her to the hospital, and they were going to make her all better. I said this over and over to her as I rubbed her back and stroked her head. I watched my mommy's blood trickle down the steps like red rain.

Then someone was there. Someone was trying to pull her away from me. I looked up. It was the same officer from the hospital. I stared at him and grabbed my mom around the waste tightly and pulled her even closer to me.

"We're fine! She just needs to go get a checkup!" I yelled at him.

Another officer was trying to take me now, a woman this time. I wouldn't have it. I think I was yelling, but everything felt foggy, as if I were watching it happen to someone else. I know I needed to keep my mom safe and with me, and nothing else mattered.

"You can't take my mommy! I'm taking her to the hospital so they can give her some Band-Aids! I shouldn't have fallen to sleep. It's my fault." I was crying now, begging these strangers to leave us alone. "Please stop pulling on her! She's very weak, and you're going to hurt her!"

The officer from the hospital bent down so we were eye to eye.

"Little One, how about you and I take you and your mommy to the hospital together in that ambulance right there?"

He pointed in the direction of the street where there was a

big ambulance sitting.

"All right, but I don't want all those people looking at her," I said pointing to a crowd of people that were staring up at us.

What if we put your mommy on this comfortable bed that has wheels, and we lay this blanket over her nice and gently just so they can't stare at her? Then you can ride with Officer Riley here in the other ambulance and we can all meet at the hospital. Does that sound like a plan?" he asked.

I was trembling. "I have to go with her. I can't let go of her. I just can't. If I do, I'm afraid I won't ever see her again. Just let her rest a little while longer please?"

I laid my head on my mom's and starting rubbing her back explaining to her that she was going to get a checkup and everything was going to be all right. I told her how sorry I was that I had fallen asleep, but we could stay here as long as she wanted. I would wait for her to tell me when she was ready.

Suddenly there were more people surrounding us. I felt a pinch in my arm, which made me look quickly to my right, and there was a person, a black woman.

"Hi, sweet pea," she said in a soothing voice. "We're going to take really good care of you, so don't be afraid."

"What about Mommy?" I asked before everything went dark.

When I woke up, I knew right away I was in the hospital. I knew by the smells that I have never experienced anywhere else, not to mention the constant beeps and rings that chimed through the hallway.

I was confused. Didn't I leave here and go home already? I knew I had gone home and laid down with my mom while she rambled on about the hardware store. She talked more than she ever had, and all of it was about the hardware store. I had spent my life wishing she would talk to me, and now I remember wishing she would stop. I remember that she finally agreed that she would come to the hospital to get a checkup with me. I know she did. I know I left here and went home to my mom.

At least I thought I did. Did I dream it?

Did I still need to plan my escape?

My mom would never leave me at a hospital, so it must have been a dream.

When I turned my head, it shocked me to see there was a nurse sitting in a chair reading a magazine right next to my bed.

"Good morning, sweet pea. I hope you slept well," she said.

She was an older black woman with her hair wrapped in a bun made up of hundreds of tiny braids. She introduced herself as Athia, and she was looking forward to meeting me later, but right now she needed to get the doctor and let him know that I was awake so he could say hello.

What was the big deal that I was awake? And "sweet pea"? Why did that name make my stomach feel funny? Even when I said it to myself, I thought I was going to throw up. She left and the doctor walked in a few seconds later, and he didn't look as happy as he usually did.

"I'm feeling much better, and I think I'm ready to go home now," I said.

He wrinkled his forehead and gave me a fake smile with his lips puckered inward as if he had just sucked on a lemon. He looked down at the floor for a second.

"That's great news. I'm so happy to hear you're feeling better," he said.

When he looked at me, his eyes kept flicking to the top of my head. I reached up to touch my head, and I noticed my hair was wet. I know I hadn't taken a shower since I had been there so I asked the doctor.

"Little One, can you tell me what happened yesterday?" he asked.

"Sure," I said in the happiest tone I could muster up, trying to prove to him I was all right. "I came in and gave the woman behind the desk a note, and you gave me a test that could see right through my head."

I tried to sound very impressed because I remembered how proud he was of it.

"I have something wrong with my head...I forget what it's called... but it's not too bad. You told me that only time will heal it, and I should be very careful with it. I have no breaks in my face, which is very good. I had a policeman come in, and so did a crazy lady named Johnny. So how's that? Pretty good for hitting my head, huh?"

I smiled. That must have convinced him.

CHAPTER FIVE

"Now it's your turn, doctor," I said, "Why is my hair all wet?"

"I'm not quite sure, but I will look into it for you. How does that sound?" he asked while lightly scratching his head. "You're going to have a new doctor today, isn't that exciting?"

"Why? Where are you going? Why do I need a different doctor? You're my doctor," I said.

"Well, I will be here to check up on you, of course. How could I leave my favorite patient? I just have a lot of work in my office to do and they want me to get it done, so I asked for some extra doctor help. I only get the very best doctors for my favorite patients, so don't you worry about that."

He said this with his usual smile, which made me feel comfortable again, and I smiled back at him.

"I promise when I'm all done in a day, maybe two, I'm going to stop by and check in on you," he said.

"I hope you're done quickly. I'm going home, and I would like to say goodbye to you. Maybe I should say it now so I don't miss you?" I asked.

"No, Little One, I'll be back soon. I wouldn't let you leave before I said goodbye. I promise you that," he said with another smile.

"That's good, but before you leave, can I ask you one more thing?" I said.

"Of course you can! Anything at all," he said.

"Is my head really okay? Because I just looked down at my pillow and it's kind of red."

The doctor looked down and grabbed my pillow gently from my bed.

"No worries, Little One. Your head is just fine."

He reached up from the closet and grabbed another pillow to replace the one he had taken.

"The people in the laundry must have accidently washed this with something red," he said, looking at the pillowcase for quite a while. He seemed sad again.

"Are you all right, Doctor? I didn't mean to upset you. I was just worried about my head. I was afraid it was bleeding, but if it's just a washing mistake then it's okay, right?" I asked, trying to comfort both him and myself.

"Yes, yes, of course it is. I will talk to them and have them check for that red cloth or sock or whatever it was that snuck its way into their laundry," he said, rolling his eyes and making me laugh. "Maybe the nurses can give you a nice hot shower today. Wouldn't that feel nice?"

Then before I could answer, he touched the tip of my nose. This made me smile again. He explained that he thought I needed just a little more rest, and asked me if that would that be okay.

"Yes, Doctor," I said. "That would be okay. I'm extra tired today." As I laid my head back down on my new pillow, I fell back to sleep, remember what Mommy said, that they might keep me an extra day and not to worry.

Shortly after I woke up, I was given a warm shower by one of the nurses. It felt wonderful and I was hoping my mom could get one too because the water pressure here was so much better than ours. I had some toast and with a tiny bit of butter on it. Later on a woman I had never seen before walked into my room.

"Hello! My name is Doctor Katherine," she said.

She reached out and shook my hand as if I were a grown up. I was beginning to like that gesture – the officer had shaken my hand as well. Doctor Katherine had brown hair that she wore wrapped tightly behind her head and glasses with small, black frames on a no-nonsense face. Her lips seemed annoyed, and the dark-red lipstick she wore probably didn't help them to look any friendlier, but her eyes said something totally different. They were a soft blue and looked almost childlike, hiding behind her glasses. They wouldn't have matched the rest of her at all if it hadn't been for her tiny build and the dimples that were on each of her cheeks when she talked.

"She's a lady child," I thought to myself, a bit of both.

"Now it's your turn," she said with a tiny red-lipped smile as if we were already friends. "Would you mind helping me out and sharing your name with me?"

What was I supposed to say? I wondered. I don't have one. So I took the only route I knew.

"I don't remember it," I said. I don't know if they told you, but my memory isn't that good. I hit my head and I got my stories all mixed up last night."

"I see. Well, that's perfect because I happen to be the kind of doctor that can help you with your memory. I work with children, but I don't try to fix what hurts in their bodies, things that you can usually see like bumps and bruises or scrapes. I fix what you can't see with your eyes, like feelings of anger, sadness, and confusion, and other things, like memory. I help with the invisible things. Does that make any sense to you, sweetie?"

"No," I said. I squinted my eyes at her. "How do you know what's wrong with someone's insides unless they tell you?"

Was she like the Johnny lady, just wandering into my room?

"That's what I do as a doctor. I fix things that you can't see. Can I try to give you an example?" she asked.

I nodded my head yes without saying anything about how I thought she might be crazy. She then asked me to place my hand in hers, which I reluctantly did.

"Now, you can see your hand, and it's in mine, and I can also see it and feel it, yes?" she asked.

"Yes," I said, watching her closely.

Then she put out her other hand and asked me to put some confusion or sadness into it. I gave her my mush face, which was when I squished my upper lip until it almost reached the tip of my nose.

"Well?" she said. "I don't see or feel it in my hand. Where is it?"

"I can't put confusion or sadness in your hand!" I said.

"Why is that?" she asked with a straight face.

I looked at her closely. "I can give you my hand, but I can't give you confusion. It's not something I can hold. It's not a part of my body, and it's not like I carry it in my pocket because it's up here." I pointed to my head.

She sat back in the chair and slanted her head to the right just slightly and waited there silently. Then I put it all together and suddenly understood.

"That was a neat way to get me to understand what kind of doctor you are," I told her. "You're really good at explaining things. Do you have any more games like that you want to play?"

She giggled, which also sounded childlike.

"No," she said showing her tiny smile again. "I don't have any more right this minute, but I will." She winked.

"Okay then, I'll ask you something. Why are you here for me?"

This time I slanted my head just like she did. "I don't need help with anything in my head. I just got banged up, that's all, and that's the only reason I have a problem with my memory."

"Maybe we can just talk a little bit and get to know each other?" she asked.

"That would be nice, but I won't be here long. I'm going home soon, but it was really nice to meet you. I hope you have a nice day," I said politely.

Again I got a head tilt, but this one was different. It was a "you're not leaving until I say your leaving" head tilt. It had all kinds of authority to it. That made me a little upset. It was my room, and she had walked in without my permission or my doctor.

"Can I be honest with you?" I said tilting my head to the same extreme as she was, which was very uncomfortable for me, but I wanted to look rude so she would leave.

"Your red lip stick makes you look mean, and your eyes are much nicer than you make your face look. I thought you should know that."

I did it. I was rude, and it felt horrible. My stomach started to feel icky, and I hated myself the whole time. She wasn't moving, though. What was going on? That was the meanest I had ever been. That was all I had in me!

"Thank you for telling me. I was thinking about a new look, actually, and your honesty helped me to convince myself to go ahead with it."

She looked as if she was completely happy with my comment and implied that I had actually helped her!

"Holy moly," I thought, "That completely backfired on me."

Secretly I was relieved that I didn't hurt her feelings, and my stomach instantly felt better.

"Sweetie, did someone tell you that you were going home?" she asked.

"My doctor said my head would be fine, and that I just needed some rest. I got some so... so I'm good to go," I told her.

"What's the last thing you remember about your home, sweetheart? Can you tell me a little about it?" she asked in a calm voice. "We can think of it as another game if you want."

She looked at me for my approval. I looked at her for quite a while, trying somehow to make her feel uneasy and wanting to change the subject, but that wasn't working at all. She was a tough cookie.

"Let me help you a tiny bit, okay?" she asked. "I ask a question and you try to get it right. Can you tell me what the weather was like outside when you left here and went home to see your mommy? Was it cold or warm? I know the answer, but can you take a guess at it?"

My head was suddenly spinning, and I couldn't believe what she was saying. Who cared what the weather was like! She not only knew about my mom, but it really creeped me out that she knew what I had silently planned. She was like the witch in my Snow White storybook: She had a magic mirror, and she could see Snow White and everything!

So, I told her my plans to sneak out and go home to my mom. I told her how I hadn't left yet and how creepy I thought it was that she knew my plans when I never told them to anyone.

"You don't remember leaving here and going home, sweetie?" she asked.

"No, I never went home," I repeated. "I told you I had *planned* to leave, but I've been too sleepy, so I haven't left yet."

I pointed towards the chair that my clothes were on to show her that I was going to change into them so I could leave, but the chair was empty. My clothes were gone.

"Where are my clothes?" I asked slowly slipping into panic. "My clothes were lying on the chair over there... they're gone now, and I want to know where they are," I said, getting slowly louder as my panic escalated. "How did you know about my plan and how did you know about my mom or where we live? No one knows that! You're a witch aren't you? How do you know anything about us?"

My voice was beginning to crack with emotion, fear, and confusion.

"Sweetheart, I'm not trying to scare you. I'm not a witch, I promise. I only want to see if anything I mentioned jogged your memory a little, that's all. Please don't be upset."

She placed her hand gently on mine. "Let's talk about happy things, okay? What's your favorite thing to eat in the whole world?"

I pulled my hand away from hers quickly. "Why don't you tell me? You know everything else about me!"

I tried to get as far to the other side of my bed as I could.

"I know why you have the eyes of a kid!" I yelled. "You probably ate one! I bet you live in the woods in a cookie house, don't you?"

I kept on saying things that didn't even make sense to me.

"Don't be afraid of me. I'm trying to help you," she said.

"That's exactly what a witch would say!" I yelled back at her again loud enough that a nurse came in.

"Is everything all right?" the nurse asked.

"No, it's not," I yelled. "I don't want her in here! She's a witch, and she needs to get on her broom and go!"

"This is too much for you sweetheart," the witch said. "I will come back in a day or so, and we can start again. You can even ask around to make sure I'm not a witch." She smiled at me.

"How long have I been here?" I asked in a frightened voice.

"Sweetie, I think you need some more sleep before you have any more information put into your little head," said the witch.

I was curled up against the top of my bed at this point, not only wanting to know how long I had been asleep, but now I had to accept that witches were real. Were goblins, trolls, flying monkeys and The Cheshire Cat real too?

"You need to get some quality sleep, sweetheart, and the nurse is going to help you do that, okay?"

The witch nodded to the nurse, who stepped out and returned in seconds with a drink of water. She told me it would help me to calm down. I thanked her because my throat was very dry. I continued to stare at the witch doctor, but I also started to slowly slide into a more comfortable position in my bed.

"Well, I've never left, so you're wrong. I've been very sleepy," I said. My voice sounded like I was talking from somewhere very far away. I was so tired I could hardly keep my eyes open. "My mommy is going to be very worried."

When I woke, I remembered the witch doctor. I knew that I had to get out of there and go home. I didn't have any clothes, so that was the first thing I had to figure out. I got out of bed. I was a little woozy, my head felt fuzzy, and my mouth was very dry. I looked out my door, and there was a nurse with her back to me. I could hear different voices all over the hallway, but I saw no one. I walked slowly down the hall and ducked into an empty room every time I thought someone was coming.

Then I saw them. They were lying on a chair just like mine had been. Someone else's clothes were draped over the chair and shoes underneath. I had never taken anything that wasn't mine before, but I needed to go home, and I need clothes in order to do that. When I got home I would change, bring these clothes back, and the other kid would never know they had been missing.

I walked quiet as a mouse into the room, took the clothes and shoes, then I realized the room was empty, so I changed quickly. Whoever owned these clothes was a giant. I had to roll the jeans up four times, and the sweater almost reached my knees. I carried the shoes, not wanting to make any noise until I was near the exit. When I went to open the door, it was locked. As I made my way slowly and quietly down the hall, I found out all the exit doors were all locked. I thought this was a hospital, but it seemed more like a jail!

I tried to press the buttons on the huge doors that read "elevator," but they didn't work either. I waited in an empty room across from one of the locked doors. As soon as someone opened them, which I hoped someone eventually would, I would sneak behind them. It felt like hours passed when a nurse and a man with white clothes were pressing the buttons on the elevators. The buttons didn't seem to be working for them either.

"This is going to take forever," the man said. "Wanna take the stairs?"

That's when I finally escaped. Once he swiped a card that was connected to his belt, the door opened and closed slowly, which allowed me to follow them through the door without them noticing. I stayed behind for a few minutes so they were ahead of me. Once I was on the last floor by the exit I snuck into the bathroom and filled the toes of the shoes with toilet paper to make them fit better so the walk home would be easier. This was a trick my mom had shown me a long time ago. I headed to the exit. Mom wasn't by the dumpster as planned, so I just kept walking, hoping no one stopped me before I made it around the corner.

As I got closer to home I could almost feel my mom's arms around me. I missed her so much and I hoped she wasn't too worried. I had a feeling that I had been gone much longer than we had planned. I walked up the steps and I started smiling knowing I had succeeded in returning home, and most importantly, I could hopefully convince her to get a checkup now. As I turned the doorknob and opened the door, my smile quickly faded. My heart pounded loudly as if it were going jump out of my chest. Confusion washed over me like a cold bucket of water.

It was empty. Our apartment wasn't just empty, it was naked. There was no furniture and the ugly carpet was gone. Everything was gone. It was as if we'd never existed. The walls were white and clean, which was something they had never been. I yelled out for Mom and my voice echoed, but she didn't answer. I opened my room. Everything had been taken. I walked into the bathroom. The sink, shower, and toilet were gone. It was as if someone or something had erased any evidence that my mom and I were ever alive. That we'd ever snuggled there ate, slept, had lessons there, or even loved each other there. I was looking around slowly, remembering where what little we had used to be.

Then I thought of something that raised my hopes: The hardware store.

"She has to be there," I said out loud as I walked towards the fountain.

As soon as I put some distance between me and the empty room that I used to call home, I heard a siren. It was getting closer. As I looked back, it stopped in front of our apartment. A police car stopped and someone ran up our stairs.

They must be looking for me. But how did they ever get

our address in the first place? I started to walk as quickly as I could without bringing attention to myself. I was determined there was no way I was going back to the hospital without my mom. It was beginning to get dark, and I hoped that I hadn't missed the closing of the store.

Once I reached the fountain, I watched it as my mom always did. I saw the old man go in the backroom, and I walked through the front door, and within seconds I was lying on the blow-up mattress in the old tent. I barely breathed, afraid the old man would hear me. I had been lying there for only a few minutes when I heard him fiddle with his keys. The lights turned off. Shortly after, I heard the door close and the key turn in the lock. I waited for his car to start and peeked out of the tent to watch as his car lights went by the building. I could finally take a full breath without the fear of being caught.

Mom wasn't waiting for me like I had so desperately wanted her to be. I felt sick like I was falling and this was all a bad dream. I started crying, and I didn't stop until I thought I was going to throw up. I was confused and missed her so much that it hurt. Where could she be? What happened to our home? Why was it gone? Why were the doors at the hospital locked? It was a hospital, wasn't it? I was having quite a large conversation with myself like I'd always had with Mom, except this time I was the one that wasn't answering the questions.

I looked around the tent. I was so thirsty I could barely swallow, and I remembered the old man said the canteen was what campers used for water. It was empty. I found the bathroom past his little office in the back where my mom had taken me when we were here before. I filled the canteen completely and drank from it, feeling the cold water soothe my dry throat. I filled it once again to take back to the tent with me. I looked in the mirror. I looked nasty. My bruises were all sorts of dark purple, green, and several shades of blue. My eyes were bloodshot. I walked back to the tent and lied down again. My thoughts started swirling and preventing me from thinking about one particular thing. I slowly scanned the tent, which was to be my new home until my mom came for me.

CHAPTER SIX

I looked at every tiny detail of the tent: The little table the canteen sat on, the slightly larger table that held camping stoves and lanterns that were still in the box. My eyes locked on a pink and black backpack that was sticking out from under the green plastic tablecloth that covered most of the table except for its metal legs. Was another kid hiding in here too?

I got up and pulled it from under the table and unzipped it. The backpack was filled with clothes... new clothes. Sticking to the Velcro straps of the backpack was a winter coat with the tags still on it, and as I peered farther under the table, I found a pair of winter boots. All the clothes as well as the coat and boots were for a girl, and they looked like they were my size. Was someone else here?

I sat back on the mattress and looked at the backpack as if it was going to talk and give me answers to my questions. I had only looked at the top items of the backpack. If they belonged to someone else, I didn't want to get into their stuff. I felt bad enough about the clothes I was wearing, needing to have taken them without asking. Did some other kid really have a mom that planned on them living in a stupid hardware store too? That was hard to believe.

Wait! I sat up quickly, making myself dizzy. My mom had

talked about a backpack in my dream. Can something you dream about actually appear? What was happening? Did I hurt my head worse than the doctor thought? I thought hard about my dream, about anything else she said to me. I went over the parts of it that I could remember. The store's opening and closing times, that the owner was very particular, that I wouldn't have to remember everything because she wrote it all down and put it in my *backpack*.

I sat on the floor and began to empty it. The bag was loaded with an assortment of clothes – socks, panties, jeans, and sweaters – each folded tightly and small so they all fit. It was packed, and it was all meant for me! Inside was my favorite book, *The Velveteen Rabbit,* along with all my other storybooks. My workbooks, toothbrush and toothpaste, along with tiny soaps and shampoos were all in there too! There was a tube of something with a note attached that read, "To hide your bruises, my love." I smelled the paper and held it against my chest because I knew my mom's hand had written that note, the hand I wanted so much to be holding.

On the bottom there was another piece of paper. I was shaking. I didn't want to see my mom's instructions on that paper. It wouldn't be a good, warm feeling like the other note had been, but I knew I had to read it. If her writing was on this note, it would confirm that I was going crazy. I unfolded it, and there they were the instructions about the hardware store she told me about in my dream.

I was crazy.

That man had hit me so hard that he had shaken my brain around and made me crazy.

"Mommy," I whispered. "What is happening? How could this be real? Why all of these new things now? When I have asked for them my whole life?"

I wasn't even excited, and I didn't care about the stupid clothes. I had been without them for so long they didn't matter. I needed my mom, that's all I wanted. Where was she? I missed her so much and I was so worried about her. Maybe she went to get a checkup and they kept her longer than she'd planned, just like what happened to me.

I sat on the floor of the tent and tried to figure out where she could be and what was going on. Maybe I should go back to the hospital to see if she was there. Then I remembered how the witch doctor knew what I had only planned in my head. I looked at the backpack in front of me that my mom had talked about in my dream. Maybe I should go back for myself. I tried to lie down for a little while, hoping my head would stop throbbing.

Then it hit me. My mom must have taken everything from the apartment! She must have gotten a checkup on her own, got better, and she not only wanted to surprise me with these new clothes, which was only the beginning. She was going to surprise me with a new house, maybe one with a porch where we could sit and eat our lunch. That's where she is, getting our new place ready! Why didn't I think about that earlier? Of course my mom would leave instructions for me. Why wouldn't she?

I smiled at the thought of her making us another home, a clean pretty one this time. The sadness and confusion were suddenly replaced by excitement. I decided that the next day I would have to figure out a way to drop off the clothes that I borrowed from the hospital. I would bring them to the woman at the desk, and she would know what to do with them. I would just tell her they belong to the tall girl on the fourth floor, and that would be that. Then I would walk by the houses that I saw everyday on our walk, and maybe I would see my mom hanging up a decoration or something. I wouldn't ruin her surprise though, I would come back to the tent until she was ready for me, but at least I would know she was all right. Maybe we could plant a flower garden in the summer like everyone else did. I felt better already.

I didn't like the smells that filled the hardware store. They were strong smells, and as I walked around I saw stuff for people's grass. It was shocking to me how many different kinds of grass seed the little hardware store carried. How many different grasses could our small town have? There were rakes and shovels, and one shelf closest to the tent was filled with different colors and sizes of paint cans. I wish the paint wasn't so close to the tent. Then maybe it wouldn't smell so bad. One shelf smelled even worse though. It was the shelf with cans to kill any bug imaginable: flying bugs, walking bugs, little ones and huge ones. I wondered if my mom knew about these. Maybe it would have helped with roaches.

I cried that night in the tent. It was too much for me to actually be sleeping in the tent of the hardware store that had taken up every afternoon of my life since I was old enough to know what was going on. I hated this place with everything I had in me. Yet, there I was, waiting for my mom inside, staring at the ceiling of the tent for hours, instead of sitting outside while she stared at it for hours. I knew it was going to be okay, and that she was going to surprise me, but it felt like I hadn't seen her in forever. I missed her so much. My head hurt, and I hadn't eaten for a while.

I thought about my dream again. The one where my mom said she left me at the hospital and admitted that she wrote that she had died in the note. Did she really do something so awful? It seemed so real sometimes. What was happening to me? Maybe my brain was broken. Maybe I should walk back to the hospital so they could help me. I would apologize to the witch doctor and ask her for her help again. I would only stay for an hour so I wouldn't miss my mom if she was getting ready to come back soon. I didn't want to ruin it for her. She would be so disappointed.

Well then, I decided. The hospital was no longer an option if it meant my mom might leave again. It was going to be amazing having a new home and living like everyone else, with a lawn, a hanging plant, and curtains in the windows. My mom could sit on the porch and wave at people as they passed. They would finally see how sweet and pretty she was, and they would be nice to her. I couldn't wait to have us be accepted and feel like we belonged there too.

My headache was getting worse, and the ringing in my ears

had started again. I put my head down. I had so many questions, and I didn't know what I should do. I felt like my head was actually going to pop off my shoulders like the top of a wish flower.

I woke later to a man's voice talking to the old man who owned the store. It sounded like Officer Quinn. He was asking if he could hang a picture of a little girl that had left the hospital and still needed medical attention.

"Of course, Officer," the old man said. "I just hate seeing pictures of little kids that are lost. It just breaks my heart."

"Yeah, she's a sweet kid too," the officer said. "We really need to find her, so keep your eyes open for me, all right, Mr. Collins?"

"Sure thing, Officer. Let me know if you find her, if you don't mind."

"I will, sir," the officer said. "Have a good day."

I looked around. My mom was still gone. I need a little more rest. I think my head was making me sleepy because I was never this tired before. By the time I woke again, the store had already closed. It was dark outside, and I had missed an entire day. Maybe I wasn't even there. Who knows? Maybe I was dreaming this, too. I felt dizzy and my entire body ached. My head still hurt and my ears will still ringing. All I needed was my mom. I didn't know what was taking her so long.

I got up to look at the picture the officer had brought. I never had anyone take a picture of me, so I was very curious how they got this one. It was a drawing, but it was like looking in a mirror. I never saw someone draw a picture that looked so much like a real photo. Underneath it listed everything about me, including the length of my hair, how I wore it in a braid, and the angel's kiss on my hand. How was I supposed to look for my mom with these pictures everywhere? If it was here in this stupid hardware store, I assumed they were probably all over the place.

I had to clean up and get ready for tomorrow, and I needed some more water to drink. It was getting hard to swallow, and I couldn't make any spit. As I passed the office on the way to the bathroom, I heard a humming noise. It was a small refrigerator, and when I opened it, I saw that it was filled with bottles of water. I took one, feeling bad that I hadn't asked permission. But I was living in his store without asking, so what was a small bottle of water? Then I remembered the clothes that I was wearing. I wanted to return them as soon as I went home that day. Another kid didn't have their clothes because of me.

I opened the bottle of water and drank the whole thing before I reached the bathroom door. It was much colder than the water from the faucet. I looked in the mirror in the bathroom. How was I supposed to change the way I looked so I could find my mom? I washed myself with paper towels. My face was still very sore, but it was getting better. I needed to wash my hair. It felt dirty, but the sink was so tiny, and I had so much hair that I had no idea how to go about it. I decided that I had to do something I never thought I would.

I took my braid, and using the top hair tie, I slid it down to right before it touched my shoulders. I walked back into the old man's office and opened the drawers of his desk. Once I found scissors, I went back into the bathroom, held my breath, and cut where the hair tie ended. My hair was so thick that I had to cut through my hair a little at a time. Finally, I heard my heavy braid thump onto the floor. My haircut didn't make me look that different, but it made me feel sad inside. I loved my long hair and my mom loved brushing and braiding it every day. Now my hair looked frizzy and wild from the dull scissors, but my head felt so light. I never realized how heavy my hair had been. I tried to cut the frizzies out of my hair.

When I was done, tears were streaming down my face. I looked at the spiky haired boy staring back at me in the mirror. I used the tube of stuff my mom left me on my bruises, and you would never know I had been hurt. I wondered why she hadn't ever used it herself if she knew about this stuff. I put some on my angel's kiss, too, because it was mentioned on the poster drawing.

"Hello stranger," I said to the mirror. "Are you ready to

look for your mom now? Will she even recognize you?"

I didn't recognize myself. I wet my hands and washed off any loose hairs that were still on my head. I wiped up the sink and the floor of any hair that I could see and flushed it down the toilet. I grabbed my braid and put it in the backpack, thinking that my mom might want to have it to remember the old me.

I lied back down on the bed again and dreamed that I was with my mom. We were going over spelling words and giggling about something. We were happy and my mom was the way I remember her being a long time ago: perfect skin and soft, golden yellow hair. Her weight was slender, but not like a Halloween skeleton. We were together and she was smiling her old smile, the white teeth and beautiful full lips to complement them. I was touching her hand and she was nuzzling her nose in my ear whispering, "I love you, my love."

I woke with a sense of peace. It took a few minutes for me to realize where I was again, and I had a horrible urge to cry, but I didn't. I was numb now. Mom wasn't here. I felt like my head was very light, not just because of my haircut, but more like a balloon that was floating around my shoulders. I was the one who was missing a piece of her puzzle now, not my mom. I was more confused than ever. I decided I had to leave as soon as the old man opened the store. I would sneak out when he went back to hang up his hat. I wrote a note with some paper and a pencil I borrowed from the old man's office and left it on the tiny pillow on the mattress, telling my mom to rest and I would be back in just a little while. I wrote that I loved her and missed her. I changed into the new clothes and put on the new boots. It wasn't snowing yet, but it had been awfully cold when I walked here the other night, so I didn't think it would be weird to wear them. Besides, I had no other choice.

As I walked through the town on my way to the hospital, everything seemed different. People were happy and smiling at me. Some even said hello. That never happened. I always got the "poor kid" look, and my mom got the awful mean looks.

Was it my new clothes? It couldn't be my haircut – that was gross. What if it was because my mom wasn't with me? After that thought, I walked with my head down every time I passed someone. If my mom couldn't get a smile or a hello from them, I didn't want one either.

I looked closely at every house that I passed. There was no sign of my mom, but there was a picture of me on almost every tree. Once I dropped the clothes off, I would look a little harder, but this headache was throbbing as if I had just been hit all over again. I had stumbled a few times. I blamed it on my new boots. I walked into the hospital as if I belonged there. I set the girl's clothes on the front desk.

"Please return these to the tall girl on the fourth floor. Thank you," I said, and turned and left a little quicker than I had entered.

I heard the woman say, "Excuse me? Hello? One second please!"

I ignored her and kept walking. As I passed the Chinese restaurant, I remembered that they were my favorite people. They were always so friendly, and they always smiled at both me and my mom. It was too early for lunch, but I had never left there without them offering me a free eggroll or a sample of something. I had to give it a try because I was beyond hungry. I was right, and when I left, I was happily eating a fresh, warm eggroll that they were preparing for lunch. The woman at the counter gave me a handful of cookies too. They felt bad that they weren't ready for lunch, but as usual, they showed kindness and offered me free food. They had no idea I needed it so desperately.

As I walked by the all the houses we passed every day, I walked slowly and looked at each one for any sign of my mom. She wasn't at any of them. I heard music in the distance and remembered that it was the time of year when the town square started its festivities for Christmas, which lasted for more than a month. I turned and started to walk in the direction of town, knowing it would okay because I would need to pass the houses once again on my way back to the tent. I wanted to go there, not for the things I loved to do with my mom, like watching all the moving dolls through the window or looking at all the beautiful Christmas trees, but I hoped they would be giving out free food so I could stock up my pockets in case my mom wasn't coming back for another day.

Once I reached the square, there were more pictures of me. It gave me a strange feeling to see my face all over the place, like the old me was dead and gone, not just hiding and afraid of being recognized. Suddenly I was lifted off the ground and I was sitting on Santa's lap.

"Ho ho ho," he said. "You lucky girl, you're first in line! What can Santa get for you this Christmas?"

I stared at him and asked him if he was really real and could really do magic things, or if it was just a ploy to take hard working people's money? He gave me an odd look, squinting his eyes as if the sun was blinding him.

"Yes, young lady, Santa is very real. I live at the North Pole with Mrs. Claus, and I have a lot of elves that work hard all year to make the toys I deliver on Christmas Eve to all the girls and boys around the world. Now what would you like more than anything?"

"Why haven't you ever come to my house before?" I asked looking directly into his huge happy eyes.

"Well, maybe I didn't have the right address!" he said beginning to squirm in his chair.

"Okay Santa, I'll believe in you if you give me one thing. I need my mom to come back tonight, tomorrow is all right, too, but soon."

He stared at me as if I had said I wanted a pony or something. He was Santa – all he had to do was find my mom and ask her to come get me.

"Are you lost, sweetheart? I can get you help. I think I just saw a few policemen around here a few minutes ago," he said turning his head.

"No, I'm not lost, but if you could please find her and ask her to come get me that would be great, Santa. Thank you," I said as I jumped off his lap.

A small elf was staring at me the same way Santa did as he handed me a candy cane. As I walked away I heard him tell Santa, "Geez, we should let the cops know about her. Something isn't right. That poor kid needs a mulligan."

"What's that?" Santa asked.

"You know, a do over," the elf said, "a second chance."

I stopped and turned quickly, but and as soon as I took a step, I stumbled, almost falling into a group of people in front of me with little books, singing Christmas songs and smiling. When I finally got through the crowd, Santa and the elf were gone. When I looked around, my heart sank. It was getting busy and more people had begun to show up at the square. I was short and everyone seemed extra tall, blocking my view. I wanted to know where to find this mulligan. I needed it, whatever it was. A second chance would change everything. My mom wouldn't have gotten sick, the crazy man wouldn't have gotten into our apartment, and my mom and I could be together right that very second.

After looking for quite a while, I finally found Santa again. I stood in a very, very long line waiting to see him. I had to ask Santa and his elf about the mulligan thing. There were ten kids ahead of me when they said that Santa was going to have a cocoa break. They went down the line and handed us each a candy cane and told us he would be back in an hour. I didn't have an hour to wait. I had spent half my day standing in line. I had to look for my mom and not miss the closing of the store. I had two candy canes and some cookies though, so at least that was something.

CHAPTER SEVEN

Walking back towards the hardware store, I looked at every house even closer than I had earlier. There was still no sign of my mom. I walked back to the tent hoping that she would be sitting there waiting to take me to our new home. I lay there on the mattress, praying my mom was close to getting me so I could leave this place forever. I appreciated the thought she had put into it for me, but I still I hated it. I felt as if this place robbed me of being a normal kid. What would things have been like if she hadn't spent every day staring at this building? It had taken so much of my life already, and I was only eight. I was wondering if our lives would have been different if that wasn't all she ever wanted to do every single day. Would we have done fun things? Would we have talked more and laughed more? Would my mom and I have gone to the park? Would I have been able to play or know what it was like to be on a swing set? Suddenly I wondered how long she had been planning this. How could she have known years ago that we would be separated? Why would you plan on your kid living in a hardware store when they were barely old enough to walk?

After the store closed, I filled the canteen again before I lay back down and waited for a tap on the door. I was hoping tonight was the night that Santa would find her and tell her she needed to come get me. I would have sat by the door, but I barely had enough energy to walk. I was weak and my head was throbbing again. I was no longer hungry. The candy canes were still in my coat pocket with the Chinese cookies. My stomach got icky at the thought of eating them, even though all I'd had to eat all day was one eggroll. Thinking back at the houses I saw this morning on my way back from town, I wondered which one Mom chose. I wondered what it would be like to be a neighbor to someone and maybe live next to a kid my age. Maybe my mom would let me play with them. I started to feel sleepy and struggled to stay awake to hear my mom, but tiredness took over, and I fell into a deep sleep.

The next morning came and went. My mom wasn't there, and as hard as I tried, I didn't have the energy to get up and leave the tent. I just needed a little more sleep. When I woke again, the day had passed, and the hardware store was closed. Night had arrived, and I was still alone. I closed my eyes and slept. I dreamt that my mom was outside, knocking to get in.

When I opened my eyes, I didn't know if I had really heard her, but I had to check. I stood up and wrapped the sleeping bag around me. My legs were shaking as if I had walked 1,000 miles. I stood outside the tent and started to feel dizzy as if the floor was getting closer to my face. When I reached my hand out to steady myself, I hit one of the shelves holding cans of paint and knocked several over on my way to the floor. When I looked up, I saw red paint running down the shelves, hitting each one until it was one large puddle on the floor in front of me. I saw my mom's blood run down the steps, and I remembered where I had left her. I struggled to get up, and I unlocked the store's door. I stumbled to the fountain in my t-shirt, jeans, and bare feet, slipping and falling on the ice that the cold winds had begun to form on the pavement.

I needed to make it home. I had to help my mom. She was bleeding. I was fighting off the exhaustion and headache that were trying so hard to prevent me from going home. I refused to let them win. I could feel my feet being sliced beneath me. They were beginning to go numb, and yet burnt at the same time. My knees hit the ground so many times that they were stinging something awful. Each time I fell, I tried to stop myself with my hands, which only skidded and shredded against the icy walk as if they were made of wax. I slipped and fell for over a mile before I reached our apartment. I fell up the stairs, and the pain surging through my body became unbearable.

My mom wasn't on the stairs. I couldn't take it anymore, and I started screaming for her.

"Mommy!" I yelled weakly, not having enough strength to hold my head up straight. "Mommy, let me in! You need me!"

The door opened, and I heard a woman scream, "Oh my God!"

She picked me up and wrapped me in a blanket.

"Mommy, is that you?" I asked through tears.

"No, sweetheart," a woman's voice said.

She held me close to her and slowly rocked me as she talked on her phone to someone. She smelled like something, like warmth. I could see her face and that she was crying. She was so pretty. I reached up and touched her face with two fingers.

"Don't cry. It's okay. She'll be back soon," I said. "Are you her nurse? Did she finally get a checkup?"

I told the woman that I had left my mom here on the steps, and I needed to bring her for a checkup.

"She was bleeding so badly," I cried. "I only had to get her some Band-Aids. I don't need a silly house. I only need her."

There were flashing lights dancing on the ceiling of the apartment. My mom would have loved them.

"They're so pretty," I told the stranger as she continued to rock me softly.

I heard someone talking. It was the officer. He was kneeling in front of us, saying everything was going to be all right. I looked at him, and he looked foggy. His voice sounded as if he were talking from a place far away. I asked the officer if, when they were done giving my mom a checkup, they could help my head because it hurt really, really bad.

"Only after Mommy's checkup though, right, Mommy?" I

whispered. "You first."

I let the smell of warmth and the soft rocking drift me far away.

When I woke again, I had a needle in my arm. It was pinching me and making my arm hurt. My hands and feet were bandaged thick with white cloth. They were both throbbing, and my knees felt like they were on fire. When I removed the blanket, I could see that they were bandaged as well.

I was in the hospital again. The soft pillow my head was laying on, the white sheets on the bed, and the clean smell in the air confirmed it. What was going on? I looked to my right and saw the nurse that was so nice. Athia, I think her name was.

"Well, hello there, sweet pea! How's baby girl feeling this morning?"

"I don't know what's wrong. Why I am here again?" I asked her.

"I'm going to get the doctors, and they can help you with all your questions, okay sweetie? I'll be right back," Athia said as she left, smiling at me.

I liked Athia. She always gave me a feeling in my tummy like she knew me better than I knew myself. She could make anyone smile and feel special. When Athia returned, the lady doctor that made me mad was with her, but she looked different this time. Her hair was down and it was cut differently, framing her chin. She no longer wore glasses or red lipstick anymore, but a soft pink color. Beside her was Doctor Pierce, who smiled at me. They sat down next to each other.

"Hello sleepy head. How are you?" Doctor Pierce asked.

"I'm not that great, seeing as how I'm back here again with a needle in my arm. Why does it go up to that bag?" I asked as I pointed to the one hovering from a pole over my left shoulder.

"That needle is helping to give you medicine, food, and vitamins that you need so you can get your strength back," he replied.

"What do I need medicine for? I'm not sick," I said.

"You are a tiny bit," he said, pinching his fingers close together. "You're suffering from something called 'Post-Concussion Syndrome.' Your head started to hurt more and more each day, didn't it?"

I nodded slightly.

"You became weaker not only from the concussion, but from something called malnutrition. That's when your body isn't getting enough food or vitamins. The needle in your arm is helping you to get all of those things, plus helping to prevent your hands, feet, or knees from becoming infected," he explained.

"What happened to them? Why are they all wrapped up?" I asked.

"Do you feel strong enough to talk for a few more minutes? If you do, I can explain all this," he said.

"Yes, please? I need some answers. I'm so confused," I said with my voice slightly cracking.

"You walked for a long time in your bare feet on the sharp ice, Little One. I'm sure you must have fallen several times by the cuts you have on your hands and knees. You have deep cuts and a small case of frostbite on your feet, which is caused by being exposed to freezing weather for too long, but luckily it isn't too severe and will heal in time. You can't walk on them for a little while, but they will be fine, and so will your head. The headaches should be gone completely by the end of the day too. Won't that be nice after suffering all this time?" he asked, touching the tip of my nose, something he had done before to make me smile, and it worked again.

"Yes, Doctor, I can't wait for it to stop hurting. I can't seem to remember when my head didn't hurt," I said. "I need some help with putting the invisible part of my head together too, so I think I need your help." I looked at the witch doctor this time. "You look very pretty," I told her. "I'm sorry for being so mean and rude to you. I won't be like that to you this time, I promise. Will you help me?"

"Of course I will help you, Little One, and thank you for the compliment," she said with a friendly, pink smile. "Can you tell us what you do remember that you didn't remember before?"

She looked a little more serious with her eyes squinted slightly as if she were waiting for me to say something important.

"I think I remember most things, but I don't know if I remember them the way they I should. They're kind of mixed up, like when you drop a pizza box upside down, and you open it and the toppings are all mixed up, but you know everything's still in there," I said pointing to my head.

"That's a very interesting description, Little One. I like it! I have never heard that before," she said.

I started to explain everything to them: The years of watching the hardware store; the backpack and note in the tent; the haircut I gave myself so I wouldn't be recognized; and how I remembered the paint spilling. I told them about the walk home in my bare feet.

"I thought she was bleeding on our steps where I had left her, but that's where things get all mixed up," I said. "The last thing I remembered was a strange woman rocking me, and there were lights on the ceiling, that's it. There are more pieces, but nothing that I can really explain or put together. I guess we'll have to wait for my mom to explain it."

They both listened to every word I said.

"Did she finally get her checkup?" I asked, "She was so weak and she had been sick for a long time."

Then my thoughts started to wander. I must have been staring for a while when I heard the lady doctor ask in a soft distant voice what I was looking at.

"Red rain running down the steps," I told her, my voice barely a whisper.

"What was red rain, sweetheart?" she asked.

"Her blood. She cut herself really bad. I didn't have time to get her the checkup that she needed. I feel asleep. I was so tired and my head hurt," I heard myself say.

I heard something that sounded like someone clapped their hands together once loudly and I jumped, feeling as though I had just woken from a deep sleep.

"Are you all right?" the lady doctor asked me. "Do you have anything else you need to talk about?"

I looked at her and wondered what she talking about, but then remembered I needed to know where my mom was.

"I'm really hoping she's here with a vitamin bag that's helping her to get better too, or maybe I can't find her because I think she wanted to go camping really bad and I refused to go with her."

Doctor Pierce stood up and played with the bag above my head and I became very sleepy. I wasn't sure how long I had been sleeping when I finally opened my eyes again, but the first thing I noticed was that my head didn't hurt. I couldn't remember the last time I didn't have a headache since that crazy guy hit me. I was very relieved as I lay there appreciating my head being pain free and the quiet that my ears were finally bringing me. My thoughts went quickly to my mom. If she were here, she would have come to see me already, wouldn't she? If she were camping, she had been gone a long time. I warned her about all the things in the wilderness. I hope she listened to me. If she wasn't here and she didn't go camping, I didn't know what to do. I didn't know where else to look.

"Good morning, sweet pea," Athia said as she walked into my room. "How did baby girl sleep last night? I bet you'd like some raisin toast and juice. How's that sound to start you out this morning?"

"Hi, Athia! That sounds good. I never had that before," I replied.

"Well, I will be right back so my sweet pea can try some," she said leaving as quickly as she appeared.

Raisin toast was delicious, and I wanted to have it with every meal. Athia said she would see what she could do. A few minutes later Doctor Pierce and Doctor Katherine, whom I decided I had to quit referring to as the witch doctor if she was going to help me, came in together again.

"Good morning, Little One," Dr. Pierce said.

"How are you today?" Dr. Katherine asked.

I told them both that my head felt amazing. I slept well and I told them how much I loved raisin toast. Then I asked before they had a chance to reply if they had found my mom yet.

"Please tell me she's here," I said.

I looked back and forth at them. I would accept an answer from either one of them as long as I got one. I explained that I was out of ideas and needed their help. They just stood there, silent, looking at me with sad eyes. And not the "poor kid, you're wearing such ugly clothes" sad eyes like the people gave me on our walks. They were the saddest eyes I had ever seen.

"We have something to tell you, Little One," Dr. Pierce said. "But before we do, we need you to know that we are all here for you, and you will get through this, all right?"

I ignored their sad faces. "Doctor Pierce, I need you to please tell me that my mom is here and she's getting vitamins just like me."

He sat on the edge of my bed and gently held the tips of my fingers poking out from the bandages.

"No," he said as he looked up at me. "I'm sorry to have to tell you that your mommy isn't getting any vitamins, Little One. She went to heaven because she was just too sick and weak. No one could have saved her, not even all the doctors and the nurses in this hospital."

I stared at him and I knew I must have heard him wrong. "No Doctor, my mommy, she's blonde and has blue eyes, like dark blue marbles. She was weak and just needed a checkup and some Band-Aids, that's all. She's wearing a thin, long-sleeved white t-shirt, jeans, sneakers, and probably just a thin jacket. I know she was bleeding badly, but she just needed some Band-Aids. Maybe she went camping...she kept talking about it. Can you just look around and find her for me, please?" I begged.

"I know who your mommy is, sweetheart, and I would give anything to be able to bring her to you. I really would, but I can't," he said. "She didn't survive. She needed much more than a checkup and some Band-Aids. Your mommy died and went to heaven, and I am so sorry. You did the best you could for her, sweetheart. You have to know that, but no one could have helped her."

It was as if his lips were moving in slow motion, but I couldn't hear him. I took my wrapped hands, which seconds ago were too sore and stiff to move, and placed them over my ears. I sat there with my numb hands over my ears and rocked back and forth, wanting to forget his words.

Then something strange happened. I was screaming. I was screaming louder than I had in my entire life, but there was no sound coming out. There were hands on my shoulders, and they were trying to hold me. I had no idea what I was silently screaming. Maybe it was the sound of me shattering from the inside, and that's why I couldn't hear anything. It wasn't like a glass that hits the floor and breaks, making a loud noise, but like a million silent pieces of me scattering inside of myself never to be whole again. She was dead.

My beautiful mommy was dead.

I was on my side, and there were bars on both sides of my bed, as if I were a baby and might fall off. My eyes felt swollen and my throat was on fire, but I didn't care. Once again, I had lost track of how long I had been sleeping. Had I slept an hour, a day, or maybe a few days? I didn't care. I didn't care about anything. I was staring at the wall that faced the hospital hallway. I just couldn't believe I would never see her again. We would never go on our walks to the stupid fountain that I complained about so much. Now I would give anything in the whole world to walk to the fountain with her. I started crying, and my tears wet my pillowcase. Athia was there next to my bed. She was saying something to me, but all I heard was a whooshing sound.

Days turned into nights over and over. I was washed with a sponge and went to the bathroom in a pan in my bed. I still didn't care. I slept constantly, wanting to disappear into the sleep that kept me far away from reality. I was fed through the needle in my arm. My doctors came in trying to reach me, yet I had convinced myself I was invisible. I wondered what they did with someone after that person died. Does that person just disappear and go directly to heaven, or do they have to hang around for a while and make sure God is all right with them coming? Does someone from heaven come down and give you directions on how to get there? Or maybe there's a bus that only they can see, and it's filled with a bunch of other people who died, and they all go together so they can talk to each other on the way there? What if the doctors were wrong and they confused someone else for my mom? They hadn't. I knew that in my heart, but I couldn't let my brain accept it completely. I wanted to be with her. I held my breath, hoping I would die, but I wasn't good at it and after a few seconds, I gasped for air. The thought of actually dying scared me.

But the thought of living without her petrified me.

The next morning Athia came in my room as usual.

"How's baby girl doing today?"

I rolled away from her and tried to escape back into another deep sleep when suddenly Athia had her hand on my side and rolled me back, making me look at her. My eyes went wide with surprise.

"Sweet pea, I know the pain in your heart is something so bad that you can never imagine it ever getting any better, and that it will feel like this forever, but it won't," she said. "Time will help you to heal. Time and happy thoughts, that's what keeps our hearts beating and healing. I need to tell you something Athia believes, sweet pea. I'm no fancy doctor and I'm talking to you not as a nurse, but as a mama. I have five children of my own, so I know how mamas think. I know you're a fighter, that's what you are. Your mama's not sick or weak anymore, sweet pea, because the angels healed her, and she's watching over you from above every second. She is sitting on the edge of one of those fluffy clouds. Would she want you to give up at eight-years-old when you have a whole life ahead of you? What would your mama tell you if she could whisper in your ear right this minute? How about you start fighting for yourself, for your own life and happiness? I know that would make your mama smile. You think about that."

Athia kissed my forehead and left. I thought about every word Athia had said. I asked myself what my mom would say to me if she could whisper in my ear. I knew she wouldn't be happy with me right now. Athia was right. She would want me to get better and have a happy life. Was she really all better, sitting on a fluffy cloud watching over me? It was a nice picture to have in my head, and it made it a little easier to begin accepting that she was gone, that I wasn't going to become invisible, no matter how hard I tried.

First, I needed to accept everything that had happened. I could feel it all the way into my bones, all the memories, the good, bad, and the horrible ones. The reality that she was never coming back, that she was gone forever fell on me like a weight. There would never be another snuggle time, and I would never be able to hold her hand again. I started crying, not keeping it inside anymore. Athia came in and sat next to me and gently rubbed my back. I saw Doctor Katherine in the doorway, and somehow I knew that seeing Athia with me, knowing I felt close to her and trusted her, that she knew I was in good hands, and she left. I knew she would be back, but for tonight I had Athia. I knew that night while my tears were overflowing that I wanted my mom to be happy at what she saw when she looked down at me. I just had to figure out how that was going to happen without her.

The nurse removed the needle from my arm as soon as I started eating on my own again. She gave me a small amount of Jell-O. I was still hungry, so she brought me something called oatmeal that was mixed with some milk and raisins. She told me it was pretty watered down so it didn't upset my tummy. I wasn't a fan. I didn't want her to go to any more trouble, but she insisted on trying one more thing and returned once again with a wonderful thing called Lucky Charms. If they'd let me, I would have had it for lunch and dinner as well.

Shortly after breakfast Dr. Pierce came in and welcomed me back. He told me how happy he was to be talking to me again. He didn't mention my mom, which I was grateful for. I wasn't quite ready to talk about her. He started to explain what he had been doing to treat my hands and feet.

"Your hands are healing nicely, I'm happy to say, and I can start to take the bandages off soon. I can take a layer off today, in fact," he said with a smile, happy to be giving me some good news.

He slowly removed the bandage from my hands. They were still bright red and had a lot of cuts all over them. He put some cream on them with a long Q-tip and gently wrapped them back up again, but this time with fewer layers.

"Doctor, do my feet look like that too?" I asked, worried about what I had done to them because the bandages were twice as thick as they were on my hands.

"Your feet were in pretty bad shape when you arrived. We warmed them slowly because they were extremely cold, and then we treated the cuts and blisters. We put an antibiotic cream on them and then loosely wrapped them. They seem huge, but the bandages on your feet are different than the ones on your hands. They're lighter and let more air in," he said.

He answered every question and never seemed bothered either. That was new for me.

"Your knees no longer have any bandages, and they seem very happy," he said.

"Doctor, knees can't be happy," I said, smiling at him slightly.

"I am a professional, Little One, and if I say knees talk, knees talk. That's why they like to tell jokes to your funny bone," he added, trying not to laugh, but he couldn't stop himself, which made me laugh at his silliness.

I started talking to my mom as if she were still here. I knew she was gone now, but it helped me to slowly get used to not having her around me. It made me feel better believing she could hear me. I told my mom everything the doctor said, in case she was busy when he came in.

"Did you get to eat in heaven?" I asked and told my mom about Lucky Charms.

CHAPTER EIGHT

Later that same afternoon Dr. Katherine came by, just as I knew she would.

"Would you mind some company for a few minutes?" she asked while standing in the doorway of my room. She usually just came in and sat down.

"Sure, Dr. Katherine. Come on in," I said.

"I just wanted to check in on you and see how you're doing," she said. "I noticed you're talking and letting not only Athia, but other nurses wheel you to the shower and the bathroom. That's great news!"

"Yeah. The shower feels great and to be able to have my hair washed... well, what's left of my hair... feels good too. I feel bad for the nurses and Athia. They have to wrap my hands and feet with plastic every day before I can shower and they brush my teeth for me like I'm a baby because of my hands. I can't make a grip yet," I said.

I tried to show her, but she convinced me not to, telling me I might hurt them.

"Don't feel bad about the nurses helping you. They care about people. That's why they chose to become nurses, so don't feel bad about that any more, but it's nice that you think about them and how they feel," Dr. Katherine said.

I couldn't wait until I had use of my hands again. I didn't tell her about the potty situation. I went to the real bathroom now, but still needed help. She stood and asked me if I had anything I wanted to talk about.

"It's hard but I am trying," I said. And that's all I told her about that.

"I know you are doing your best. We're all very happy that you're back. We missed you. Would it be all right if I stop by tomorrow and we talked again for a little bit? Just a simple talk," she said.

I nodded, wondering to myself if she could really keep it simple.

That night after dinner Athia asked me if I was ready to watch one of her favorite shows. I sat up a little when she turned on a television on the wall in my room. I had never had a television. The show was called *Bewitched* and it was just starting.

"Do you know this show?" she asked as she fixed my pillows so I was comfortable. "I'll check back in just a bit after the show and see if you need a snack or some juice."

Then she was gone. I watched the show, and I don't think I blinked once. I sat there with my mouth open in awe of this mom and her little girl. They could do magic. The mom, Samantha, and her daughter, Tabitha, who was just two or three years old, were witches, good witches. They could make things move and people appear. Tabitha only had to touch the tip of her nose and she could make a cookie go from downstairs all the way to her room and land in her hand. She could even make a stuffed animal float across the room and land in her arms. The mom could do a whole lot more because she was older, and it took just a twitch of her mouth. It was the most amazing thing I had ever seen. When it was over, Athia came in with a cup of apple juice and something called fruit cocktail.

"Athia, is that show on a lot?" I asked, not wanting to wait long before I saw it again.

"It's on the same time every day. I'll make sure that it's

turned on for you when I'm not here so you don't miss it. How's that sound?"

"Thank you Athia. Not only for the show, but for what you said to me the other day. I did listen to you, every word," I said.

"I'm glad you did! It's nice to come in here and see your little face talking and smiling. Sweet pea, you are going to have a very nice life. You have a lot of healing to do on the inside and the outside, but you will heal. Once you do, you will become a butterfly and spread your wings and see and do things that you never imagined you could. When you leave here, which won't be too much longer, you better come back and tell Athia all about your new exciting life. You'll do that now, won't you?"

"Of course I will, Athia," I said and hugged her for a very long time.

Athia had become more than a nurse to me. She was a friend, and she felt like she could be part of my family, or maybe it was more like I wished I were a part of hers.

"I talk to her a lot," I told Athia. "I tell her about my day, and how I'm feeling, and how much I miss her. Do you really think she can hear me from all the way up in heaven?"

"I am absolutely positive, sweet pea," she said. "There is not a doubt in Athia's head."

That was all the confirmation I needed.

Doctor Pierce was explaining to me that Dr. Katherine was an outstanding doctor and a very, very good person.

"She has helped a lot of children, and they all seem better after her visits. Just remember she's on your side and she's a great listener," he said.

"Thanks, Doctor. If you trust her, it makes it easier for me to trust her too. I think you're a great doctor, too. I just have to ask you a question between you and me. I have to know, is she a witch? You can tell me."

His eyes got wider than I had ever seen them, and he leaned forward, laughing out loud.

"No," he managed to say through laughter. "Doctor

Katherine, I assure you, is not a witch. I had her take a special witch test before she was hired, and she failed horribly, but that's just a secret between you and me, okay?"

I smiled and I agreed, feeling much better that she wasn't a witch, or since she failed, that she wasn't a very good one.

"Why would you ever think that she was?" he asked, wiping a tear from the side of his eye.

"She always seems to know stuff that no one else does, and she's a doctor that works on your head, but not the way you do," I explained.

"Well that's a very good explanation. Now I can understand your question better," he said, trying very hard to act serious.

Then he sat up straight in the chair and said without laughing, "I still swear to you that she is not a witch in any way. And I was only kidding about the witch test. There are no witches, Little One, only in storybooks and on television. She will be a great help to you through this hard time if you let her. She is truly a great doctor in her field. I can fix things that I see, but her job is much harder. She has to fix things she can't see, like feelings, memory, and emotions. You have to be really good to fix those things," he said.

"I think I'm ready to ask you some questions if it's all right with you, Doctor?" I said.

"Of course it is. I will help you with whatever I can," he said with a comforting smile.

"What happened to my mom? Why she is…you know… gone? Why did she get so sick that no one could help her and how did she get cut so badly?" I asked.

"Little One, your mommy didn't take very good care of herself. She became too thin and needed some special help that she should have gotten a long time ago on her own, so don't think that you could have helped her. She became weak, and her body kind of shut itself down and stopped working. She didn't cut herself either, sweetheart. She was so thin and weak that one of her veins kind of broke. Our veins hold all our blood so it may have looked like she cut herself," he said, once again answering all of my questions.

"I couldn't have helped her even if I had brought her here sooner? Even if I knew where the Band-Aids were?" I asked, close to tears but fighting them back as hard as I could.

"No, no matter what you think you could have done, I need you to listen to me. It's very important that you believe and understand what I'm saying. No checkup or any Band-Aids of any kind could have saved her. I'm sorry, but you have to lighten that load on your small shoulders and know that there was nothing you or anyone could have done for your mommy. She was too sick. Do you understand what I'm telling you?" he asked.

"Yes," I said, losing the battle with my tears.

Doctor Pierce handed me tissues and continued talking.

"I can't tell you how sorry I am about your mommy and how hard this must be for you, but we are all here for you and as I said before, Doctor Katherine is excellent. You should give her a chance."

"I will, Doctor. I will try really hard to let her help me."

He asked me if I wanted him to stay for a while. I told him that I thought I needed some time alone, and I thanked him for his long talk with me and answering my questions.

"Anytime. Anytime at all," he said.

He told me he would see me soon and left me to my thoughts

Trying not to call her the witch doctor any longer was difficult for me. She stopped in for a few minutes every day, each visit getting longer by a few minutes. If it weren't for Doctor Pierce, I would have been sure she was indeed a witch, due to her ability to get me to talk about my mom without her asking and without me realizing until it was too late.

"How are you doing with all your emotions?" she asked.

"I'm doing all right. Thank you for asking," I said politely.

"I remember when my Grandma went to heaven when I was about your age. We were very close. We made the best chocolate fudge you could ever imagine. I think I still have the recipe somewhere. I should make some and bring it in," she said, looking upwards as if she were writing an invisible reminder in her head. "I talked to her about everything. Even though I knew she couldn't answer me back, it felt good to believe that she heard me. She seemed to help me through a lot of hard times."

She smiled slightly. "You know, sometimes I catch myself talking to her to this day, and it still makes me smile."

"I do too," I said, freely regurgitating all the information that I swore I would never give up so easily or quickly. "I talk to my mom all the time and tell her about everything, even what I eat throughout the day. It makes me feel good too. She never cooked, but I bet if you could have taught her, she would have been able to make chocolate fudge too."

Then I caught myself. There it was – the witch move. She was so great at it, but it didn't seem like a trick. She really seemed to remember her grandma, and I didn't know what fudge was, but for some reason, I suddenly wanted some.

"I bet your mom would have too," she agreed. "You know what? Maybe I'll make a batch and bring some in tomorrow. How's that sound?"

"It sounds delicious, and I don't even know what it is," I replied excitedly.

"Well, after tomorrow you will!" She said she enjoyed our talk, and she would visit tomorrow with her special snack in hand, and she left.

It was hard, but I had to admit I was enjoying her visits more each time. I even was starting to feel like I felt better, maybe even lighter, after each one. She was really good. The next day she walked in, and I had my first taste of chocolate fudge. It was beyond delicious, smooth, and creamy. I could've eaten the whole pan myself.

"So what do you think of my tasty treat?" she asked, already knowing the answer by the smile on my face and my chocolate-covered lips.

"Your grandma would be very proud of you," I said, making her smile, which revealed her chocolate-covered teeth. That made me laugh, and then she laughed, and we both laughed really hard together. That was something else about

Doctor Katherine: She was very generous. She not only made the small pan of fudge for us, but she made several so all the nurses could have some. It reminded me of the nice Chinese people that always gave me something to eat when I went in.

CHAPTER NINE

A few days passed and I was so happy when Doctor Pierce announced that the bandages from my hands could be removed completely. They were still sore, but nothing like they had been. The fresh air felt good on them, and Doctor Pierce said they had healed nicely, just as he'd suspected. My feet, however, would take a little while longer. I was all right with that and was happy to wiggle my fingers again, even though they looked pretty bad with their scaly, pink skin, but I was told that would go away in time.

As Doctor Pierce was saying goodbye, Officer Quinn knocked and asked if he could visit for a few minutes. He and the doctor said hello and shook hands as they passed each other in the doorway. I told him he could, and he sat down in the chair by my bed. I hadn't seen him in a long time.

"I brought you something that might make you smile," he said, handing me a small bag that I hadn't noticed when he walked in.

I took the bag and asked him what it was.

"You need to look inside and find out," he said with a huge smile growing on his face.

I reached in and pulled out the cutest white teddy bear I had ever seen. I forgot that Officer Quinn was there for a second as I held the bear gently with my sore fingers and rubbed his soft fur on my cheek. Then I felt embarrassed, and I quickly thanked him.

"He's so cute! I've never had a stuffed animal before," I said.

"Never?" he asked, and by the look on his face, I could tell he immediately regretted asking me. "Well, now you have your first, and he's kind of heavy, so I thought he would be really good company to hold at night."

"He's awesome! Thank you, Officer Quinn," I told him. "You didn't need to, but I love it."

"You can call me Quinn if you want. You don't need to add the "officer" every time unless you want to," he said.

But my mind was already wandering elsewhere.

"Do you get all the messed up kids stuffed animals?" I asked.

"You're not messed up, and no, I have never bought anyone a stuffed animal before, but I'm glad you like him," he said.

"Why me, Quinn? Is there something wrong with me more than the other kids you know?" I asked.

"No I just saw that little bear and thought you might like him. I was assigned to finding the guy that hurt you and your mom. We caught him and put him in jail. I thought you would want to know," he said.

"So he's in jail, and he's never going to be able to hurt anyone again?" I asked, making sure I understood what he was telling me.

"No, he won't hurt anyone again," he said.

"He won't ever be able to find me?" I asked.

"Nope, never," Quinn said confidently.

"Quinn, I think my mommy gave him a whooping, and I hit him in the head really hard. If you break a bone with a bat, would it sound like a tree branch snapping?" I asked.

"Yes, it could sound like that," he replied.

"It was my mom. She was protecting me," I said.

"You two were quite the team, fighting off a crazy guy," he

said with a smile.

"Quinn, she was the best," I said. I knew that my tears were back, and I tried to wipe them away, but I couldn't keep up with them.

"I didn't mean to upset you, sweetie. Honest, I didn't. I'm sorry," he said, trying to comfort me.

"No, it's okay. My tears don't tell me when they're coming," I said, wiping them with the tissue he handed me.

He stood up and wiped his hands on his pants nervously, like he didn't know what to do with a crying kid.

"I'm going to go grab a coffee so you can have a few minutes of privacy, okay? I'd like to wait for Dr. Katherine anyway, but would you like a hot chocolate? I'll ask the nurse to make sure it would be okay," he said.

"Hot chocolate? That sounds really good. I would love to try it. Thank you, Quinn!"

He looked at me with his head tilted as if he had a question, but instead he said he would be back in just a few minutes.

As he started to walk out I said, "Quinn, don't be sad. My mommy wouldn't want someone she didn't know to feel sorry for her. That's just the way she was."

He nodded, smiled and left to get his coffee.

When he returned, he said they were making fresh coffee, and he would rather wait a few minutes because it was much better that way.

"How much do you know about what happened?" I asked.

"Everything I need to know," he said, looking at the floor.

"So Quinn, what do you think about my new haircut?" I asked with my head tilted to one side.

"You did a fine job cutting it all by yourself. I do feel bad that the poster I hung up at the hardware store that made you cut it all off. You look good though. It looks good," he said.

"You're lying," I said, smiling at him.

"What? Why would you say something like that?" he asked.

"Okay, put your hand on your chest and then say you think it looks great."

I stared at him while he wiggled in his seat and used the

excuse that he was trying to "break that habit."

"Do it and say it," I said, trying hard to keep from laughing, knowing it was making him wiggle in his chair. "You can't lie can you?"

"Nope, I haven't lied since I was a little kid. Did it once, I got a spanking, and I couldn't ride my tricycle or play with my friends for two whole days. I never forgot it," he said with a proud smile on his face.

"What did you do to get a spanking and stuff?" I asked.

"I went into the street with my tricycle when I thought my dad wasn't looking, and then I fibbed about it when he asked me if I had. My dad told me to put my hand on my chest to make sure I wasn't fibbing to him every time after that and it stuck, I guess," he said.

"It's a good thing, Quinn. I won't pick on you anymore. I swear."

He was smiling and left in search of some fresh coffee. A few minutes after he left, Dr. Katherine knocked at the side of my door and asked if she could come in and that I had a visitor. I didn't have any idea who would want to visit me since I didn't know anyone, but I agreed. She came in and sat down with another woman. This woman was beautiful. She had soft brown hair that sat on her shoulders and brown eyes the color of root beer. She looked so familiar, but I was having a hard time remembering why.

"Do you remember this young lady, Little One? Take your time," Dr. Katherine said.

It wasn't her beauty, her hair, or her eyes that made me eventually remember her, but the way she smelled, like no other smell I had ever known. Warmth, she smelled like warmth, and not like the kind you get from a blanket or a winter coat, but the kind that makes you feel good inside. The way I felt when I got to snuggle with my mom. I looked at her, every inch of her face, and there it was.

"You were at our apartment," I said.

"Yes!" the doctor said, and put her hands together, smiling. "Good job, sweetheart! This is Miss Kendal Jameson."

"I hope you don't mind me visiting," Miss Kendal Jameson said.

"No, it's okay." I said, still trying to inhale her scent without anyone noticing. "I'm very sorry for all the trouble I caused walking into our, I mean your, apartment and everything."

Without any warning, I started to feel a little angry.

"I'm sorry, but I don't know how you moved in so fast," I said. "It was like we'd never lived there at all. How long did you wait to move all our stuff, anyways? Where is it? Was my mom even dead yet?"

"Maybe this isn't a good time," the doctor said.

Kendal spoke up quickly. "It isn't my apartment. I didn't move in there, sweetheart. I was helping a friend of mine who rents places out. I was painting, and it just happened to be me there that night. That's all. I'm glad, too. If I hadn't been there, I would have never gotten a chance to meet you."

I just stared. I wasn't sure how I really felt.

"Maybe this wasn't such a good idea," Doctor Katherine said again, leading Kendal slowly toward the door.

"I really thought my mom was waiting for me there." At the sound of my words, they stopped moving. I continued. "I knew she was sick, and I wanted to make sure she was all right. I gave myself this ugly haircut so no one would catch me before I could find her, but she was already gone. I didn't know that. I thought she went home again, and that's why I walked in. I had no idea how much time had gone by. My head was kind of messed up. It wasn't your fault, and I'm sorry I was rude to you."

I realized I was rambling and stopped myself.

"You don't have to apologize. I just wanted to stop by and see how you were doing," Kendal said with easiness to her voice.

When she spoke all I could think of was how well she must read storybooks with that voice. She started to walk back toward me and you could see the nervousness on Dr. Katherine's face.

"You don't like your haircut?" she asked.

"Umm, no, not really. I used a pair of dull scissors, and I used to have a really long, pretty hair all the way down my back, but now I'm a big frizz ball," I said, running my fingers through what little hair I had.

"I can help if you want," she said. "I have my own hair salon, and when you're ready, you can have someone bring you over, and I will fix you right up. I promise, no more frizzies, and it will be my treat."

For real?" I asked her. "You can fix this?" I pointed to my head.

"Easy peasy, no problem," she said as she gave me her card.

"Can I go?" I asked Dr. Katherine. "Can we please?"

"Well, I will have to ask Dr. Pierce and Miss Margaret, but I'm pretty sure we can take a trip to Miss Jameson's salon next week. Thank you. That's very generous of you, Miss Jameson," Doctor Katherine said.

"Please, call me Kendal, and I'm looking forward to your call! Maybe some pretty pink polish on your fingers and toes too," Kendal said as she smiled and clapped her hands with excitement.

Kendal was saying her goodbyes when Quinn walked in. I introduced Quinn to Kendal and told him about our salon plans. He removed his hat, set down one of the cups he was carrying, and he shook her hand. His cheeks were getting very rosy, and he stumbled over his words. She looked at the curls that had been hiding under his policeman hat and handed him her card.

"I can help you control those pretty brown curls of yours too," she said flashing her beautiful smile at him.

He knocked over his coffee and it splashed all over the floor. He mumbled apologies and left quickly to get a mop.

"What's wrong with Quinn?" I asked the doctor. "He's acting really weird, more than usual."

She just smiled and looked down. Kendal was attempting to leave again when Quinn returned with a mop in his hand.

"It was nice to meet you, Officer Quinn," she said. "Maybe you'll stop by so I control those curls of yours a little?"

"Yes, thank you. It was nice meeting you again, and the curls, well, they... yeah, I think they would like that. I mean, yes, I think that's a good idea."

Kendal giggled, said goodbye to us again, and left. I was staring at Quinn with a big smile on my face.

"What's wrong?" he asked handing me my hot chocolate.

"So your curls would like that? I said. This time I was tilting my head. "You couldn't even talk around her! What's wrong with you? Is it because she's pretty, nice, funny, and smells really good? Is that why you got all gooey?"

I giggled.

"I didn't get all gooey," he said. "I'm fine, just fine."

But he had a huge smile.

"How's your coffee?" I asked, staring down at the brown puddle on the floor.

Then we both busted out laughing, and Quinn's face got even redder.

"Now let's not pick on Officer Gooey anymore. He has police work to do," Dr. Katherine said as we laughed even harder.

Once we were settled down, Quinn he got back to his job. He had a yellow envelope with him, and he pulled out a picture and showed it to me, asking if it was the man that hurt my mom and me. My insides felt like they were suddenly being shaken from the inside.

"Yes, that's the crazy man," I said.

He then pulled out another picture of a woman and asked if it was my mommy. It was her! A beautiful picture of her. It made my heart ache and tears started to stream down my face again as I reached for it and held it to my chest.

"Yes, yes, Quinn. This is my mommy!" I said. "Isn't she the most beautiful person you've ever seen?"

Quinn and Doctor Katherine both agreed that her beauty was extraordinary.

"How did you get this?" I asked as Quinn handed me

several tissues. "She never took pictures. We didn't have even one at our place. This is exactly what she looked like before she got sick."

"This is a picture that she had taken for a job she had a while ago," Quinn said. "It's the only one we could find besides her high school picture. Maggie Sullivan didn't have a lot of pictures out there of herself."

"Who's Maggie Sullivan?" I asked wrinkling my nose up and looking at Quinn.

Doctor Katherine asked me what I thought my mom's name was.

"Her name was Mommy. She told me I named her," I said.

"Little One, your mommy's name was Maggie Sullivan, and she was 27 years old," Quinn said.

"Maggie...Maggie. That's such a pretty name. I wonder why she never told me." I said.

"A lot of kids only know their parents by mommy and daddy instead of their real names," Dr. Katherine said.

"How about your daddy?" Quinn asked.

"No, my mom said I didn't have one, but I do know that my skin is darker because I'm part spinach people."

I was proud that I remembered that, but they looked very confused.

Suddenly Dr. Katherine smiled, grabbed my hand, placed it in hers, and said, "I believe what you mean is that you're part Spanish."

"Yes, that's it! Mommy was extra white, and I'm not because I'm Spanish. That's right! Thank you. Oh, and I had angels kiss me when I was born, see?" and I raised my hand to show her.

"You certainly did, you lucky girl," she said.

Quinn was looking at my hand like he had the first time he saw it, like it was a cockroach or a bug that was creeping him out.

"Why does my angel's kiss bother you, Quinn?" I asked.

"It doesn't bother me. I think it's very unique and very special. You're a very lucky girl to be kissed by an angel," he said and stood up. "Well, I'd better be on my way."

"Quinn, thank you for the bear. I love it, but I don't like hot chocolate, I'm sorry," I confessed.

"Actually, they were out of hot chocolate, so I got you chamomile tea. Hot chocolate is much better, I promise," he said, and BOOM! His hand was on his chest.

He quickly removed it, and I laughed and told him I wouldn't tease him about that anymore. I wasn't going to promise that about how he acted around Kendal though. I noticed he didn't put his hand on his heart when I asked him about my angel's kiss. He told me I could keep the picture of my mom, and that I was very welcome for the bear.

"Goodnight Dr. Katherine, and goodnight, Little One," he said. "I'll see you both soon."

Once we were alone Dr. Katherine wanted to make sure that bringing Kendal in without notice hadn't bothered me. I let her know that I didn't mind. I liked Kendal. There was something about her... I couldn't put my finger on it, but she was different – in a good way.

"I just want to remind you that it's going to take a very long time to come to terms with what you've been through and what your little eyes have seen. So if you feel like you're ever having an extra bad day, that's okay. We can talk it out," she said.

"Can you explain why I couldn't remember things, you know, about my mom, for so long? I still don't have anything together where it should be. I still feel like there are parts missing," I told her.

"Well, our brains sometimes try to protect us. They don't think we can handle certain things, so it uses its shut-off switch. Does that make sense to you?" she asked.

"It does. I hated being confused all the time. I thought I was going crazy," I said.

"You're not crazy, sweetheart. You're going to be just fine, and you know what? Tomorrow I'm going to have you move to the lower floor with all the other kids. Then once Dr. Pierce gives his okay, you'll be with Miss Margaret and out of this hospital. She'll find you a nice home with good people to stay with while Officer Quinn looks for any other relatives you might have out there. You'll still see me twice a week for quite a while though. You don't mind that, do you?" she asked.

"No, I like our talks now. I haven't had a lot of practice talking to people. It was always just me and my mom. Talking with everyone here is the most I've ever talked to anyone besides my mom. I don't really believe that I have anyone else out there. Except... my mom did say we couldn't celebrate my birthday until a special guest arrived. I've never celebrated, so I don't think they ever arrived," I told her.

"Did your mom ever mention a name, or if it was a man or a woman?" she asked.

"No, she only said we had to wait for a special guest," I said.

"Well, I will make sure that Officer Quinn is aware of that. When it comes to having a family or not, it always has to be checked out thoroughly so we know for sure. We don't want anyone to miss out on knowing you are their family, now would we?" she asked and placed her hand on mine again. "So tomorrow we'll plan on a room change?"

"Yes, that's fine," I said.

"I'm very proud of you. You're a very special child," she said and lifted my hand. "I guess that's why the angels kissed you."

She tucked me and my teddy in, turned on the television, and told us lunch should be ready soon. Once I was alone I held my mom's picture and traced every line and curve of her face with my finger. I felt like she was actually sitting with me. She was so beautiful.

"Mommy, I miss you so much. I hope you're in a happy place with angels and God and Jesus and his mommy Mary and stuff. I hope the clouds are nice and soft for you and that you're all better again. I hope they're right and that you're proud of me," I whispered to her.

I explained the mulligan thing to her and what the elf had said when I visited Santa in the park. That maybe a do-over would bring her back, and we could start all over and keep her healthy. Looking deep into her blue eyes, I started crying, knowing I would never hear her voice again or feel her face or hair. I held her close to my chest and closed my eyes, trying to remember how she smelled and the sound of her voice.

Athia walked into the room, bringing me back to the present. *Bewitched* was on, and I got lost in another amazing show. And after lunch, I started thinking about mulligans again. Did other people know about mulligans, or only Santa? Would I need to find him again? What if there was only one and someone else found it before I could?

I didn't know what to do.

CHAPTER TEN

I moved to my new floor the very next day. This time I had a roommate. A curtain divided our beds, so I couldn't see her face, but the nurses had been going in and out of the curtain all day. I was about to ask the next nurse about my neighbor when the lady I called Johnny walked in and sat down next to me.

"How have you been?" she asked. "I hope your feet are healing as well as your little hands and knees did."

"Yes, they feel better. They throb and ache once in a while, but the doctor said I should be able to walk on them in a few days," I said.

"That's very good news. I'm very sorry to hear about your mommy. We are all here to help you through this, okay? That's something I always want you to know. You're not alone," she said.

"Thank you, Johnny, I mean..." I stopped myself, not wanting to be mean.

"You can call me Johnny. I don't mind a bit," she said, laughing at her new name. "I'm going to explain to you what I do and why I'm here, okay?" she asked.

"Yeah, I have been wondering... who are you?" I asked.

"I am your social worker. I work for child protective

services. That means that from this point on, you are my responsibility to take care of and protect you in every way," she explained.

"Like a guardian angel?" I asked.

Johnny chuckled. "I've never had it put that way, but yes, I suppose you could see it like that!"

"I hope you're better than the ones me and my mom had. They didn't do their job very well," I said.

"I can promise you that I'm very good at what I do and have helped hundreds of children through the years," she said.

"What happens when I leave here, Johnny?" I asked.

"You will go live with a woman named Ruthie. She has what we call a transition home for children. They stay with her until everyone is sure that they don't have any family out there. Once they are sure, then you are put on a list to be fostered or adopted by a family," she explained.

"How does that work, Johnny? How do people decide if they want you in their family? I don't want to be treated like one of those puppies or kittens at the park," I said, starting to get upset.

"Excuse me?" Johnny asked with her eyes squinted in question.

"I went to the park with my mom once where they were all in cages. People would look at them and say things like 'this one is brown, but I want a black one. This one's too small. I want a bigger one. This one has brown eyes, or I want one with blue eyes.' I'm not a pet, and I'm not going to let people check my teeth and look in my cage."

Johnny stared at me with her mouth slightly opened and now her forehead was wrinkled up.

"That's not what adoption is like. Not at all," she said.

"That's what it was called at the park. It said 'pet adoption,'" I said, getting angry at the thought and remembering how dumb some of the people acted towards the animals. I looked her directly in the eyes, unwavering. "I'm not interested in any of that."

"My sweet girl, you need to understand that at eight years

old, this is what's going to happen, and it will all be fine. I know it's scary, and there's so much happening at once. Your little life has changed without your permission. I understand that, and I will be there for you to make sure that you will be safe, protected and happy," she said. "There are no cages, and I promise you, no one will be checking your teeth. I think we need to give this some time and let these thoughts settle, okay? I will be back tomorrow to talk some more." She stood up and smiled. "I can't wait to see how pretty your hair turns out after you see Miss Jameson."

Then she left. After a few minutes my heart came down out of my throat.

"This isn't how it was supposed to be, Mommy," I whispered. "It was supposed to be you and me in a house, not me in a stranger's house without you."

Lunch came and went as well as another *Bewitched* show, which Athia stopped by to watch with me. It was such a nice surprise since I was now on a different floor than the one she worked on.

"I was afraid I wouldn't see you anymore," I told her.

"You didn't think you could get rid of me that easily, did you, sweet pea?"

That made me feel warm inside. She made sure the nurses on my new floor knew what time to turn on *Bewitched* for me, and then she had to leave, promising to scoot back down again the next day. As the nurses continued to go back and forth to the mystery kid behind the curtain, I used the television remote to watch other shows that I didn't like half as much as *Bewitched*. While I watched, I played with my mouth because my teeth felt funny. I knew that feeling. I was about to lose another tooth. I had already lost two from the crazy guy, but I wasn't happy about this one because it was my front tooth. With this hair and a missing front tooth, I was going to look like those pumpkins with their crazy faces that sat on sidewalks and porches in the fall. At least when the people looked at my teeth at adoption, they would walk away quickly. The thought made me giggle out loud.

While I was eating dinner, exactly what I thought would happen did. My front tooth fell out just as I bit into a soft warm roll. I took the tooth off my plate and wrapped it in my napkin. What bad timing. At that instant, Quinn knocked.

"Hi Quinn," I said, trying to hide the gaping whole in the front of my mouth with my lips.

"Hi... why are you talking like that?" He asked in a worried voice. "Are you all right?"

"I lost a tooth. That's all," I said, still trying to hide the gap.

"You're a lucky girl! The Tooth Fairy is going to come to see you!" He said.

I frowned. "What is a Tooth Fairy?"

"You have no idea what the Tooth Fairy is?"

I shook my head slowly no. He shrugged.

"Well, when you lose a baby tooth, you wrap it in tissue or a napkin," he said, pointing to mine, "and you place it under your pillow before you go to sleep. Then the Tooth Fairy, who is this teeny, tiny little person the size of your pinky finger with gold wings made from tiny jewels, flies in, takes your tooth and replaces it with a bright shiny new quarter."

My mouth was open and my eyes were wide. Quinn started laughing and assured me he wasn't crazy. My eyes followed him around the room as he flapped his arms and made a lot of animated gestures to show me what this Tooth Fairy person would be doing. It would have looked silly for any grown man to do, but Quinn with his policeman clothes and gun on his belt made it even sillier. There were two very pretty nurses standing in the doorway watching him. When he noticed them, his cheeks turned red and he dropped into his chair.

I was shocked by what he had just said. Was it possible my mom had lost her baby teeth late in life and her teeth were going to come back nice and white? Could she have her beautiful smile back again? Maybe she had made a deal with the fairy thing so that instead of quarters, she had brought those clothes for me. Or maybe she got so many quarters that she had enough to buy all my new clothes?

Then I looked at Quinn and wondered why he kept coming

around if they caught the crazy guy. Maybe my guardian angel got fired and God had sent Quinn in its place. Why else would someone seem to care about me when they didn't even know me? Were there other people like Quinn, but my mom never let me meet them? I wondered what his parents were like. Did he have a mom and a dad? Where did he live? Maybe he had one of the houses that I always I wanted me and my mom to live in, the ones with the porches and real dinner tables. I couldn't ask him, not yet anyways. I thought it would be rude to ask him about his life when I hardly knew him. Suddenly a nurse walked in, smiled, and disappeared behind the curtain.

"Who's back there?" I asked.

"Another little girl," Quinn said, his happy face changing to one that looked sad.

"What happened to her?"

"I can't give out that information, sweetie. Everyone deserves their privacy, including children," he replied.

I felt brave, so I decided to ask one of my questions. "Why are you still visiting me, Quinn, when you already found the crazy guy and put him in jail?

"I volunteer from time to time on this floor." He lifted the tag that hung in front of him that read "volunteer." "I read books to the younger kids and teach them not to be afraid of policeman."

He picked up the books that had been sitting on the floor that I didn't notice when he walked in. I suddenly wanted to know what had happened to my backpack with all my books, clothes, and other things. I couldn't believe that I had just noticed it missing after all this time. Quinn stood up and walked in my bathroom and walked back out with my backpack.

"You might prefer your own books. They're all still here, safe and sound. I have something else for you, too."

He reached in the front pocket of his shirt and pulled out my mom's watch and handed it to me. I held it as if someone just handed me the whole world in my hands.

"My mommy's watch," I said softly. "Thank you so much,"

I said softly, and I slipped it on my wrist.

"You're welcome." He smiled and watched me admire the watch. "You have your appointment with Miss Jameson tomorrow, isn't that right?"

I looked up and nodded. "Yes, and I can't wait to see what she can do with this mess!" I pointed to my hair. "Want me to say hello for you?" I said, smiling, remembering how goofy he had acted before.

"No... Actually I saw her myself today." He lifted his hat, showing his newly cut and controlled curls.

"You look great, Quinn! Wow, she must be really good to take care of those crazy things."

I quickly apologized, not meaning to say out loud what I had been thinking. Quinn just laughed again and said he still had a few more stories to read, but he would like to stop up tomorrow to see my new haircut.

"I hope you do, Quinn," I said, smiling at him.

"Make sure you put your tooth under your pillow tonight so the Tooth Fairy can come!" he said.

I rolled my eyes and promised I would do exactly that. After he left, I wrapped my tooth and placed it under my pillow, shaking my head at Quinn's goofy idea of the little fairy tooth or whatever he called it. I laid there thinking that until the hospital I had never been in a real bed with clean sheets and a fluffy pillow, not to mention having a room with cockroach-free walls and shiny floors. It was strange that a place where you go when you're sick was making me feel better in more ways than I had ever expected.

The next day was the day I was allowed to get out of the hospital and see Kendal. Dr. Pierce checked my feet and said I needed a wheelchair because my feet were still not ready to be walked on. But this wouldn't stop Dr. Katherine, who said that I was so tiny she could carry me from the wheelchair to wherever Miss Jameson needed me to be. She helped me get dressed for our special day. She pointed out my lost tooth, adding how adorable I looked. I explained about Quinn's fairy person and she just stared at me.

"What's wrong?" I asked.

"Well, did you even bother to check under your pillow?" she asked.

I scoffed. "No, I guess I was too excited about today... and besides, I don't think I believe in that fairy thing. I've lost a lot of teeth, and I've never had her visit me before."

"Maybe she just didn't know where to find you," Doctor Katherine said.

Yeah, right. That was Santa's excuse. Just to make her happy, I reached under my pillow and pulled out the napkin I had placed my tooth in.

"Aren't you going to open it?" Dr. Katherine said.

I unwrapped the napkin, and I couldn't believe what I was looking at. My tooth was gone, and there was a shiny coin covered with some colorful sparkly stuff.

"I can't believe it! She's real! I have a coin, my very own coin!" I said with my eyes wide, never taking them off the fairy dust. "I can't wait to tell Quinn!" I said excited at the thought of not only telling him, but also showing him.

"We'd better get going or we're going to miss our special salon day," Doctor Katherine said, picking me up gently and placing me in a wheelchair.

I was happy once we reached Kendal's salon, which was called The Serenity Salon. I had never been in a car before, and we had to pull over every few blocks so I could get some air and let my head and stomach settle. Thank goodness Kendal wasn't far from the hospital!

When we got there, we were given hot chocolate with whipped cream and a tiny candy cane sticking straight up out of the middle. It was a million times better than the tea Quinn had given me. It tasted like Christmas in a glass. Dr. Katherine went to the nail and toes area and placed her feet in hot water with bubbles. She closed her eyes and sipped on her hot chocolate with a big smile on her face while a lady started rubbing Dr. Katherine's feet and ankles. I sat in a big black chair that spun around and went up and down. I was so short they had to place another small chair under me like a baby. I was embarrassed, but Kendal assured me it was often used for smaller women and even some shorter men. That made me feel much better.

Then Kendal washed my hair. I thought I was going to go to sleep. It was something I had never felt before. Mom would have loved this. I wished she could have shared this day with me. When I was placed back in my chair, I smelled flowers and asked where they were coming from.

"You silly," Kendal said. "It's a special shampoo I use for my favorite customers."

It was so much better than the smell of the hospital. I hoped it would stay in my nose for a very long time. She turned me around so the huge mirror was to my back and I could only see Kendal clicking away with her scissors. I could also see Dr. Katherine, who looked as if she had fallen asleep. I asked Kendal how she made Quinn's crazy curls behave so well. This time she was the one whose cheeks got red.

"Are you all right, Kendal? Your face is very red," I said in a teasing way.

"I'm fine, sweetie," she said with a hint of a giggle in her voice. "I had to use a special cream rinse and a hair product made to tame crazy curls like Shamus's," she said.

"Who's Shamus?" I asked.

Kendal stopped clicking and said, "Shamus. That's Officer Quinn's first name, like mine is Kendal and yours is…?"

"I don't remember my name yet," I said, still embarrassed that I didn't have one and quickly changing the subject back to Quinn so she didn't feel uncomfortable. I especially didn't want her to feel that way with scissors in her hand working on my head, which was already in gross shape.

"I never knew that. I always call him Quinn," I said. "He's pretty special in some way, isn't he?"

I had meant to keep that to myself, but I said it out loud without thinking.

"He is a very nice man," Kendal said

She kept clicking away with those scissors and just smiled.

After something called a "blow dryer" was used and a little bit of product, Kendal spun me around. I couldn't believe what I saw.

"Kendal, is that really me?" I asked, not believing that the kid in the mirror with the awesome haircut could possibly be me.

"That's you, beautiful! How do you feel now?" She squeezed her hands tightly together and smiled.

"I feel like I would have cut my hair a long time ago if I thought I would look this cool."

Kendal clapped her hands and asked for everyone's attention so they could witness my new look.

Dr. Katherine finally opened her eyes and said, "Holy...! How did you...? Kendal! She looks amazing!"

The customers and other stylists all clapped and complimented me. I felt amazing and grateful, so incredibly grateful. Dr. Katherine and I must have said thank you thousand times. By the time we left, I had a new haircut, pink nails, and pink toes, which they were able to do without getting a drop of polish on my foot bandages. Dr. Katherine had red toes and her nails looked just like candy canes. "Whimsical," she called them.

"I thought I would have a little fun," she said.

Back at the hospital it was slightly past lunchtime, and after several compliments from the nurses, they said they would bring me something to eat shortly. I still couldn't get over how different I looked. What a day. First, a visit from the Tooth Fairy, and then a special salon visit to Kendal's. I sat up in my bed and told my mom all about it, not wanting to leave her out and knowing how happy she would be for me. As I looked at her picture, my heart felt heavy, knowing that I would never hear her voice again. I told her about the Tooth Fairy and thanked her for giving up her teeth for my clothes and how much that meant to me. Then I put her picture on the table next to my bed and tried to stay happy about my amazing day.

When I was done with lunch, Johnny walked in, and after a few compliments about my hair, she got right to business. She repeated again what she had told me last time about adoption and about going to live with Ruthie.

"Sweetie, Ruthie has been my dearest friend since we were both your age. I trust her with my life, so I know you will be safe with her. I have never met a child in all my years that hasn't loved Ruthie. You know, she even has children who, after they grow up, come back to visit her. They introduce her to their fiancé's making sure that she approves, and others bring their children back to meet her. Now does that sound like someone to be afraid of?"

"No, she sounds very nice, but you don't understand, Johnny. It wasn't our plan. We were supposed to be together, my mom and me. We were supposed to meet, and we would live in a house together. Now that I have to go alone, it's hard for me to feel all right in my stomach, and the Ruthie lady, she doesn't sound scary, but it's all scary, Johnny!" I said.

"Sweetheart, I know all this is frightening and confusing, but I promise you with every step you take, you're walking towards a new life filled with happiness, a home, family, school and friends. Doesn't that sound a little exciting? Just a teeny weenie bit?" She put her fingers together and putting them close to her eye making it look as if she was using them as glasses.

"Yes, Johnny, my mom would want me to be happy, and I will try. I promise," I said, hoping I could believe in my heart what was coming off my tongue.

"Fantastic! Now get some rest and we'll talk again tomorrow."

She got up, smiling, winked at me, and went behind the mystery curtain, and began talking to whoever was back there.

"Mommy," I whispered, this is all going to be okay, isn't it? You don't mind me going to live with this Ruthie lady, do you? I can't live in this hospital for the rest of my life!"

After I finished my dinner, I tried to wait up for Quinn so he could see my new hair, but it had been an extra-long day, and I was so tired that I feel asleep.

105

CHAPTER ELEVEN

My mom and I were sitting at our new house with a huge porch and plants hanging from their brightly colored pots. We were laughing as we watched them twirl in the breeze. She looked beautiful again, the way she used to. She was perfect and we were happy and together again. I was telling her how I found the mulligan and that's how she was healthy again. She was so proud of me. I told her how my name was Tabitha now, and I could do magic with just a touch of my nose. She said she loved the name Tabitha. I touched my nose and changed her jeans into a long dress with sparkles all over it. She spun in circles and looked like a princess. We laughed like we never had in the past. She waved and said hello to the people that passed by our house. They all smiled and told her how pretty she looked. I turned my clothes into a dress just like my mom's, and we grabbed hands and spun together, the sparkles from our dresses glinting in the sun, making tiny rainbows dance beside us. I looked into her eyes. She never looked so happy.

Then things started to change. I saw a spot on her nose and tried to wipe it off. Then another appeared and then another. But they weren't spots. They were roaches. I touched my nose with one hand, trying to make the magic come back, and swiped bugs off my mom's face with the other, but I couldn't keep up. Cockroaches crawled all over her. I touched my nose again and again, but nothing happened. The laughter was gone, and we were back in our old filthy apartment. Blood dripped from my mom's nose. It started to rain inside, a thick red rain, and the room began to flood with it. I tried to swim and save my mom at the same time, but the rain was rising above my chin and running into my eyes until I couldn't see anymore. I was drowning and the thickness of the rain dragged me down, farther down. My mom was gone, and I started to scream for her, but she wouldn't answer.

"Mommy!" I screamed. "I won't stop! I won't give up"

Someone was shaking me. I woke to the sound of my own screaming. Someone was holding me tightly against their chest, trying to restrain my hands and rocking me slowly while I sobbed. I opened my eyes and saw Quinn. He was rocking me, telling me it was all right, that he was there, and he was going to keep me safe. He placed my teddy bear in hands, but never stopped rocking me as I cried for my mom.

When I opened my eyes again, the mystery girl had poked her head around the curtain. Her head was wrapped with thick bandages and her face was covered with bruises and several cuts. Her eyes were almost completely swollen closed with only a sliver of movement behind them.

I closed my eyes again.

We were so happy. We were spinning our beautiful dresses. I was magic, and she was so proud.

"My name is Tabitha," I said.

"You need to go back, Tabitha," my mom said.

I could feel Quinn rocking me. She was gone. I didn't want to be awake again. I wanted to be back with my mom. I touched the tip of my nose, hoping there was still some magic left, and fell back to sleep.

When I woke once again my eyes felt puffy, and I was still in Quinn's arms. He was sound asleep. Dr. Katherine was in the chair next to my bed and stood up when she saw I was awake. She carried me to a wheelchair wheeled my out to the hall.

"Are you all right?" she asked. "Shamus stopped in to see your haircut, but found you in the middle of a horrible nightmare. He asked the nurses to call me. He held you for hours until he fell asleep, and I didn't have the heart to wake either one of you. You looked so content and he had been working a double shift. I just sat here working on my papers watching over a child and a big policeman."

"It was about my mom," I said, looking down to stop the tears from coming. "I was with her and we were so happy. I miss her so much... I..." But I couldn't continue.

Dr. Katherine placed her hands on my lap and told me that as horrible as my dream was, it was good for me to dream again. I had to know that the bad was gone when I woke up. I had to know that it was over now and I had to think about today.

"But we can talk about that nasty old nightmare as much as you want until you're ready to put it behind you. I do have one question though." She paused. "Little One, does the name 'Tabitha' sound familiar?"

I looked at her and thought about my dream, and how much my mom had loved that name, the name of the magical little girl from the TV show. I made a decision.

"Yes, yes, it does," I said with my toothless smile, and the happiness in her face was something I hadn't seen yet, not even at the salon.

"Well, it's a pleasure to meet you, Tabitha," she said, and she put her hand out to shake mine as if we were meeting for the first time.

It was an amazing feeling. The freedom of having a name was something I could have never imagined. I was officially somebody. I was going to add an "M" to remind me to never stop looking for the mulligan thing, whatever it might be.

"My name is Tabitha M. Sullivan," I said proudly.

"What does the 'M' stand for?" Dr. Katherine asked.

"I don't really know that part, but hopefully it will come to me one day," I said. I didn't want to tell her about the mulligan.

Dr. Katherine explained nightmares to me. "You will most likely have more bad dreams, Tabitha. You should know that, but you also have to know that you will survive them and that we can deal with them when you wake up."

I wiped my eyes. "It's just that she was so real and alive."

"Your mommy will always live in you, and you will always feel her right here," she said and pointed to my heart. "That's where we keep our best memories of the ones we love."

I looked in at Quinn sound asleep in my bed. "I can't believe he stayed all night. He never let me go and I felt... Doctor Katherine I never felt safer in my whole life than I did knowing Quinn was holding me, and not because he's a policeman, but because it was Quinn," I said.

"Tabitha, I've known him since he was a boy, and he's definitely somebody very special," she said with a smile.

"Can I tell you something silly?" I asked her. "I think sometimes that God or my mommy sent him to me because my guardian angel was fired and Quinn was hired instead." I felt kind of embarrassed for saying that, so I added, "I know that's silly..."

"That's not silly, Tabitha," Dr. Katherine said. "I think it may be one of the sweetest things I've ever heard. How would you like to go to the cafeteria with me and have breakfast this morning?"

My stomach gurgled and we both laughed.

When we came back from breakfast, Quinn was gone. He left a message with a nurse that he had an important case to work on and would be back in a few days, but that my haircut looked wonderful... that it made me look like the beautiful Tooth Fairy he had told me about.

"He's a wonderful young man," Dr. Katherine said. "I wish there were more like him. Now let's get you back in bed so Dr.

Pierce can check your feet to see if the new medicine has helped at all."

When Dr. Pierce unwrapped my feet, he smiled. He seemed very happy with what he was seeing, just as I had hoped.

"Your feet have healed nicely and much quicker than I had anticipated. I'm very impressed with the new ointment. I think you'll be able to start your journey into your new exciting life within the week. Now, let's get you up and try out these little feet, shall we?" he said.

The thought of leaving the hospital gave me huge butterflies in my stomach, but I did as Dr. Pierce asked, and I stood with Dr. Katherine holding one arm and a nurse holding the other. As I began to walk for the first time in what felt like forever in the special booties they gave me, my legs felt weak and my feet burned the way my shoulders did when the sun shined on them too long in the summer.

"That burning feeling is fine and to be expected," Dr. Pierce said. "You did quite a job on those little feet. The fact that all you have is a little burning is a miracle in itself."

After I walked in the booties for a few uncomfortable minutes, he slipped some special pads under my feet and then placed a pair of slippers on me. They made a huge difference, and I almost felt like I could walk for miles... if it hadn't been for my leg muscles, wobbly from not being used in a long time. I would have to do leg exercises every day to strengthen them, but that didn't bother me. What scared me was leaving the safety of the hospital. Leaving the care of the doctors that had become more like my friends, leaving Athia who was the closest thing to family I had, and the thought that I would probably never see Quinn again made my shoulders feel like I was carrying a thousand pounds. My life was going to change again, and it was going to be in the hands of a stranger. I was petrified.

Dr. Katherine had been right when she said that the nightmare I had wouldn't be the last. None were as bad as the first one, but each time I woke crying. However, unlike the first time, I was able to wake myself and after a few minutes, know it was a bad dream and that I was all right.

The nurses and other people I had come to know during my stay had begun stopping by and congratulating me about finally being able to leave the hospital. They also called me by name, which was going to take a lot of getting used to, but it was also awesome every time I heard it. I acted excited about it along with them, except Athia. She knew. Athia always knew.

One night she sat on my bed and held my hands in hers. Then she slipped a necklace around my neck. It was a cloud she had bought me.

"Now, sweet pea, I don't want you to be afraid. I heard you're going to Miss Ruthie's house. Is that true?" she asked.

"Yes, Athia, that's where I'm going until they're sure I don't have any family looking for me," I replied.

"She's a wonderful woman, that Miss Ruthie, hair as red as roses. You're going to love her with your whole heart. Never met a soul that didn't. Now every time you get sad – which you will, it's just a natural thing to do now and then – you put your tiny fingers around this cloud and close your eyes and imagine that is your mama's cloud in heaven and she is watching over you," she said, squeezing my hand.

"Athia, how can I thank you? I don't think I could have gotten through this without you. I love you, Athia." I wrapped my arms around her and hugged her until my tears stopped.

"So, what you're saying is you're going to break your promise, sweet pea?" she asked.

"What? Not to you! Never!" I replied.

"Then no more tears. Each time you come to your appointments to see Dr. Katherine, you ask for me, and I expect a happy hug. No tears! This isn't goodbye. This is 'see you soon'." She kissed my forehead and grabbed my face in both hands. "Just so we're clear, I love you too, sweet pea."

She walked out, leaving me feeling better as always.

I decided if I were leaving, that I would take a chance and introduce myself to the mystery girl. Still wearing my special footpads and slippers, I hopped out of bed and slowly walked around to the end of the curtain.

"Hello! My name's Tabitha. Would you want to talk or hang out and watch television together?"

She hit a button that made her bed rise up so she was almost sitting straight. It was really cool. I wondered if mine did that. I made a note to check. She looked at me and this time I could see her eyes. They were cotton candy blue. They were almost frightening and beautiful at the same time. I tried to look directly at them instead of all her bruises and cuts, which took up most of her face and looked horribly painful. In a weak, yet creepy voice she began to talk through her teeth like a snake, reminding me of my mom when she was angry.

"Why would I?" she asked.

"Why would you what?" I asked, confused, thinking that what I'd asked was pretty simple to understand.

"Don't you have enough people giving you attention already? Why do you need mine too? Are you going to have that cop rock you to sleep again like a little baby?"

She kept her teeth together when she talked, but I could still understand her. I was shocked at her response and not really sure what to say.

"I just had a bad dream that night, and he just happened to be there, that's all," I said, trying to figure why she seemed to be so angry with me when I had never met her before. "I just wanted to ask you if you wanted to hang out, but I guess you don't, so I will leave you alone. I hope you feel better soon," I said, and I meant it. She looked like she must be in a lot of pain.

"Go away. Leave!" she said, sounding like a snake.

"I am leaving! I just wanted to say hello and... well... get better," was all I could think of to say.

I walked back to my bed, not thinking too much about what had just happened, except that she reminded me a lot of my mom, but in a bad way. The way she talked through her teeth gave me the shivers. I hated that. She was angry, but I knew I couldn't have done anything to her. I had never met her, and I didn't even know her name. I guess if I were that banged up, I would be in a bad mood too. I had been injured before, but I wasn't that bad. I'm sure she was hurting something awful. Maybe that's how people treated my mom, and that's why she never bothered to talk to anyone. If the mystery girl was the first person I had ever met, I don't think I would have talked to anyone else either.

The next day Johnny was sitting in the chair next to me when I woke up. She smiled and offered me a plate of the same stuff that she had when I had met her the first time.

"If I have to live with this new name you've given me, you can at least try it," she said.

"Is it for breakfast?" I asked, not overly excited with having someone talking to me before I was completely awake.

"It's for anytime. It's delicious! Just try it," she said.

"Johnny, I'm not even awake yet. How long have you been sitting there?" I asked.

"Long enough to fill out your release forms," she said in an excited voice. "You get to leave this place today! Isn't that wonderful?"

"What? The doctor said tomorrow?" I said.

"We all had a long chat, and they said you're doing wonderful with things, and it was time you got on with your life and out of this hospital. Well, I'm going to let you wake up and grab myself a cup of coffee. I'll be back in just a few minutes, kiddo." She walked out, leaving her pan of whatever on the table next to me.

I couldn't leave. Quinn wouldn't be back yet. I picked up my mom's picture and talked to her as I did every day, tracing the lines of her face and asking her to help me with whatever they had planned for me. Before I knew it, Johnny was back and she had brought company: Dr. Pierce and Dr. Katherine. I thanked them both and told them how special they were. Before Dr. Katherine left, she handed me a pan of her grandma's chocolate fudge.

"Thank you! I love this stuff," I said, licking my lips.

"Don't open it until you get to Ruthie's though, so she can have some too," she said. "See you in a few days."

She smiled, kissed my forehead, and left.

"She knows Ruthie too?" I asked Johnny.

"My dear child, everyone knows Ruthie," and then she said it was something she called "go time," but not before she made me eat her yellow pan stuff. I was super surprised at how incredible it tasted. It was buttery and sweet. I never had anything like it. When I asked for another piece, I thought Johnny was going to fall off her chair laughing.

As we walked out of the hospital, my feet felt heavy. I didn't get to see Quinn. Johnny and I drove for quite a while. I hadn't been in a car before except for Dr. Katherine's when we went to Kendal's salon, and I was feeling like I was going to throw up again. Johnny pulled over several times and let me get out so I could breathe some cold air. Every time we pulled over she would say it wasn't much farther. As we drove through streets with giant trees and high driveways with houses as big as the castles in my story books, some even bigger, I wondered where exactly Johnny was taking me. All the homes were decorated for Christmas and Johnny must have noticed my delight when she said I would have to see them at night when all the lights were on.

We pulled up to a huge house on a hill. The driveway was up so high Johnny had to drive up pretty fast in order to get to the top. It was made of all brown and gray bricks with red shutters. There were bushes that circled the house, each the exact same size as the next. There were a million windows. It was so tall I had to bend backwards to see the roof. There was a Christmas wreath on the front door, and with the small amount of snow on each window, it looked like a fairy tale house come to life.

"Are you ready?" Johnny asked. She picked up my bag and took my hand, giving it a gentle squeeze. We walked up to the door, which was difficult with the ice that formed, and being on a slant made it worse. Johnny rang the doorbell. I had never heard a doorbell before. It was something awesome and odd to me at the same time. It wasn't a bell or a ring, but music that went on and on.

The door finally opened, and there stood a woman. She was

tall and looked strong, but not in a tough way. She looked like a beautiful queen, a queen with power. Her hair was short and red like roses, just like Athia had described it. Her eyes were light blue, and her smile was friendly and warm. She wore a light blue blouse, a dark-blue skirt and pretty cream-colored shoes with a tiny heel. She was elegant.

"Hello, my name is Ruthie. Welcome to my home," she said, and grabbed the bag from Johnny's hand and waved us in. "Come on in and have a seat. I just put on some tea water and baked some oatmeal raisin cookies."

"It smells amazing in here, Ruthie, and thank you for making my favorite cookie," said Johnny.

Oatmeal? Yuck. Not one of my favorite things.

"Of course, Margaret, don't be silly." Ruthie set down the suitcase and smiled at me.

I remembered I was holding Dr. Katherine's chocolate fudge and explained to Ruthie what she had said, which made Ruthie smile and stare at the fudge.

"What a lovely, thoughtful woman Katherine is. I really need to give her a call," she said.

"Ruthie, you'll be seeing her soon because Tabitha has two meetings a week with her," Johnny said.

"A visit is much nicer than a phone call any day! How exciting!" Ruthie said and began cutting pieces of the fudge while talking to me. "I hope you like tea and oatmeal cookies as well my dear."

She was looking at me with her big blue eyes.

"I had camel tea before," I said.

I must have made a face of dislike because Ruthie laughed and said she was not a fan of chamomile tea either.

"What is your favorite flavor of all flavors?" Ruthie asked.

"I guess I like chocolate and candy canes," I said, still shy and afraid to offend this new person.

"Excellent! Why don't we all sit around the table so you and I can get to know each other, and we'll figure out exactly how you like your tea? I just happened to have peppermint tea, which I think you'll enjoy. If not we'll try something else."

We did just that. She sat down several tiny teacups and told me that she brought out her fine china for this special occasion, having a new guest to keep her company. It gave me a special feeling to sit in her kitchen with its bakery smell. It was painted a light yellow and the floor was made out of what looked like shiny wood. The window at the end of the table was quite large and had a curtain on it with little yellow, blue, and red birds all over them, just like the window across the kitchen above her sink. In the corner was a black thing with one pipe going into the ceiling. Ruthie would open it now and then and place a piece of wood in it and make the whole kitchen toasty warm. She had a machine called a "dishwasher." It cleaned the dishes for you like magic! I couldn't wait to see it work. She must be rich to live in such a place, and I had only been as far as the kitchen.

I had a piece of fudge, which was amazing, and then I tasted my first oatmeal raisin cookie just to be polite. It tasted nothing like the oatmeal I had tasted before! It was very, very good. I could have eaten them all. We tried tea with sugar, with milk and sugar, with only milk, with milk and honey, and finally plain, which was what I liked best. I couldn't believe someone had that much patience to try that many combinations of something to see what one person liked. Johnny sat there as if she had seen it a million times. They laughed and teased each other like I imagined old friends would do, like I hoped to be able to do someday.

"Ruthie, are you a queen?" I asked.

"Excuse me, sweetheart? A queen?" Ruthie replied with a tilt of her head.

"Yes, a queen," I repeated. "This is a castle, isn't it? In most castles there's a king and a queen and sometimes a princess."

She smiled at me and said, "No, dear. I am not a queen, but that would be fun wouldn't it? This is a very large house, I admit. It belonged to my husband's family, and when they passed on, they left it to my husband and me," she explained.

"The king?" I asked, this time tilting my head.

"No, no, Tabitha. There isn't a king or queen in this big old house, but I can see how it must remind a little one of a castle," she said.

"Are you married?" I asked.

"I used to be, and then he got sick and went to heaven. I found myself alone in this huge house. I had no children of my own, so that's when I decided to open my home to children that didn't have anywhere else to go. Suddenly my heart was happy again, and so was I," she replied.

"My mommy got sick and went to heaven too, Ruthie. Maybe they know each other in heaven," I said, trying to make her feel better. I added that she was a very, very special person and that Ruthie would have liked her. "Johnny would have too," I added, not wanting to leave her out of the conversation.

Ruthie looked confused. "Johnny?"

When I explained the story of why I called her Johnny, Ruthie laughed until she had to put a napkin over her mouth and wipe her eyes.

"Oh, I love it! I just love it! She eats so much of that cake that she should be part cornbread by now," Ruthie said.

"Not you too! Really, Ruthie? Don't you fall for that silly name, too!" Johnny said.

"I'm sorry, Johnny," Ruthie said and belted out a loud laugh. I laughed out loud with her, and Johnny just rolled her eyes and sipped her tea as if we were no longer there.

"Well, I see you two are going to get along just fine," Johnny said as she stood up and looked down at me.

She told me she would see me soon, and I wasn't scared like I thought I would be. I was quickly comfortable with Ruthie. There was something about her, a warmth and happiness that she seemed to wear like clothing. We walked Johnny to the door, and Ruthie handed her a cup of something called rock salt to sprinkle on the walk on the way to her car.

"I should make way more money than I do for this domestic labor," Johnny said jokingly.

"I don't want to see my best friend slide into the street on her bum, now do I?" Ruthie asked, grinning like a mischievous child.

Johnny hugged me tight and told me she would be back soon. Ruthie and I watched as she made her way down the steep driveway, shaking the cup of salt as Ruthie had asked. We went back to the table and drank more tea and ate many, many more cookies.

CHAPTER TWELVE

"Well, my child, you must have some questions for me, am I right?" Ruthie asked.

I thought for a few seconds. "How long do you think it will be before I find a home?"

"Why are you in such a hurry to leave? Don't you like my cookies?" She giggled, putting me even more at ease.

I smiled. "I have never been in a real home like yours. It's so clean, warm, and there are no bugs on the walls."

Ruthie smiled and explained that it didn't matter what a house looked like, only love could make a home, nothing else. I told her about the house my mom and I would have had if she had stayed healthy. Ruthie listened to every word and never seemed to be bored by it.

"That's sounds like a lovely home," Ruthie said. "I especially love the colorful planters – a very good choice by you and your mommy."

I was surprised that I so easily talked to her about my mom. I was talking to Ruthie as if I had known her my whole life. It was as easy as eating one of her cookies.

"Would you like to see the rest of the house and the bedroom where you'll be sleeping? Maybe you can give me some decorating ideas," Ruthie said. "I was thinking of changing a few things and brightening the place up a bit. Would you be interested in helping?"

My eyes got huge. "Yes! Of course I would, Ruthie! That would be awesome!"

I stood up and slowly walked behind Ruthie with my bag in hand. We walked into a large room with a huge table that had ten chairs set around it.

"This is the dining room. I used to need this when I had a house full of children, but now it's only used on special occasions," Ruthie said.

It had a soft brown rug that took up the whole room and a light that hung above the table that had hundreds of tiny lights dangling from it. There was a tall cabinet with all shapes, colors, and sizes of plates and glasses. There were pictures of old people on the walls. It was a happy room, a room that you would enjoy eating in and most likely laugh in because you would like the people you were with.

The next room had a couch, two big stuffed chairs, a TV, and a table with a glass top that you could see right through to the floor. It had a fireplace, a big shelf filled with books, and a huge round rug in the middle on the floor. There was a wall covered from top to bottom with pictures of kids, babies, and grown-ups. Some were wedding pictures and others were of whole families. Ruthie saw me staring at the wall and told me that they were all the children she'd taken care of over many, many years. There must have been hundreds of them.

"They may have not been my God-given children, but I know that he certainly sent them to me to watch over in their time of need, just like he sent you to me."

"Wow," was all I could think to say.

Next was a small bathroom, clean and painted a pretty blue. I realized that I hadn't yet seen a Christmas tree. I asked Ruthie about it.

"I haven't put up any traditional holiday decorations in years, except on the front door, because I used to have many children that were raised in several different traditions. Many didn't celebrate Christmas or holidays, and I didn't want to confuse them," she said. "I couldn't keep up with them all and make each of them happy, so instead I always do the same thing. I make a huge Christmas dinner and we celebrate the true meaning of Christmas – not gift giving – but laughter, good food, and being surrounded by those that mean the most in your life."

Ruthie sat me down in her living room and asked what my Christmas traditions were with my mommy. I told her that I didn't have any and how my mom never really cared about it. I added that it didn't matter because Santa never found our address anyway. I shrugged my shoulders. I told her I had always wanted a tree and how the white ones were what I thought heaven was lined with.

"I could see heaven being lined with white trees. That would be beautiful," she said.

She put her arm around me and we made our way upstairs. There was another beautiful bathroom on the right. The hallway walls had beautiful paintings on them. I was looking at one of a little girl on a tire swing that was tied to a tree and daydreaming about how happy she looked when Ruthie spoke, making me flinch and bringing me out my thoughts quickly.

"I like to paint," she said. "It relaxes me."

"You painted all these pictures?" I asked, my eyes huge, which made Ruthie laugh.

"I did, and I'm glad you enjoy them," she said.

Maybe she didn't know how terrific they really were. I knew she must be a queen, like a secret queen, and she had promised not to tell anyone. There was no way this wasn't a castle, either. I was thinking about all the beautiful things that Ruthie had in her house along with more than one bathroom and a magic dish machine.

She asked me if I'd like to take a bubble bath when I was settled.

I looked up at her. "I have never taken a bubble bath."

The closest I had ever come was when Mom tossed me in the fountain. I didn't tell Ruthie about that.

She told me that bubble baths were one of life's most

enjoyable pleasures, and she was sure I was going to love it. We continued our tour down the hallway, and Ruthie showed me where her room was. It was exactly like her: warm and cozy. It had a big bed covered by lots of pillows on top of a thick blanket. There was a picture of a young couple on her wall, and I asked Ruthie who they were. She smiled.

"My husband and I on the day we were married," she said.

They looked so young and happy. She was so beautiful in a long, white dress and veil and he was handsome. They were a perfect looking couple. It made me sad that he was taken from her.

The next room had four beds with white blankets. It was painted blue, and dark blue curtains hung from the windows.

"This is for the boys," she told me.

Then there was a room that had tiny little boxes with bars. Balloons were painted all over the walls.

"This is room for the babies, right?" I asked.

"That's right," she said, and I was relieved that I knew something.

"This is a really cute room. Did you have a lot of babies?" I asked.

"I did, and I still have one now and then when a baby needs a home and a warm bed. I love a baby's smell. It is a little scent of heaven," Ruthie said.

We kept walking. The next room had four beds in it as well. It had pink walls, pink and white blankets, striped pillows and matching curtains.

"For the girls this time," she explained.

Then there was another large bedroom with a big bed, cozy blankets and pretty pictures on the walls.

"This is for adults that might need a warm bed from time to time or a family member when they stop in and stay."

Then she opened another room with one bed with a beautiful, light purple blanket, white walls, flowered curtains, and several pink and purple pillows. It was amazing.

"This is your room. Since I don't have any other children right now, you get to stay in the special room, you lucky girl!"

She took my bag from my hand and placed it on the bed. I was shocked that this was where I was going to sleep, in this amazing room. I couldn't believe it. I was going to be a secret princess, even if just a little while.

"Go ahead and get acquainted with your room, and I'll start your bubble bath for you." Ruthie closed the door behind me.

I touched the bed as if it would disappear. I sat on the very edge, and I could feel the softness of the mattress. The curtains had tiny purple flowers on them, and there was a dresser with real yellow flowers in a vase sitting on top of it. I was dreaming... I had to be. I felt like the real Tabitha from *Bewitched*, as if I had touched my nose and all my wishes had come true. I reached into my bag and took out my mom's picture. I sat it up against the lamp so she could see the princess room.

Ruthie knocked and asked if it was okay to come in.

"Yes, of course. This is the most beautiful room I have ever seen. Are you sure it's okay for me to sleep in it?" I asked.

"Of course it is!" Her eyes went directly to my mom's picture. "Who might this beautiful young woman be?"

"This is my mommy." I said, looking at the picture along with Ruthie. "Isn't she something special?"

"Well she is beauty at its best, Tabitha. Do you need a frame for her picture? I'm sure I have several extras if you would like one," she said.

I hesitated. "I don't want to be a bother..."

"Nonsense! It's no bother at all," she said. "Now, let's get in that tub before it gets cold and all those bubbles go to waste."

I followed her into the bathroom, and I couldn't believe it. We weren't in one of the bathrooms I had seen earlier. We were in another one. She had three bathrooms! In this one, the sink was dark green marble, and the walls were a beautiful light green color with a plant hanging from the ceiling. The tub could fit four or five people, and it was filled with water and bubbles just for me.

"Would you mind staying since I've never taken a bath

before? You could sit and we could talk, maybe, if you don't mind?" I asked, a little nervous about this new experience.

"No one has ever heard me turn down a good conversation!" Ruthie said.

She turned her back yet held my hand and helped me step up and over the tub, not turning around until I was comfortably sitting safely on the bottom of the tub and surrounded by bubbles. I stretched out and sunk down into the hot water all the way up to my neck. This must be what a swimming pool was like. It was magical. It felt like a million tiny fingers were massaging me and the scent was something I had never smelled before. Ruthie said it was a flower named gardenia. I never wanted to get out, not ever.

Ruthie used a plastic pitcher to wash my hair, and I told her all about my haircut at the hardware store and about Kendal. Ruthie was amazed at all of it. After she rinsed my hair, she sat back on a bench next to the tub.

"So what do think about bubble baths?" she giggled.

"Oh," I said. I closed my eyes. "They're better than I could have ever dreamed."

I asked her if she thought I would ever have a normal life.

"Everyone has a different definition of what normal is, just like people have different ideas of what food taste good," she said. "Margaret loves sweet potatoes, but I have a hard time looking at them because I dislike them so much."

"What is 'normal' for you, Ruthie?" I was curious.

"I think to be happy, healthy, and safe, and to love and be loved in return is my personal normal," she replied.

"I like that," I said. And swishing my fingers through the bubbles, "I have another question."

"Go ahead."

"There's this girl," I said and rolled my eyes. "She was in my room at the hospital. She's really banged up pretty bad, and she's the angriest person I've ever met. She was so mean to me! Why was she like that?"

"Sometimes, Tabitha, the meanest and angriest people are the ones that have been hurt the worst, and they're also the loneliest because they won't let anyone past the invisible wall they have built around them," she said.

That made me think about my mom and how she would change from my sweet mom to one I didn't really know. Maybe she was really scared about what was happening to her. I felt so sad that my mom didn't have someone like Ruthie to talk to when she was scared. That she had an invisible wall.

"What is an invisible wall?" I asked.

"It's not a real wall made of bricks," Ruthie said. "It's a way you feel inside. It's a way some people protect themselves from being hurt." she explained.

I thought about that for a second. "Maybe I'll stop and see that girl when I have my appointment with Dr. Katherine. Would that be a bad idea Ruthie? Maybe I can help her climb over her wall."

"It's never a bad idea to show kindness, but you also have to respect someone's wishes of privacy as well," Ruthie said. She smiled and picked up a huge towel. "Now, let's get you out of that tub so you don't catch a chill and then we can get you some dinner."

I put on fresh, new pajamas that Ruthie had waiting for me, and they fit perfectly. Then, she handed me a pair of pink slippers, which also fit, even with my special footpads. Ruthie placed a fluffy purple robe around me and tied it in the front. I now knew what it was like to be a real princess, and I expected to wake up from this dream any second.

Dinner was the first real homemade meal I had ever had. We ate at a table with real plates and silverware. Ruthie served chicken and biscuits. It was made of peas, carrots, and celery mixed with chunks of chicken in thick gravy spooned over flaky biscuits. Ruthie told me to eat slowly, and while I did, she told me funny stories about other kids that had once sat in my chair. I ate until my belly was full. Then I watched Ruthie load the magic machine with all the dirty dishes and turn it on. She said I could open it in the morning and see what the machine had done. All of a sudden, I was so sleepy, so Ruthie took me upstairs and tucked me into my princess bed. I was asleep before my head sunk into the pillow.

The next morning came quickly. When I sat up, the first thing I noticed was the shiny gold frame that my mom's picture was placed in. "Thank you, Ruthie," I said out loud, smiled, and said good morning to my mom's picture. There was a smell coming from downstairs that made me want to run, not walk, to the kitchen.

Ruthie was facing the stove, and without turning around, said "Good morning, glory! How did you sleep? Were you comfy cozy?"

"How did you know I was here?"

She laughed and told me she could hear the pitter patter of a child's feet from ten miles away. When she turned around, she had a plate filled with all kinds of things whose smells made my stomach.

"This morning I made some pancakes, eggs, and breakfast sausage."

She placed the plate in front of me, poured some melted butter and warm syrup over the pancakes, and placed a small glass of orange juice down next to the plate.

"You've never tasted any of this, am I right?"

"No, but I can't wait to," I said with the fork already in my hand.

Ruth laughed and sat her plate down. I closed my eyes after my first bite.

"Who taught you how to cook like this?" I savored every flavor in my mouth.

"My grandmother was teaching me to bake and cook by the time I was tall enough to see the top of the stove," she said with a smile.

I shoved another forkful of everything in my mouth. Ruthie laughed and offered me some tea while she poured herself another cup of coffee.

"Thank you for my mom's frame, Ruthie. It's perfect. It means a lot to me that you did that," I said.

"You are more than welcome, Tabitha. I'm glad you liked it."

When I put my fork down, I had cleaned my plate of every bit of food. Ruthie was shocked.

"Where are you putting all that food? Should I check your pockets?" she said and winked at me. "We'll get some meat on those bones quicker than I thought."

She beckoned me to the magic machine. I opened it and couldn't believe my eyes. Each and every dish was clean, all without a human touching them Ruthie laughed with joy to see how exciting I found her dishwasher to be.

"Today I thought you and I would do some shopping," she said.

I just stared.

"Are you okay, Tabitha?"

I threw my arms around her neck and clung to her. She had made me feel like an ordinary kid, even if it would just last a little while. Without saying a word, Ruthie hugged back as if she knew exactly what I was trying to say.

I told Ruthie about how I got sick when I was in a car.

"Just say the word, and we will pull over for some air, so don't worry about a thing," she said.

We drove to the biggest store I had ever seen. Ruthie said it was called a "mall." It had over 50 stores in it, along with lots of restaurants, coffee shops, and even places that did your hair and nails. It was hard not to run ahead of Ruthie to the entrance door. The first store we went to had paper in every color and design, notebooks, and fancy pens with feathers coming out of the top of them. We came to a section with hard-covered books with blank pages in them, each one with a different color and design on the outside.

"Pick one out, Tabitha. It's to keep your thoughts, good or bad. When you put them on paper, it makes more room in your head," Ruthie said.

I never thought about being able to make room in my head. It was pretty full. I picked out a notebook that was covered in tiny purple flowers, almost identical to the ones on the curtains in my room at Ruthie's. Ruthie walked me over to another section filled with pens. She reached up and asked if I liked one particular pen that had four colors of ink in it so I could change it any time I wanted. A color for each mood, Ruthie explained. You just pushed a button on top and the color changed to blue, green, red, or purple. It was the coolest pen ever.

Ruthie also reached up and grabbed some colored pencils.

"In case you want to draw pictures on some of the pages instead of words," Ruthie said.

And onward we went.

The next store had an upstairs and a downstairs. We stood in front of stairs that moved by themselves and came out of the floor. People would just put their feet on them and the stairs would just carry them away without them moving their feet at all. Ruthie called it an "escalator." I wasn't a fan. I didn't like these stairs, and if I was going upstairs, I wanted my feet to do the work.

"You will be fine, sweetheart! What we need is up these stairs." Ruthie told me. "I will be right beside you."

I flashed back to my mom saying those exact words before that horrible day. I needed to get rid of that thought as quickly as I could. So, I shook my head really hard, hoping that the bad thoughts would be crushed inside my head. Ruthie gave me a strange look and asked me if I was all right.

"No, I can't. I'm sorry, but they scare me," I said.

"There are a lot of new things you're going to see and experience. You can't let fear hold you back, sweetie. I would never let anything hurt you," she said. "If I carry you, will that help?"

I thought about what she said, and then I thought about these stairs that came out of the ground. After a few minutes, I grabbed Ruthie's hand, held my breath, and stepped when she stepped. Up we went, leaving the bottom part of the store behind us while we floated up and up until we reached the top.

"One, two, three... jump," Ruthie said. And I stepped off with her at the same time. We were once again on solid ground.

We walked to the back of the second floor where there

were all kinds of things called "suitcases". I didn't have any suits, so I had no idea why we needed a case for one.

"I thought it would be easier to carry one suitcase than your backpack and hospital bag. This way all your things are in one place. Sound like a good idea?" Ruthie asked.

I finally understood the suitcase idea, but then I was thinking that I would have to get rid of the backpack that my mom had given me. Ruthie must have seen the concern on my face.

"You can put your backpack in the suitcase so it stays nice and safe," Ruthie said.

I walked up and down the aisle trying to find the perfect suitcase. Then I saw it. I picked it up and ran to the end of the aisle to show Ruthie. It was a black suitcase with the bright pink letter T on it.

Ruthie smiled, "That is perfect. Hey, I'm starving. How about you?"

I couldn't believe it after the breakfast I'd had, but I was, too. We stopped at a cafe to eat lunch and do something Ruthie called "people watching." It was exactly as it sounds. We watched people as they went by. It was amazing how many different people passed by in such a short time.

"See how the world is made up, Tabitha? It's filled with so many different types of people. It's a wonderful thing, our world," she said as she ate her chicken salad, and I ate my first grilled cheese sandwich with tomato soup. My tummy was very happy.

Our last store looked like it was made for school. It was filled with workbooks and every kind of crayon, marker, and chalk you could imagine.

"This is a school supply store, Tabitha. You'll be starting school soon, so we're going to stock up," Ruthie said. "And we'll get some crayons, too, just for fun."

I really believe Ruthie bought one of everything from the store that day. We left with three huge bags that were almost bigger than me.

CHAPTER THIRTEEN

Back at home, Ruthie explained how writing sometimes helps get through hard times. She showed me a stack of books similar to the one she bought me. She explained that after her husband died, she still had so much to say to him, so she wrote him letters in these books and pressed rose petals from the first rose bush they'd planted together, along with the first fall leaf she caught in the air each year. There was one for every year he had been gone.

"Fall was his favorite season," she said. "Anyway, I think its tea and cookie time! I made some chocolate chip cookies this morning while you were still sleeping."

The next week went by so fast that it all blended into one huge day. Ruthie worked with me every day with workbooks, flashcards, and short stories that she had me read and then write one page after each one.

The day finally arrived for me to see what a school looked like from the inside. It was nothing like I'd imagined, not at all. In my mind I saw bars on the windows and walls painted gray and covered with roaches. I imagined the children dressed in the same depressing color with dark circles under all their eyes and the blank look like my mom used to have toward nighttime. Mom had always insisted that schools would steal my brain and keep me from her forever, but she was so wrong. The walls were painted bright, happy colors. There were homemade Christmas decorations and cut out snowflakes hanging from the ceiling and taped to the walls. Kids were wearing colorful clothes and laughing and being goofy with each other.

"Am I going to go to school here, Ruthie?" I asked. "Can I start tomorrow?"

"We have a little red tape to get through before I can answer that for sure, Tabitha. I am sure that you will be attending school, but I can't guarantee it will be this one."

We met Mrs. Biren, the person in charge of the school.

"It's very nice to meet you, Tabitha," she said with a welcoming smile, and she shook my hand.

She turned to Ruthie. "It's always a pleasure to see you, Ruthie." She kissed Ruthie's cheek. "Can I show you around today, Tabitha? I hear this is your first time in a school. How exciting for you!"

I nodded. "I would like that very much, Mrs. Biren!"

I asked Ruthie how many times she had been to this school that Mrs. Biren knew her well enough to kiss her cheek and call her by name.

"Oh, many, many times, Tabitha. Too, many times to count, my dear."

The tour of the school was more fun than I had imagined. There was a gym, where I saw kids doing exercises and running after balls. It seemed like so much fun that I wished I could have joined them. Everyone ate lunch in the cafeteria. Kids stood in line with trays and picked out what they wanted from the food laid out behind a huge counter. It smelled really good, not as good as Ruthie's, but still, good. The playground was filled with kids swinging and jumping and running. Some kids were playing on a board that went up and down with a kid on each end.

There was one thing that I had never seen before, and I wanted to ask Ruthie later if we could go back and try it after the tour. There was a big castle, and you could climb to the top with steps and come back down on a slide that came out from the side of it. Kids would run up the steps, disappear for a second, and then shoot out on the slide like a gumball. I had to try it. Mrs. Biren seemed to read my mind.

"Tabitha, would you like to play on the castle for a few minutes while Ruthie and I talk?"

She didn't need to ask me twice! I looked at Ruthie for her approval and I was at the castle in a split second. I climbed up and slid out of the castle over and over until my feet started to burn from all the steps. It was so worth it. I had never had so much fun, and I was blending in as a regular kid! Mrs. Biren said she had no doubt that I would make several friends there.

She led us to a classroom and we sat in the back to watch and listen. The class was reading out loud from a big book, and every time they got stuck on a word, the teacher would help. I looked around at all the kids. They were just like me, except I was extra small, but that was the only difference. I was feeling better about making friends and fitting in. I had never thought school or playing with other kids would ever be an option.

As we left the classroom to continue on our tour, one girl turned and smiled at me, and so did the teacher!

"Mommy," I thought, "I hope you're excited for me. I know you would like it here. I just know it. I love you and miss you so much."

Lastly, Mrs. Biren showed us the art room where Ruthie and I got to be part of the class. They were making the snowflakes that I had noticed in the hall. A girl came over and introduced herself as Emma. I was pretty sure she was older than me. I could tell by the way she acted, and I think she wore a little bit of makeup.

"Can I show you how to make one?" she asked.

I welcomed her assistance and she was very nice. After we folded the paper as small as we could, we took scissors and cut little triangles all over the paper.

"Okay!" Emma said excitedly, "Let's see how you did! It's time to unfold your snowflake!"

Slowly I unfolded my paper. Emma put her hands close

together in anticipation. When I was finished, it was a perfect snowflake, and Emma clapped her hands and congratulated me on my amazing artwork.

"Thank you for your help, Emma," I said happily.

"You're welcome, Tabitha! I hope to see you again soon!" And just like that, she was off to help another kid.

"Ruthie, I'm going to ask in my prayers tonight that I get to come to this school. I really like it here. I really, really like it," I said.

"Well I hope you can come here then," Ruthie said and squeezed my hand.

Emma came back over and told me I could take my snowflake with me as a reminder of my visit to Hobbes Elementary School. It made me smile. After we left the art class, Mrs. Biren wanted to know if I was ready to take a placement test to see which grade I would fit best. It was several pages of a little bit of everything, and I tried to finish it with the correct answers all while being timed. When I was finished, Mrs. Biren said I did very well and she was impressed with my skills. After looking over my test she decided that I would do quite well in the third grade.

I walked out of the school with a huge smile on my face, and I couldn't wait to start school. I couldn't wait to write all this down in my book. I decided green was going to be my happy color, and this was definitely a green day.

CHAPTER FOURTEEN

A few days passed. We went to the hospital for my appointments, and Dr. Katherine was impressed with my progress. Ruthie said it wouldn't be much longer before I was assigned a school. I wanted so much to go to the one we'd visited. I thought about how much excitement my mom was missing not being here. I also thought about how to find a mulligan so I could give her a second chance, like the elf had said. I would find it as soon as I knew what it was.

One night while eating dinner, the doorbell rang. Before Ruthie could get up to answer, the door opened and in walked Quinn. I couldn't swallow my food, I was so shocked to see him standing there in Ruthie's kitchen.

"Well, look at that! Two of my favorite girls having dinner together," he said with his goofy smile.

"Quinn!" I yelled and jumped up from my chair straight into his arms. "You found me! You found me!"

"Well, that's what I call a nice hello, but I knew you were here, silly. You thought you were lost? Never again, you little weirdo," and he hugged me back just as tight as I hugged him.

With me in his arms, he walked over and kissed Ruthie on her cheeks and gave her a huge hug.

"Where in the world have you been?" Ruthie asked.

"I've been busy at work... busy, busy."

Ruthie instantly had a hot plate of pasta and meatballs in front of Quinn, who sat me down next to him. I was trying to figure out why Ruthie had never mentioned Quinn, or why Quinn had never spoken of Ruthie, but why they seemed so close.

"How have you been?" he asked me after he put his hand over my head and complimented me on my new haircut.

"I never got the chance to say thank you for staying with me the night of my awful dream, Quinn. It was very nice of you," I said.

"No worries, sweetie. I needed a nap anyways," and he smiled and winked at me.

I told him everything without leaving out a single detail. I told him about the bubble baths, Ruthie's cooking, and spending the whole day at school.

"That's fantastic that you've experienced all of those fun things already," Quinn said, "Especially school. You're smart, and you'll make lots of friends. You'll love it there – that's the school I went to. "

"You go to Hobbes Elementary, Quinn? Do your parents live near here?" I asked.

"Well, I'm a grown man now, sweetie, and I live in my own house, but yes, I went to Hobbes when I was a child and I loved it," he replied.

"Shamus, do you want more bread?" Ruthie asked Quinn.

"No Mom, I'm good. Thanks, though. This is delicious as usual," he said.

Mom?

"You called Ruthie "Mom"! Is she your mom?" I asked with huge eyes.

"Tabitha, go in the room with all the pictures on the wall and see if you can find anyone that looks familiar," said Ruthie.

Look for someone I knew? Everyone I knew I could count on just about one hand. Quinn had just called Ruthie "Mom"... and she fosters kids... so... and there it was. I saw it. I should have figured it out a half hour ago. Duh!

I slowly pulled the small footstool over, removed the picture from the wall, and walked into the kitchen staring at it. I sat down opposite Quinn, next to Ruthie.

"It's you," I said. "You're on the wall."

It wasn't his eyes or his crazy curly hair that made me recognize him, but that goofy smile.

"Quinn why are you on Ruthie's wall? Is she really your mom, or did something happened to your family?"

He wiped his mouth with his napkin and said, "When I was little, even younger than you, five-years-old actually, my parents, my older brother Ronnie, and younger sister Evie went to heaven while I was at a baseball game with my friend's family. They were the only family I had. My grandparents had already passed on, and I had no aunts or uncles. I was sent here to Ruthie, just like you were. I was her first foster kid. After a year she adopted me and made me her son and part of her life forever."

Quinn saw the look on my face and said, "There's nothing to be sad about, okay? I am blessed to have Ruthie, and yes, what happened to my family was awful, but because of Ruthie I had a wonderful childhood." He reached his hand across the table and grabbed Ruthie's.

"I feel so guilty," I said. "I lost my mom... but you lost... your whole family." I could hardly get the words out. I felt like I was filled to the top of my head with guilt.

"Tabitha, I have Ruthie, and I had an amazing childhood growing up here, and quite a nice one so far as an adult. You can't feel guilty or weigh one loss against another. A loss is a loss," he said.

I didn't know how to feel. "You're always so happy. You're never sad," I said.

"You need to understand that when I was little, I was confused, frightened, and angry. I wanted my family back more than anything. I thought if I hadn't gone to the baseball game, I could have saved them. Ruthie was patient, kind, and helped me through a million feelings I had. I'll tell you a secret: Dr. Katherine was my doctor, too, and she helped me a lot."

I thought my eyes were going to bug out of my head, but after a while, I agreed. I then remembered how she said she had known him since he was a boy. Now I knew why.

"I know I will see my parents, my brother, and sister someday in heaven, but I also know they are happy for me and the life and people I've been blessed with," he said.

"How did you lose them all, Quinn? Did they get weak and unhealthy like my mom and Ruthie's husband?" I asked.

"No Tabitha, they were in a car accident."

I told him that he couldn't have helped them, and that if he hadn't gone to the baseball game, he wouldn't be here with us.

"Without you, Quinn, that would have made us all feel lonely inside and not know why," I said.

Ruthie began to look upset.

"Ruthie, did I make you sad?" I asked.

"No sweetheart, you did just the opposite."

I crawled into Ruthie's lap and asked her if I could grow up there with her, and if she would adopt me, too.

Ruthie placed both her hands gently on my face, "No, my sweet child. I'm much older now, and I only take in children that need a place to live for a little while, not permanently."

I immediately looked at the table trying to find something to focus on so I wouldn't cry.

"I'm too old to raise a child again," she said. "But no matter what, I will always be here for you, and you can stop over and have tea and cookies with me anytime. How's that sound?"

My insides felt like jelly and I wanted to cry. I wanted Ruthie to say "yes" so badly. I wouldn't have to be scared, or wonder who was going to want me, or if anyone would anymore. I would be safe and happy with Ruthie. I already was, and I couldn't imagine after being with Ruthie ever having to go somewhere else. I smiled at her the best I could, not wanting her to know how crushed her answer had just left me, so I tried to ease the worry that I saw building in her eyes.

"If you throw in a bubble bath, you have a deal," I said.

Ruthie's shoulders lowered, and her eyes grew big and bright again. She kissed my forehead.

"You have a deal."

Quinn was looking at Ruthie and me, and reminded me that I might have family out there somewhere that couldn't wait to have me in their lives.

"There are also so many people that have so much love to give to a child, and that is their only wish in life," he said.

I tried to smile and look interested in what he was saying even though I was still a ball of jelly.

"Tabitha, you know what?" he said. He squinted his eyes and leaned forward, just a little. "There are secret passages in this house." His eyes grew wider. He whispered, "They're in the basement."

I started to feeling creepy until he added, "We used to play in them when we were kids, and I'll have to show them to you sometime."

I was relieved and smiled at how he made the basement sound scary and then switched it so quickly to something fun.

"It's been a long time since I've been down there, but it would be fun to see it again. Are you with me, Tabitha? Do you want to go into the secret basement passages where you can be a pirate whose ship is stuck on a rock or an astronaut that's stuck in space?"

I looked at him as if he were crazy, making him laugh at me. I still didn't have any urge to go down there, but maybe I would change my mind.

"Mom, that was delicious as always, thank you. After I let this settle for a few minutes, maybe we should have some of that banana cream pie you have in the fridge."

"How on earth did you know I made that pie, Shamus?" Ruthie asked with her head tilted.

"I am a police officer, Mom! I know everything." He made his hands fly around, acting like a magician.

I was staring again, wondering if he was serious. I sniffed the air a few times, pointed accusingly at Quinn, and said, "You saw Kendal!"

His eyes got huge, and he leaned back as if he were afraid of me. "How did you... how could you...?"

"I can smell Kendal a mile away! She's the only person I know that smells like warmth!"

Quinn narrowed his eyes. "My God, you're right I couldn't figure it out, no matter how hard I racked my brain. It's warmth! She smells like warmth if you could bottle it," he said, running his fingers through his curls.

"Exactly," I said and folded my arms and grinning.

"You can smell her from across the table?"

We just stared at each other. I was waiting for an answer about Kendal and he was waiting for an answer about my smelling ability.

Ruthie broke the silence and said, "Are you two going to talk about smelling things, or are you going to have some pie?"

We both agreed that the best answer was pie.

"So, did she tell you how much fun we had at the salon?" I asked Quinn while we were inhaling the pie, another new food I could add to things I had never tasted, but couldn't wait to have again.

Quinn didn't seem to hear me, so I asked him again. He looked distracted, as if his brain had left for a minute. Then he finally answered.

"She did, and she said that Dr. Katherine really relaxed, so much that one of her employees thought she may have fallen asleep for a second," he said as he laughed.

"It was a great time, "I said. "I still can't believe what she was able to do with my hair. And look at my nails! My toes are the same color, too!" I held out my pink fingers. "Hey, are you boyfriend and girlfriend now?"

"Tabitha, that's a pretty personal question, don't you agree?" Ruthie asked.

"Ruthie, you really need to meet Kendal. She's amazing, and she smells so good," I said.

I closed my eyes and imagined Kendal standing in front of me.

Ruthie smiled sideways, "What makes you think I haven't met her?" She slid off her shoes and wiggled toes that looked like little candy canes, just like Dr. Katherine's fingernails.

"Ruthie! You did meet her!" I said.

"She sent me a very nice note and her business card, so I thought, why not be a little silly?" She giggled.

"Yeah, Dr. Katherine called it whimsical, I think," I replied.

"Kendal's quite a beauty, Shamus, and just as sweet," Ruthie said.

She looked at Quinn, who I suddenly realized hadn't known that his mom had met his girlfriend without him knowing about it.

"So, Kendal and I think St. James is a beautiful place for a wedding." Ruthie took a sip of her coffee.

Quinn dropped his fork and started choking. Ruthie laughed hard and patted him on the back.

"I'm just kidding, Shamus! We said nothing of the sort. Your name wasn't even mentioned," she said. "Although, you're not getting any younger, and I would love to have a grandchild before I'm one hundred." She winked at me.

Quinn gave Ruthie a wide-eyed look, which made her laugh with joy. When he got his composure back, he said that he was too busy and that women need a lot of attention.

"I'm not sure I am ready to have another person share my life completely, not for a while anyways, Mom," he said.

Ruthie rolled her eyes and told him he was up to his ears in nonsense. I suddenly remembered that the Tooth Fairy had come to visit me, and I had never gotten to tell Quinn.

"Quinn! The Tooth Fairy left me a shiny new coin with pretty fairy dust all over it, just like you said!" I told him.

"See, I told you she would come and visit you, silly," he said with a smile.

"I know, but it's hard to believe in a little fairy that carries heavy coins around with her," I told him.

"She doesn't carry them around with her. That's what the wand is for," he explained.

"Oh, I see. That makes more sense now." It finally came together for me.

"So are you?" I asked again.

"Am I what?" he replied.

"Are you going to marry Kendal?"

Ruthie and I couldn't hold back our laughter, watching how quickly his face turned redder than an apple.

CHAPTER FIFTEEN

The next morning I could hear Ruthie and Johnny talking in the kitchen, and just like any other morning at Ruthie's, I could smell something wonderful cooking for breakfast. I said hello to Ruthie and Johnny and gave them both a good morning hug. Johnny said she had good news for me.

As I sat and ate the sausage and waffles that Ruthie set in front of me, Johnny told me that since it was still unknown if I had any relatives, they were unable to put me on the family foster or adoption list just yet. However, school was mandatory and she had signed me up that very morning to start Hobbes Elementary in two days.

I jumped out of my seat with food still in my mouth and hugged Johnny tightly, then danced my way over to Ruthie and spun around in circles, so overly excited that my hopes of going there had come true. They were both smiling and Ruthie was clapping for me because she knew better than anyone how much I wanted to go to that school.

Suddenly I stopped dancing and chewing, and I'm pretty sure I stopped breathing.

She was a giant, almost as tall as Ruthie's shoulder, and Ruthie was pretty tall. She had spiky hair, closer to white than blond, and it stood straight up on its ends. Her blue cotton candy eyes stared out from her black and blue face.

The mystery girl was standing in Ruthie's doorway, staring at me with her arms folded in front of her, her eyes narrowed as if she were a snake ready to strike. I looked at the table quickly and for the first time, noticed a plate of half-eaten breakfast beside my own.

"Tabitha, this is Tori. She'll be staying with us for awhile," Ruthie said. She walked over and kissed the top of the girl's head. Ruthie only had to bend slightly to reach her head. Compared to me, Tori was huge.

"Tabitha, huh? Are you sure Samantha, Darren, and your grandmother Endora aren't around?" she asked with her eyes glued to mine as if she wanted me to turn to stone.

"That's right! I loved that show! I haven't seen it ages," Ruthie said.

"I know somebody who watched it every day," Tori said still looking through me, not at me. Her feelings hadn't changed since we'd met at the hospital, and I still had no idea why.

"Ruthie, Tori was in the other part of Tabitha's room for a little while, but they never met... or did you?" Johnny asked looking at both of us.

"Yeah, we met for a few seconds, but that was it," Tori said. She finally took her eyes off me and sat down to finish her breakfast.

"Tori won't be able to join you at school, Tabitha, for another week or so. But when she does, she'll be in a higher grade because she's two years older than you."

My eyes got a little wider. She was ten years old? Double digits! No wonder she was so tall. She was almost a grown up!

"Unless of course, Tori gets a foster family or adopted by then," Johnny added.

Tori laughed and rolled her eyes. "That's funny, really funny."

"You know, it's possible Tori. You've had wonderful foster families, and you were almost adopted twice. How's that solid food going for you so soon after having your jaw unwired?"

Johnny asked.

Her jaw was wired? Holy moly! Gross! Why? And what was that like? Then I realized that that was why she had talked like a snake through her teeth – she had to.

"Johnny, I'm fine, and I really don't feel like talking about my personal life in front of a stranger, if that's all right with you."

I perked up and smiled. "Hey! You call her by the name I gave her, Tori! It's pretty funny, isn't it?"

Tori looked at me as if I were something she had stepped in. "*Margaret,* can you please leave my private life between you, me, and Ruthie?"

"Yes, of course, Tori," Johnny said. "I'm sorry, and I completely understand."

I wanted to crawl under the table. Tori still hated me and didn't even want to acknowledge that I was excited, unless she was just trying being nasty. My happy home with Ruthie was about to change with no warning, and my feelings of happiness and excitement had already turned to the feeling of invisibility. Tori's overwhelming presence made me feel smaller than I already was. I was afraid I was shrinking before their eyes. No one else seemed to notice Tori's dislike for me. Maybe they were used to different kinds of kids having to meet each other over the years. Little things like Tori seeming to hate me was something they had probably seen a billion times.

Maybe it wasn't a big deal, I thought with a little hope awaking in me. Who knows, maybe by the end of the day we could be talking and stuff. I crossed my fingers behind my back and sat back in my seat at the table.

"Well, I'm sure you'll get to know each other better when Tabitha moves her things into the girls' room along with yours, Tori," Ruthie said.

"No, that's all right Ruthie," Tori said in an urgent voice. "Let her stay in her room. I don't mind being in the bigger room by myself. I like to be alone. Really, Ruthie, it's fine," she said.

"Now Tori, you're not new here. You have stayed with me

more times than I can remember, and you know I'm a stickler for the few rules I have. If there is more than one child in this house, a room will be shared. It helps children get to know each other, and it's good for them. So Tabitha, you will be moving your things into the next room when breakfast is over. I want you to take the bed across from Tori's."

I was no longer hungry as I watched Tori's reaction. She looked as if her breakfast had turned into nails, and her upper lipped turned into a snarl as she chewed. I felt as though I were going to throw up and my knees felt weak.

Once I was done with my breakfast, I excused myself and started the frightening, nerve-wracking, and intimidating journey toward sharing a room with Tori. I picked up my mom's picture and rubbed the cloud necklace that Athia gave me and asked Mom to watch over me. I told her that Tori really hated me and I knew she was used to people being nasty to her, but I wasn't. I told her I would try to act like her and pretend like it didn't bother me. I kissed her picture and gathered what few items I had and walked into the next room where Tori was already standing.

I sat my stuff on the bed across from her as Ruthie had instructed. Tori kept her back to me, which was better because her eyes made me feel uneasy. Then she ruined it and had to start barking orders at me.

"Don't touch my stuff, don't talk to me for any reason, and not just in this room, but in the whole freaking house, got it, toddler?"

I was silent. If she didn't want me to talk to her, I couldn't possibly answer her because that would require me speaking to her.

"I said, got that, toddler?" This time she repeated it in a little louder voice, but I was still silent.

I put my mom's picture on my dresser, placed teddy safely under my pillow, put my clothes away, and exited the room.

"How was that mommy?" I whispered and smiled slightly, knowing I hadn't let her get to me, at least not this time.

Ruthie was putting some cookies in the oven, and Johnny

had already left when I came into the kitchen.

"How excited are you for school, Tabitha?" Ruthie asked with a big smile across her face.

"I can't wait, Ruthie. I can't believe I can actually go there. I'm not sure I'll be able to sleep tonight," not adding that it would be partly because Tori would be sleeping in the bed next to me.

"Do you need any clothes for school or are you all set for right now?" she asked.

I thought about each piece of clothing I had and then what the kids at school had been wearing. I was pretty sure I was all good for right now. I would feel guilty wanting more clothes since I was convinced my mom gave up a lot to get me the ones I had, and Ruthie had done so much for me already.

"All right, but if you do end up needing something, let me know, and we'll get you whatever you need," Ruthie said. "Your teacher will give you a list of school supplies, so we can stop and get them after school."

"Where will Tori be when you drive me to school?"

"She'll be with us, and while you have your appointment, she'll wait with me in the cafeteria, just like you will when she has hers," she said.

"Ruthie, I can take a bus to school. I don't have to have you and Tori drive me every day," I said.

"I like to drive the children that are in my care, sweetie. It's not a bother! I rather enjoy it. When you are fostered or if you have family somewhere out there, I'm sure you will be able to take a bus or do whatever you and your family decides, though. How's that sound?" she asked.

"Isn't Tori old enough to stay home alone for a few minutes?" I asked.

"Tabitha, Tori has been injured quite severely, so, no, I can't leave her alone, at least not for quite a while. I know there's friction between you two, and it doesn't take a rocket scientist to know Tori's the girl in the hospital that was so mean to you, am I right?"

I slowly nodded my head and told her that it was going to

be awful living here now, that it would never be the same. I could feel the tears start, but I fought them off. Ruthie sat in the chair across from me and held my hands.

"Tabitha, the world is full of adjustments that have to be made all the time. Some are good, and some seem awful, but they are all learning experiences. Not everyone is going to be nice. Some people are going to be difficult."

She looked down and stared at my hand.

"It's an angel's kiss, Ruthie. Mommy said they knew I was special, so they kissed me before I was born to remind me," I told her.

"That's a bunch of crap," Tori said from the doorway. "It's a stupid birthmark. Maybe it's to remind you how many people kiss your ass."

"Tori, apologize to Tabitha for talking to her that way, and to me for using cuss words in my home," Ruthie insisted in an annoyed voice.

"I'm sorry, Ruthie. I will try to remember to watch my words," she said.

"And what do you have to say to Tabitha?"

She looked at me, raised her upper lip, and left the kitchen. Ruthie stood up as if she was going to go after her to make her apologize.

"Please, Ruthie. It will only make it worse. I'm fine, really, and I don't care what she says," I said.

"Okay, Tabitha. I'll tell you what. I'll bend the rules this one time. Why don't you grab your things and move back to your room again."

I jumped up and hugged her. "Thank you, thank you, thank you, Ruthie! I would never be able sleep in the same room as her, never!"

"Never say never, my child," Ruthie said as she kissed the top of my head.

I went upstairs and, without saying a word to Tori, who was lying on her bed reading a book, I packed my things and went happily back to my room. I didn't see Tori again until dinner. She walked into the kitchen, said hello to Ruthie, and sat as far away from me as she could. Ruthie made stuffed shells covered with cheese and sauce.

"Ruthie, did you make me my favorite dish on purpose?" Tori asked.

"I did, Tori. It's a welcome back dinner," Ruthie said and smiled as she placed a plate of bread on the table.

"Thank you, that means a lot to me," Tori said and actually smiled, which made her look less evil.

Just before Ruthie sat down, she realized she forgot the Parmesan cheese and went to the refrigerator to get it. As soon as Ruthie's back was turned, Tori unscrewed the top of the salt shaker and poured it all over my dinner. She sat back down, took her butter knife, and slowly slid it across her neck, pointing at me while she did it. By the time Ruthie returned to the table, my heart was racing out of my chest. Not only had Tori ruined my dinner, but I think she'd threatened to kill me if I told Ruthie.

"This is amazing, Ruthie," Tori said as she closed her eyes, enjoying her special dinner.

"Tabitha, don't you feel well? You haven't touched your dinner," Ruthie said.

I stared at her. I didn't know what to do, so I said I had an upset stomach asked if I could be excused.

"You poor thing! Of course, go rest and I will bring you some ginger ale and toast in a few minutes," she said.

I walked upstairs, knowing that my time here would no longer be happy. My feet suddenly felt like heavy bricks. I told my mom what Tori had done at dinner and asked her to help me stay strong like she was when people were mean to her. Ruthie walked in a little while later with a big glass of milk and a plate covered with a towel. She sat down next to me on the bed.

"While clearing your plate, I noticed it looked a little more sparkly than the dish I had first placed in front of you," she said.

Tears began to run down the side of my face, and I tried to hide them from Ruthie.

"You don't have a tummyache, do you, sweetheart? Tori poured salt all over your dinner, am I right?"

I was afraid to say anything because Tori had threatened me.

"Well, I can take care of her while you eat your dinner the way it was intended," Ruthie said, and uncovered a fresh plate of stuffed shells with a slice of her homemade bread. I sat up and took the plate.

"Thank you, Ruthie. I'm starving," I said, wiping another tear that had snuck down my face.

"Sweetheart, I won't have this nonsense in my home. If one child prevents another from being able to eat her dinner, I will take care of that immediately," she said.

"Ruthie, please don't say anything to her," I whispered. "It will be worse for me if you do, honestly. I'm fine. I will be more alert at dinner from now on, that's all," I said.

"Tabitha, you're so afraid of Tori that you feel the need to whisper. I don't find that acceptable in anyway, and you will not have to guard your dinner. This is a house of caring and love, not fear," she replied.

"But she threatened to kill me!" I made the same motion that Tori had at dinner.

"I will be handling this, Tabitha. You will not feel fear in my home. Eat your dinner, drink your milk, and I will take care of Tori." She stood up and said she would be back in just a little while.

Ruthie did return a short time after to clear my dishes.

"Things should be better from now on," she said.

I thanked her, but I didn't tell her that I didn't have any faith at all that Tori was going to change in any way. I told Ruthie I was going to read some of my storybooks before bed. But I wasn't staying in my room because I was afraid of Tori. That's what I told her. She didn't need to know.

The next morning my insides felt gooey, knowing that at breakfast I would have to be at the same table with Tori again. I sat down at the table after I gave Ruthie her morning hug, and Tori walked in seconds after.

"Good morning, Ruthie. Good morning, Tabitha. How is everyone this morning?"

I looked up, shocked that Tori had said my name and was acting so friendly.

But acting was exactly what she was doing for Ruthie. One look in her eyes, and I could see the hatred behind them. I wasn't the smartest person when it came to other people, but I was far from stupid. I ignored her good morning and without breaking eye contact with Tori, I told Ruthie that breakfast smelled wonderful. I reached over and took the salt and pepper shakers off the table and set them on the counter next to Ruthie. I wasn't going to let Tori make Ruthie's house a place of fear, just like Ruthie had said. I loved Ruthie too much to allow Tori to do that.

Ruthie talked through breakfast, and I was so grateful that I didn't have to talk or listen to Tori.

"I received a letter in the mail yesterday saying that your school is starting a new program for children in the foster system, whether they are new to it like you, Tabitha, or have been it for a long time like you, Tori. The children will range from newly transitioned into the system to those who have been adopted. They feel it would be helpful for you children to talk about your experiences and know that others are going through similar things. Maybe you can all help each other and give advice. I think it's a wonderful idea," she said, "Any thoughts from either of you?"

"I think it's great, Ruthie. I'd love the chance to talk to other kids that have been through this," I replied.

"What are your thoughts, Tori?" Ruthie asked.

"Ruthie, I'm not weak, and I don't need my hand held or to be in a room full of bleeding hearts that want their mommies and daddies, so no, thank you. I've done just fine all this time without a dumb class," Tori said.

"Well, I'm sorry you feel that way because I signed you both up for the class every Thursday after school in the gym," Ruthie said.

"Awesome, Ruthie! I can't wait to meet other kids and see

what they have to say about everything," I said. I ate my breakfast and enjoyed every bite.

After breakfast, I was brushing my teeth when Tori walked by and whispered, "I spit on your toothbrush. Enjoy it." Then she walked away.

I turned the water in the sink up high, closed the door, and threw up as quietly as I could.

The rest of the day I went over all the workbooks that Ruthie bought me, wanting to be prepared for the next day. After lunch, I walked by the bathroom. This time, Tori was brushing her teeth.

I walked backwards and whispered, "I scrubbed the inside of the toilet with your toothbrush. Enjoy." And I walked away.

I heard Tori throwing up, and she wasn't quiet by any means. When I went to my room I opened up my dresser to decide what I would wear to school the next day, and I thought I was crazy again. All of my drawers were empty. I looked under my bed and in the closet but found nothing. I yelled down for Ruthie. She couldn't figure it out either and called Tori upstairs.

"Do you have anything to do with the disappearance of all of Tabitha's clothes?" she asked.

"Why would I take her clothes, Ruthie? They wouldn't fit me. I'm normal sized, not a toddler. Besides that would be stealing, and people that steal go to jail," she said.

"Tori, you didn't take Tabitha's clothes?" Ruthie asked her, looking her straight in the eyes.

I could tell Ruthie was saddened when Tori replied, "No." She stared at Tori and bent her head down slightly. I felt so bad for Ruthie that Tori lied to her.

"Well, girls get your coats on. We have to go get Tabitha some new clothes," Ruthie said.

"Why does she need new clothes? She has what she's wearing!" Tori asked.

"She starts school tomorrow, Tori, and because I said to put your coats on. We have to go to the store," Ruthie said in an annoyed voice.

That was a tone I had never heard from her. I knew I should have been happy to get new clothes, but I was trying with all my might not to scream, cry, and beg Tori for my clothes back. I asked her with the calmest voice I had, my only defense to keep myself from crying.

"My mom bought me those clothes, Tori. They're the few things I have left from her, and I know you took them. Please give them back," I asked, never looking away from her eyes.

She smiled at me like the Cheshire cat from Alice and Wonderland, went to her room and dropped some clothes on her bed, and walked out. I looked at them. They were the clothes I had borrowed from the "tall girl" at the hospital when I went looking for my mom. They had been Tori's clothes. Was she trying to get even with me? How did she know I was the one that took them? I could explain if she only asked. I had returned hers, and I could only pray in time that she would return mine. Then I did something I wasn't proud of, but I was desperate.

Ruthie went a little overboard with shopping for new clothes. She bought me several pairs of jeans, three different sweatshirts, and four sweaters, along with so many shirts that I lost track. She held them up against me one after another and said, "I love this one! This is adorable! Oh my, so cute!"

Tori stood by, watching from a distance ticking like a time bomb. I could feel her eyes burning into me like the sun, but I didn't pay any attention to her. I didn't ask for new clothes or to go shopping. We were there because of her. You couldn't tell Ruthie was upset with Tori. She tried to include her in all the conversations, but Tori would have nothing to do with it.

Ruthie continued to shop as if she were being timed. I think she was trying to hide and calm her feelings through shopping. Ruthie knew as well as I did that Tori took my clothes, and she could hold out forever, but school was tomorrow, so shopping really wasn't a choice. I hadn't known Ruthie very long, but I knew enough to know she didn't appreciate being forced to do anything.

CHAPTER SIXTEEN

With bags of clothes in my hands, I made my way up the stairs. I heard the clanging of pans, running water, and the opening and closing of cupboard doors as Ruthie made dinner. I was afraid these clothes would disappear as well, so Ruthie let me put them in her room for now. Even Tori wouldn't dare to go there. While I was setting the table, Quinn came in after giving the doorbell a long, drawn-out ring.

"How are my lovely ladies doing this evening?" he asked with his usual goofy smile.

He was still in his uniform, which meant he had just left work and was hungry for some delicious Ruthie food.

"Why do you insist on ringing the doorbell to your own house?" Ruthie asked with her hand placed on her hip.

"Don't you remember? Installing that was my first big boy job. The guy who put that in let me hold the tools, turn the screws, and then he let me choose the song, which I have to admit I regret a little now," he said, looking toward the door scratching his head.

Ruthie gave him a hug and touched the side of his face. "Yes, Shamus, I do remember now."

When Quinn asked Ruthie why she looked stressed, she explained how we had just returned from doing some emergency shopping and why.

"Tori's here? She's out of the hospital already? That's great news! How's she doing?"

Ruthie just raised her eyebrows and Quinn said, "Oh, I gotcha. Maybe you should give Margaret a call if it gets to be too much?"

"Shamus, I'm not that old, and I can still handle a mean streak in a child. I know why it's there. I am keeping my patience, but getting everyone through it is another thing. I've had plenty of practice. It will be fine, and I don't need Margaret just yet."

Just as Ruthie finished her sentence, Tori flew into the kitchen like someone had lit her on fire. She came after me with her right arm cocked back behind, ready to strike, but Quinn stepped between Tori and I.

"Whoa, whoa! Calm down. Nobody's putting their hands on anybody else in this house! Got it?" he said in a calm voice.

"What did you do with my clothes, you stupid bitch?" Tori screamed at me. She nearly broke through Quinn, but he held her back.

"Tori, you calm yourself right this second and step away from Tabitha, do you hear me?" Ruthie said loudly.

Tori stepped back, still looking like a wild animal.

"I will not have violent behavior or any language like that in this house again, do I make myself clear?" Ruthie said in an even louder voice. That got everyone's attention immediately. "Now do you think you can state your problem in a proper manner with proper language while keeping your hands to yourself this time?"

"Ask her where my clothes are, Ruthie! She stole them once, and now she stole them again. I'm not like her. I don't have bags of new clothes and people kissing my ass every time I turn my head!" she yelled.

"Tori! The language! Please!!" Ruthie said. "Tabitha, do you have Tori's clothes?"

"Yes, Ruthie, I do," I said without any emotion in my voice.

Quinn and Ruthie spun to look at me, both shocked by my confession. Tori tried to jump again, but Quinn put his hand up. She sat down, but very slowly, giving Quinn a death stare the whole time.

"Hey, cop. Why you don't you do your job and arrest the thief? She just admitted she stole my clothes again," Tori said.

"I didn't steal your clothes from the hospital," I said. "I borrowed them so I could leave the hospital and go to my mom because I didn't have any clothes. I returned them, and that's how you got them back. I took your clothes this time, yes, but you won't get anything back until I get my mom's clothes back."

Then there was a knock, and Johnny was there. She couldn't have had more perfect timing.

"Hi everyone!" she said in a happy voice, then as she looked around, "What in the world is going on?"

Ruthie filled her in. She was shocked that Tori would steal my clothes, come after me, use more cuss words in Ruthie's house than ever before, and that I was keeping Tori's clothes "ransom," as she called it.

"That's enough of this nonsense!" she said. "Tori, go upstairs and get Tabitha's clothes, and when you come back down, Tabitha will bring you yours."

"I'm not giving her anything," Tori said. "I don't have any clothes but the ones I'm wearing, you piece of..." Feeling Ruthie's gaze upon her, she stopped herself from whatever she was about to call me.

"That was all right for me though, wasn't it?" I asked. "You don't have school tomorrow, Tori. You'll be just fine," I said, trying to use a normal voice.

Then I saw it: The anger in Tori, as if an actual firework had gone off behind her eyes.

"News flash, loser! Those clothes came from a woman, but it wasn't your precious mommy," Tori said, talking in a baby voice. I knew she was trying to make fun of me. "She wasn't your mother!"

Johnny grabbed Tori's arm and tried aiming her toward the

door. "Let's go, Tori. You can stay somewhere else instead of Ruthie's."

Tori shook her arm out of Johnny's grasp. "What? They didn't tell you, toddler? That she wasn't your real mommy? She was just some drug addict that wasn't even related to you. You're so dumb you thought she needed a checkup and some Band-Aids!"

She pretended to rub tears out of her eyes with both hands like a baby. "She probably stole you like you stole my clothes or found you in the garbage where you belong!"

The feeling in my legs and arms began to go numb and my mouth was becoming dry as dirt.

Quinn got in front of Tori and said, "That's enough, Tori. She doesn't deserve this, attacking her like this. No one is going to treat anyone else like that in this house, nobody. Do you understand?"

Ruthie stood there, leaning with one hand against the counter, not believing what was happening in front of her.

Tori turned on Quinn. "You know what, cop? This is Ruthie's house, so arrest her," she said, pointing to me, "or leave."

Quinn got a little closer and said, "It's me, Shamus, Tori. Don't you remember me? I used to bring the puppies over for you kids to play with all the time." His voice sounded hurt, almost surprised.

She just looked at him, really looked at him, as if he had just walked in. Then she looked back at Ruthie as if for verification, but still didn't acknowledge Quinn. Johnny was trying again to remove Tori without any luck. Ruthie walked over and put her arm around my shoulders.

It was all happening so fast. What was she saying about my mom not being mine? I was shrinking smaller and smaller, and soon no one would be able to see me at all. I could barely get my thoughts to stop spinning in my head. I reached out and touched the back of Quinn's arm.

"Quinn, she's not telling the truth, right? She's lying and being nasty. That's all, right?" I asked in barely a whisper.

Quinn turned to me and started to bend down so he could be eye to eye with me. I put my hand out to stop him.

"Put your hand on your heart and tell me she's lying, Quinn. That's all I need from you. Please?" I pleaded, my voice fading slowly along with the rest of me.

He just stared at me with sad eyes. I had gotten sad eyes my whole life, and I hated them. I tried to grab his arm to place it on his heart for him, but I couldn't make him to do it.

I couldn't shatter again. I couldn't go to that lonely, confusing place that you go to when you shatter. If they have to pick up all your pieces twice, can they put you back together a second time?

"Mommy, you were mine and I was yours," I said inside my head. "We were a team. I love you, no matter what," and I rubbed the cloud that hung from my neck.

She would have never let anyone get to her, no matter what she heard strangers say about her as they passed by us on our walks. She would have never let them break her. I felt a sudden strength, or at least I didn't feel like I was going to shatter anymore. I might be shaken, but I wasn't going to let Tori bully me anymore, or she would never stop. She would own me every day, making me afraid in my own skin, and I didn't want to live like that. I had to make my mom proud, and I had to make Tori know that I wasn't going to be her doormat. I squeezed Ruthie's hand, and I walked past Quinn and towards Tori.

"I don't care Tori," I said. "I don't care what you say about my mom because I know the only thing that matters is that she loved me more than I could ever explain to someone like you. Who she really was doesn't matter to me because she'll always be right here with me," and this time I was the one who put my hand over my heart.

"Tori, you might be taller, meaner, and older, but you're nasty. You're a nasty person because you like to hurt people. That just makes you sad. I'm happy about a lot of things. I got to have my mom for eight years, then I got to meet all of the special people that are in my life now, but do you want to know what I'm happiest about Tori?" I said.

I got dangerously close to her face, to where I could feel her breath on mine.

"I'm happiest of all... because I'm not you," I whispered.

I stood up and told Ruthie I was going to take a hot bath if she didn't mind, and I walked up the stairs feeling as if someone had taken over my brain and my body for the last few minutes. Tori's words were jumping around in my head, not making any sense at all. I decided I would write what happened in my book after a nice bubble bath. Red – that was the color that I would use for anger, or maybe I would use purple for confusion.

When I got upstairs, I stepped into the first bathroom that I never saw anyone use and grabbed Tori's clothes out of the tub. I left them at the top of the stairs. I didn't want to be like her, I wasn't that way. My heart was beating funny and it was getting hard to take a deep breath. I could hear talking downstairs, but it seemed so much farther away than that. As I got my pajamas out of my dresser, I talked to my mom about how she was mine, and no matter what, she would always be mine. I explained that Tori that was the crazy one. I turned and looked at my mom's picture as I always did.

Suddenly someone was screaming and crying. I was on the floor, and Ruthie's voice was there, and someone had both hands on my shoulders trying to get me to look at them. Suddenly they grabbed my face and made me look up, forcing me to have eye contact with them. It was Ruthie.

"Tabitha it's going to be all right. We're going to get another picture exactly like that one, do you understand?" she said. "It's just a picture."

"My mom... she's in so many pieces in the glass," I said. "Blood again, Ruthie." I held up my hands. They were shaking, and I screamed. It was starting all over again. "She died! How can she be bleeding again?"

"Oh my God... I didn't mean to!"

Someone was crying from somewhere far away.

"I didn't know this would happen! Honest guys, I'm so

sorry! I didn't... let me help! Tabitha, I'm so sorry!" the faraway voice screamed.

"She's all broken, Ruthie. I have to put her back together. She died... How she can be bleeding again? I don't understand," I said.

"Tabitha, I will not let this happen to you. God as my witness I won't," Ruthie said as she brought my face upwards to hers again.

Ruthie never stopped looking into my eyes, never letting me look away from hers for a second.

"This is not your mommy's blood. She did die, sweetheart. This is your blood!" Her voice was calm, strong. "You cut your fingers on the broken glass." She held my fingers up so that I had to look at them. "See? These are your fingers! Now look at the glass from the frame. It cut your fingers. This is not your mommy. It's just a picture, and it's all torn up, but we're going to get you a new one. Now tell me what I just said."

"This is my blood. I cut myself on the glass," I replied.

"Say it, Tabitha!" Ruthie said in a loud, demanding voice.

"Mom, this is too much for you. LET me..." someone said.

Ruthie told me to repeat it again.

"This is my blood. I cut it on the glass," I said, repeating her words.

Ruthie never allowed me to break contact with her eyes.

"Now, say, 'This is just a picture and I can get another one.'" She handed me several pieces of my mommy's face.

We did this over and over, maybe hundreds of times. At last I started to come out of my deep dark fog.

"I'm tired, Ruthie," I said.

"I don't care!" Ruthie said. "Tell me what happened to your mommy."

"She died, Ruthie," I replied.

"What happened to your fingers?" she asked.

"I cut them on the broken glass from the frame," I replied once more.

"What are these?" she said, holding pieces of my mom's

face in her hands.

"They're pieces of my mom's picture that got torn up, but we can get another one right, Ruthie?"

She hugged me and began to cry. She said in her gentle loving voice, "It's going to be all right. You're going to be all right, my sweet child. Thank you God," she said.

"Please don't cry, Ruthie. It's all going to be all right," I said, almost falling asleep mid-sentence. I was being lifted up. I was so tired.

I woke up in the room I loved so much that I had before Tori came to Ruthie's house. Ruthie and Johnny were in chairs next to my bed, and my hands had a few Band-Aids on them. I lay there for a few minutes and tried to remember what had happened. I slowly whispered Ruthie's words over and over again. I looked at the table by my bed.

There in its frame was the picture of my mom.

I must be crazy again. My head problem was back. Nothing had happened to the picture like I'd thought.

"Well, morning glory," Ruthie said.

"Why are you both sleeping in chairs? Aren't you uncomfortable?" I asked.

"We're fine, sweetheart. We weren't sleeping," she said. "We were having our coffee and checking up on you. How are you feeling?" She reached over and touched my shoulder.

"I have to back to the hospital, Ruthie. I'm crazy again. I thought my mom's picture got torn up, but it's right there. And why do I have Band-Aids? My head's messed up again," I said through my tears.

"Don't cry, sweetheart. You're not crazy and you never were."

Ruthie explained everything and told me that Quinn had stopped by early that morning with a new copy of my mom's picture and a glass for the frame. I felt relieved that I wasn't crazy, but it didn't help that I had gotten confused and gone to a dark place again. But Ruthie had already spoken to Dr. Katherine about this.

"She said it isn't uncommon for a child to become

confused like you did last night when they have been through something traumatic. She would like to have you come to the office later though so she can talk with you about what happened and answer any questions you might have," she said.

"Ruthie, how did you know how to get me to come back from the dark place I was in?" I asked, wanting to jump out of bed and hug her until she changed her mind about adopting me.

"I've had a lot of children who have had different problems and have had struggles with dark places, sweetheart. I haven't left a child stay in their dark place, and I wasn't about to leave you now, was I?" She stood kissed my forehead.

"Thank you, Ruthie, you know, for caring so much..." I looked at her and begged her with my eyes to say, "Tabitha, would you like to live with me until you're a grown up?"

Instead she said, "Tabitha, you never have to thank me for caring about you, child." She reached out and put her hand on mine.

That wasn't what I was asking her to say. Maybe I needed to practice talking with my eyes.

"I missed my first day of school, didn't I?" I asked. Tears started to build at the thought.

"It's all right. You can go tomorrow. One day won't make a difference," Ruthie said, waving her hand in the air.

Ruthie always seemed to know what to say.

"Johnny, you haven't said a word. Are you all right?" I asked.

"I'm fine, Tabitha, and I agree with Ruthie that you're fine as well. I'm very sorry for what Tori did to you yesterday, and if it helps, she feels horrible as well," she said.

"Tori did that to my mom's picture? Why? Why does she hate me so much? I don't get it. I've never done a thing to her," I said, staring at Johnny in hopes that she might be able to give me an answer.

"I don't know Tabitha. Tori is dealing with a lot of things. She was close to death only a few weeks ago, and I know her head isn't quite right yet."

As Johnny was talking, I noticed all of my clothes Tori had taken were returned and sitting on my dresser.

"Is she still sleeping?" I asked.

Johnny looked surprised and confused at the same time.

"No, Tabitha, Tori was moved to another transition home last night..."

I had a lot of questions that I knew I needed to save for Dr. Katherine, my confusion and feelings doctor.

"I did ask her how she knew the things she said about your mom," Johnny said. "She told me a particular nurse was talking while getting your bed ready next to Tori at the hospital before you switched floor. The curtain was closed, and I suppose the nurse made a horrible mistake and spoke about something she had no right to. I will address the situation so this never happens again. A child's privacy is as important as an adult's, and everyone has to understand that," Johnny said.

"Why didn't she seem to remember Quinn? They lived in the same house for a long time, didn't they?" I asked.

"When we were leaving last night she did look over at Shamus sitting on the couch and said, 'I remember you, Shamus. You always picked me to watch the puppies for the whole weekend,'" replied Johnny. "He always brought a puppy home when he volunteered with animals. Tori and the other children had a wonderful time naming and walking them. The child that was voted 'most well behaved' that week was the lucky one because that meant Shamus would leave a new puppy with them to be in charge of for the whole weekend. It was almost always Tori."

The house phone rang and Ruthie left.

"Johnny, it must be really hard to be responsible for a lot of kids, deciding where they should live and with who, huh?" I asked.

"Sometimes it can be stressful knowing my decision will affect whether a child will be happy, yes, but I love what I do," she said.

"Well, I bet you're awesome at it too," I said, trying to make her smile again.

"Thank you, Tabitha, I appreciate that," she said.

"I mean, I hope you are because my happiness kind of depends on you and if you mess up well..." I gave her a weird face, and she finally laughed with her shoulders relaxing away from her ears.

Ruthie came back in. "Margaret can I talk to you? There's someone on the line looking for you."

Johnny patted her pockets. "Where in the world is my cell?" She looked around the chair where she had been sitting. "It must have slipped out of my pocket." She left to get her phone call.

"Is everything okay, Ruthie?" I asked.

"I'm fine sweetheart. Are you hungry? I think we should go downstairs and have a nice breakfast."

When we came downstairs, Johnny was already gone. She never said goodbye.

CHAPTER SEVENTEEN

Ruthie and I were sipping hot chocolate before breakfast when I decided to talk to her about something that was weighing on my mind and my heart.

"Ruthie? Can I tell you something that might sound a little strange?" I asked.

"Tabitha, I don't think you could tell me anything that would sound strange at my age, but of course you can tell me anything, sweetheart," she replied.

"I asked my mom a million times why we were so different. She tried to tell me... twice... before she, you know, went to heaven. We could never talk to anyone or have any friends, and if anyone stopped us on the street, I was to keep walking and pretend that we didn't know each other. She was always afraid that someone was going to take me away or separate us."

I was relieved to talk about it and get it off my chest. It was something I think had been hiding in the back of my mind for a little while, but it was finally ready to come out."

"Ruthie, is it possible that when my mom was getting really sick, she was trying to tell me that she wasn't my mom? I never celebrated my birthday, Ruthie. I don't even know when it is because she said we had to wait for a special guest. Could she have been waiting for one of my parents to come to back?

What was she so afraid of? People don't just come up and separate moms from their kids, do they Ruthie? When they're just having a walk?"

"No, Tabitha, they don't," she said.

"What did Tori mean when she said my mom was a drug addict?" I asked.

"You have been doing a world of thinking, haven't you?" Ruthie asked. "I can't answer those questions for you because I don't know anything about your mommy or your life before except what you've shared with me. I know that you had quite an awful experience."

She reached over and grabbed a pen and paper from the drawer next to her and helped me write down all my questions and thoughts to give to Dr. Katherine at my appointment later that day.

"Now, I don't know about you, but I am starving, and my tummy says it's a waffle morning. Does your tummy agree?" she asked.

"Let me ask!" I said, pretending to talk to my stomach. "Yes, it said it's a waffle morning, Ruthie!" And we both started laughing.

After breakfast I bathed and got ready for my appointment with Dr. Katherine. I was feeling guilty about the relief I had that Tori was no longer at Ruthie's, but I still wondered why she hated me. As I was walking to my room from the bathroom I overheard Ruthie on the phone.

"Margaret, what do you mean you still haven't found her? It's been hours! It's freezing outside. ...Tori doesn't know anyone around here, does she? .... Mmm hm... Mmm hm... When is the last time they saw her? ... Did something happen there? .... God have mercy! Keep me updated. I'm worried sick."

I sat on my bed. I didn't know how to feel. Tori had been nothing but nasty to me. But I also had no idea how Tori was feeling. Maybe she was confused like I was, and she was out looking for someone who wasn't there anymore. She could be stuck in a dark place and couldn't get out, or maybe she didn't believe anyone could help her.

Then I thought about how cold it was outside, really cold. I had no idea what had happened to her to have her be so bruised and cut up, not to mention how her head was wrapped at the hospital. Johnny had said she almost died. I looked at my mom's picture and asked her to ask God, whom she probably saw a lot now, to please help them find Tori, to let her be safe and warm. Then I told her again, just so she was sure, that even though she might not be my real mother, I still loved her and she would always be my mom.

"Tabitha, are you all right?" Ruthie asked from the doorway, startling me out of my thoughts.

"Ruthie, I'm sorry, but I heard you talking on the phone, and I know Tori went missing," I confessed.

"Now, Tabitha, you should never listen to another person's private conversation." Her frown softened. "But we have to keep believing that Tori's safe and sound and they will find her soon. Now let's get you ready for your appointment."

I told Dr. Katherine everything that I talked about with Ruthie. She asked me how I would feel if any of my theories were true. I was honest and told her that in my heart I kind of already knew that they were. She looked up from her writing.

"Does that bother you?" she asked.

Dr. Katherine always told me that if I wasn't honest about my feelings, I would never be able to go forward. I took a deep breath.

"It would have bothered me a lot before I met Ruthie and Quinn. Quinn still loves his mother, who went to heaven, but Ruthie is his mom and he loves her very much. My mom loved me and I loved her. No matter what, she will always be my mom," I said and shrugged my shoulders. "I know she didn't take me, though. She was always waiting for a special guest to arrive. Maybe one of my parents?"

"I'm very impressed, Tabitha. Your thought process is very grown up for an eight year old," the doctor said. She tilted her head as if to make sure I was really all right.

Then we talked about what happened when I cut my

fingers on the broken glass from my mom's picture and how confused I was. My brain was still adjusting to what I had experienced and what I had seen, Dr. Katherine explained.

"You're still healing Tabitha, and it won't happen overnight. Look how far you've come with your nightmares – Once you're awake, you now know you're safe and that they were only bad dreams. This was your first experience with confusion since you left the hospital, and thanks to Ruthie's experience with many children over many years, she knew what to do. Our sessions together will also help you along the way," she said. "You'll be just fine."

I nodded. Her words made me feel calm.

"What else can we talk about today?" she asked.

I thought about the things Tori had said about my mom.

"What is a drug addict?" I asked.

Dr. Katherine hesitated. I told her why I wanted to know. So, she patiently explained how drugs take over a person's body and mind, making them sick and changing the way they look and act. Even though the drugs make the people sick, they can't stop taking them because the drugs have a very powerful hold on people. They are like prisoners to the drugs, Dr. Katherine said.

I thought about my beautiful fragile mom being a drug prisoner and began to cry. I imagined the drugs like tiny people, smaller than the Tooth Fairy, dressed in black with sharp ugly teeth dancing around inside my mom's brain, holding a gun at her and making her take more of them. I pictured them telling her to act mean, even though she didn't want to. I thought about how they colored her teeth yellow and brown and dark bluish grey under her eyes. Maybe every morning when I saw her throwing up, she was trying to get them out of her, but they kept hanging onto her insides and wouldn't let go.

"Why don't they just stop or get someone to help them to get away from the drugs?" I shook my head. It just seemed so simple.

"It's a little harder than that, sweetheart," Dr. Katherine

said. "Most think they're handling their lives and their addiction just fine until it's too late. They become too weak to get help, and that's when their bodies stop working."

"Then they go to heaven like my mom," I said. I stared at my feet, remembering how weak and thin she had become, barely able to get out of bed.

"You know, sweetheart, I'm sure if she could have, your mom would have never started taking drugs so she could stay healthy for you."

"I know she would have too, Dr. Katherine."

I felt sad and missed my mom a lot. I wanted to give her a hug and tell her I understood that it wasn't her fault. My brain felt clean, and I was thankful to get my thoughts out and have my questions answered. I felt stronger and a little smarter each time I left Dr. Katherine's office. I liked that feeling.

She is a good witch after all, I giggled to myself.

When we were leaving, Ruthie and I saw Quinn and another officer standing with a man who had his hands behind his back. He was beat up pretty bad. When Quinn saw us, he frowned. He looked at me and then at Ruthie as if asking a silent question from all the way across the hall. Ruthie gave him thumbs up, and his frown instantly cleared. He winked and then went on his way. Sometimes I forgot he was a real policeman and not just our Shamus Quinn.

As Ruthie and I were walking towards the exit, an old woman walked passed us, slowing as she walked by, and staring at me the whole time. Ruthie noticed and stopped walking.

"Can we help you with anything?" Ruthie asked in a friendly voice.

The woman was leaning on a walking stick, and looked much older than Ruthie. Her earrings made her earlobes droop and her face was one large wrinkle. She jerked her head up quickly as if someone had woken her.

"Oh my goodness! I apologize," she said. Her cheeks reddened. "I just... I just saw the child, and she reminded me of a child I knew years ago, when she was less than knee high. She had that same olive skin and beautiful green eyes. It's just something else, I'll tell you. I do apologize."

Her eyes rested on me for another moment. "Well, where in the world are my manners?" She held out her hand to Ruthie. "My name is Olivia LaPage. I volunteer here on Mondays and Wednesdays." She held out the badge that hung from her neck.

Ruthie shook her hand and introduced herself. I felt like a big person when I reached out my hand too.

"I'm Tabitha Sullivan," I said. I loved the way it sounded and couldn't imagine getting bored with introducing myself.

Olivia's smile left her face. "Did you say Sullivan, child?"

She looked down at her hand, still holding mine, the one with the angel's kiss.

I watched the color drain from her cheeks, leaving them as white as her blouse. Ruthie grabbed her elbow and helped ease her into the nearest chair.

"Tabitha, I need you to sit over there on that bench where I can see you," Ruthie ordered in an urgent tone.

I watched the nurse bring the woman a drink of water. Ruthie listened intently to what the old lady had to say. I couldn't hear what they were saying, but I could see that Ruthie just stared at the woman as she spoke, looking up only occasionally at me and flashing me a quick, nervous smile. The old woman shook her head and placed her hands over her mouth. Ruthie was suddenly holding the woman's hand. I wanted to yell to Ruthie not to get so close to a stranger, but I knew that Ruthie always seemed to know exactly what to do and when to do it.

After a while, I saw Ruthie pick up her phone, dial, and talk. Shortly after, Quinn came walking quickly down the hall with a serious look on his face, like someone had eaten his last piece of pie. He waved and smiled at me, then went back to his serious face. Ruthie stood up as Quinn walked over to them. Was he going to arrest that old lady? Did they have special jails for old ladies? I mean what could she have done? Steal earrings? They really loved their earrings.

Then Ruthie smiled and hugged the woman. Quinn took

her spot on the chair while Ruthie walked back to me.

"What's going on Ruthie? Why did I have to sit way over here? Why did Quinn have to come? Is he going to arrest her? Why did you hug her? You should never get that close to a stranger!"

Ruthie stopped walking and looked at me. "How on earth did you just say all of that in one breath? I'm dizzy now just from listening to you! Let's find a nice place for lunch, and I will answer all your questions as best as I can. How's that sound?"

She was going to answer all my questions.

I didn't know if I would ever get used to anyone saying that.

While we ate lunch, Ruthie kept her word and answered all my questions.

"She became dizzy because she probably didn't have enough to eat or drink this morning. I was talking to her to make sure that she was talking clearly and didn't need medical attention. No, Shamus was not going to arrest her, and yes, I did call him because I was getting very hungry and I didn't want to leave her alone. She had more to talk about and I didn't want to have you wait any longer. I gave her what is called a 'lovely to meet you hug.' Anything else I can answer for you?" she asked.

"Yes. Why are you fibbing? There's a whole hospital filled with nurses. You didn't have to call Quinn. If she was just some lady, you wouldn't have been so interested in what she had to say." Ruthie's eyes went wide, but I couldn't stop now. I had one more thing to say: "And that hug you gave her was a 'thank you' hug, not a 'lovely to meet you hug.' I've had a lot of hugs since I got here, so I'm an expert."

I took a deep breath. "So, Ruthie, why are you fibbing?"

"I did not tell you one fib," Ruthie began. I frowned, so she continued. "Now, did I tell you everything? No. There are some things I can't tell you until I hear from Shamus. We need to make sure that woman was telling the truth and that she is right of mind. But, if it eases your mind, sweetheart, nothing that she said was bad or scary in the tiniest bit."

"All, right Ruthie." I looked down at my plate. "I'm sorry I called you a fibber."

"I won't think twice of it," she said and stole a fry off my plate.

We both giggled and went back to munching on our lunch.

"So while I was waiting for you for- ev- er," I said, rolling my eyes at Ruthie. She smirked back at me. "I was thinking about Tori. Maybe she knew that I'd stayed in a tent for a long time. She seemed to know other stuff. She might have known that I was warm and safe there."

"What are you getting at?" Ruthie asked.

"Well, maybe they should look at all the places nearby that sell tents. I saw a bus when we were at the mall. I mean, you never know, maybe she took a bus to the mall, and maybe there was a tent set up there," I said.

"That's sounds like a great idea! If they haven't already looked, I'll mention it to Shamus," she said. She looked at me for a moment before speaking again. "Tabitha, when they find Tori, what would you like to happen?"

"I know it sounds strange, but I sort of want her to come back to your house because it's kind of her home. I mean, it sounds like she's been there a lot, and you guys know each other really well. You helped me from going to my dark place, so maybe, if that's what's wrong with Tori, you can help her, too," I said. I toyed with my food before looking back up at Ruthie. "She told Johnny to tell me she was sorry, so maybe it won't be as bad as before?"

Ruthie just smiled and stole another fry.

CHAPTER EIGHTEEN

I was finally at school and loving it. Everyone was nice and all the classes, especially art, were fun and interesting. My teacher, Mrs. Kaydot made learning really fun. She talked a lot about different things that the other kids had been learning about before I arrived. For me, just about everything was new, and I couldn't get enough. The rest of the week went by way too fast. I was looking forward to the week when the special class for foster kids would start.

There was still no word from Tori. Her picture was on "missing child" posters everywhere, reminding me of when mine was too. Her hair was long and curly on one side of the poster and short and spiky on the other side, the way I knew her. She looked like two different people. The only similarity was her blue eyes that seemed to jump from the picture. They were actually beautiful when she wasn't glaring.

Johnny was at the house a lot over the weekend. She didn't look very good. She had dark circles under her eyes, and they seemed puffy like she hadn't slept. I got scared and asked Ruthie if Johnny was a drug addict. Ruthie gave me the oddest look until I described what Dr. Katherine had told me about drug addicts: the dark eyes, looking thinner, and weak. Ruthie took my hands.

"Sweetheart, I understand how you could see those signs on Margaret, but I assure you that she is only exhausted from looking for Tori and is overcome with worry. Tori has been a part of our lives since she was only two or three years old, and it's very hard on all of us."

"It's my fault, isn't it?" I asked. "If I'd never come here, Tori would still be here."

"Tabitha, you are exactly where you should be, and I don't want you to think that ever again, understand? Tori's own actions were what removed her from here, no one else's."

Whenever Johnny came over, I left her and Ruthie in the kitchen alone so they could have grown up talk. I had an icky feeling in my tummy about Tori, and I didn't even know her or really even like her too much, so I couldn't imagine what Ruthie and Johnny were feeling. The weekend came and went without any news about Tori, and Ruthie was beginning to show the toll it was having on her too. She now had dark circles and I hadn't seen her eat much all weekend. I was worried about everyone.

School was a happy place for me, but now I was having a hard time enjoying it when I knew how horrible everyone I loved was feeling. Then there was this one stupid boy named Sydney. One day he called me a pollywog when the teacher wasn't listening. Then he started doing that every day. I didn't even know what a pollywog was until two girls, Jessy and Samantha, told me.

"It's a baby frog before it gets big," Jessy said.

"Yeah, I think he's making fun of how small you are," Samantha added.

It was only my fifth day, but I think I could call them my friends. I wasn't sure how that worked.

"I wouldn't let him bother you. He's just a bully and always picks on kids that are smaller than him," Jessy said.

"That can't be too hard. He's pretty big. Why does he have a problem with me?" I asked.

"It's probably just because you're new and small, and he's a jerk," Jessy replied.

That afternoon we were allowed to go outside because it wasn't too cold and most of the snow was gone. There were a bunch of us girls just standing around talking when someone walked by me and hit me with their shoulder so hard that I would have fallen to the ground if Samantha hadn't caught me.

"Aw, what's the matter? Did baby pollywog almost fall down and go boom?" I heard the dumb Sydney boy say.

I had enough. I didn't care how big he was, I wasn't taking that stuff from anybody. I knew if I did, it would never stop. So I walked up to him as quick as I could, grabbed his shoulder from the back, and spun him around.

"Why do you think it's all right to pick on another person?" I asked.

Suddenly I was yanked backwards. I spun around and saw a tall kid in a green hoodie. The hoodie was pulled low over his head as he stepped past and stood between me and Sydney. When Sydney saw the kid, his eyes got really wide and he tried to back away, but the slide was in his way.

"Excuse me!" I said, "You shouldn't pull on people either! Do you hear me? Excuse me?" I said.

I grabbed the hooded kid's arm. He turned and looked down at me. Only it wasn't a he. My mouth dropped opened.

"Tori?" I whispered.

"I'll be with you in a minute," she said.

Tori got real close to Sydney's face. The kids near Sydney backed away. Tori whispered to him, and Sydney's face turned red. When Tori backed away, Sydney was crying. He wiped his face and looked at me.

"I'm really sorry, Tabitha," he said. His voice blubbered as he spoke. "I will never, ever pick on you, talk to you, or upset you in any way again."

Then he turned to all the kids standing in the playground and yelled at the top of his lungs.

"My name is Sydney Overton, and I'm a stupid bully. I pick on kids that are weaker than me because I am a bully and bullies suck. I will never pick on anyone in this school again. I swear to God."

As he walked away, some kids just stared in shock, but a few others teased him.

He turned on them and yelled, "Oh yeah? Do you want Tori Galloway to stick your head all the way up your ass?" He pointed toward Tori.

The playground went quiet, and the teasing stopped.

"Can we talk?" Tori asked, grabbing my elbow and guiding me to a quiet corner.

I noticed a bunch of kids whispering and a few pointing at us.

"What's going on, Tori? Everyone's worried about you. Where have you been? Are you all right?" I asked.

"I'm fine. I just didn't want to be at that stupid new house with those old people anymore," she said.

"Why didn't you just call Johnny and have her pick you up? Isn't that the way it works?" I asked.

Tori stuffed her hands in her pockets and shrugged. "Anyway, I came up here to say to your face that I'm really, really sorry for what I did to you, Tabitha. I can't stop thinking about it, and I need you to know that I never meant to hurt you as bad as I did. I was just so mad and stuff."

"Why would you hate me when you don't even know me?" I said. I clenched my fists and felt my face get hot. I didn't want to cry in front of her, so I just blurted out everything I was thinking. "Why be so mean to me and then come here and stick up for me? Do you think everything is okay now because you made a stupid bully cry? Ruthie, Johnny, and Quinn are so worried that it's making them sick, and you could stop it with one phone call," I said.

Tori kicked a stone with her toe. "I was a bully to you, Tabitha, and I'm really sorry. I don't hate you, not even a little, and I don't have any excuses."

"You need to go home to Ruthie's or call Johnny," I said. Tori looked away from me at the mention of their names, but I continued. "They're really worried about you. They can help you with anything that's bothering you. You know that, you've been around them a lot longer than I have."

Tori shook her head. "Tabitha, you don't understand," she said. "I'm bad luck. Wherever I go, whatever I do, everything turns to shit. Let them know I'm fine, will ya? I don't want them to worry or get sick because of me."

"Tori!" I stomped my foot. "If you really care about them, come with me. I can call Ruthie from the office, and she'll pick you up right now."

Tori shook her head and started to back away. "I can't, Tabitha. But tell them I love them, will ya? I'm closer than you think. Let them all know that I'm fine."

"Please, Tori. Tell them yourself. Come home." I bit my lip so that I wouldn't cry in front of her.

The bell rang, and I turned to look back to the school. All the kids were running inside. When I looked back at Tori, she was walking away across the playground.

"Tori!" I yelled after her. "Please just come back! Please?"

She just kept walking.

The dam had burst and tears streamed down my face. Tori could have fixed everything so easily. I didn't understand, and I was angry, a feeling I didn't like at all. I had to call Ruthie, and maybe Quinn. Maybe he could find her. I ran past everyone to the office and asked to use the phone.

Ruthie was so relieved when I told her, but she was also confused about why Tori didn't just come back or call Margaret. She said she would call Quinn and ask to keep a look out for her near the school.

CHAPTER NINETEEN

The next day was the last day of school not only for the week, but I found out we had something called Christmas vacation for almost 14 days! When I looked around, I could tell I was the only one that wasn't smiling and dancing, even though I was enjoying the mini candy canes and the chocolates that the teacher was handing out to everyone. It also meant that the new class to meet other kids in the foster system wouldn't start until we got back. I was looking forward to that a lot, and now I would have to wait even longer.

Everyone at school was treating me a little different, in an overly nice way now, all because of Tori. I wasn't happy about that. I wouldn't answer any questions about Tori. I wanted to be Tabitha, not someone Tori Galloway had to stick up for, or someone the kids had to be nice to just because they were afraid of her.

I heard all kinds of silly things about Tori: She was really 18 and was a cage fighter, or that she was a runaway and had lived on the streets since she was five. I heard that she'd escaped from prison and had hurt two huge guards really bad. I couldn't believe the stupidity of the things they were saying. Then I overheard a group of girls say that they heard Tori had killed her whole family with her bare hands while they were sleeping and that's how she'd become a foster kid.

Great! Tori had all the kids thinking that foster kids were messed up. It made my stomach sick. It wasn't like a kid chose that. You never want to lose your family. It was so dumb. I was suddenly glad that vacation started soon. Tori had managed to ruin this happy place too.

The week was over, and Tori was still nowhere to be seen. Ruthie kept telling me that it was great news that Tori had come to visit me, and that it meant she was all right. Part of me was still very angry at Tori for not coming back. I mean, it helped them that I saw her, but Ruthie was always looking at her phone, and I would catch her staring at me for a really long time, but I wasn't sure if she was really seeing me. When I spoke, she'd jumped a little, and I knew she must have been deep in thought.

"I'm going to go write, Ruthie. I'll be down to set the table in a little while," I said.

I had to empty my head because I hated being angry. It just wasn't a feeling I liked, and I hoped that writing about it would help me get rid of it.

Later while I was setting the table, Ruthie asked me to set two more places for Quinn and Johnny. This didn't make me as happy as it usually would. All during dinner I couldn't stop thinking about Tori. I knew how much she loved Ruthie and Johnny. There had to be more to why Tori was staying away. None of it made sense. It was very cold out, and I kept wondering if she was warm. That thought alone made me so I wasn't hungry. No one else seemed to be either. They were pushing their food around their plates with their forks.

Finally, Ruthie got up. "I've got something that will cheer us all up."

She opened a cupboard and handed Johnny a beautifully wrapped gift.

"What in the world is this?" Johnny asked.

"It's just something that I have been working on for a very long time," Ruthie said. "Open it and you'll find out."

Johnny removed the wrapping and uncovered a large blue

and pink canvas with writing all over it.

Johnny's eyes grew wide. "How you did? How could you? It's every single one... isn't it?"

Ruthie nodded proudly. "Except for Tori and Tabitha, but that will be fixed shortly. I wanted you to see all the lives you've changed, Margaret, all the wonderful things you have done for so many children."

On the canvas was a signature of every child that Johnny had ever been assigned to. Some were married now with their own families and some were new like me. Johnny smiled for the first time since Tori disappeared. She hugged Ruthie and passed the canvas down to Quinn and me so we could see. There were hundreds of names and little notes.

Ruthie handed me a pen, and I found a free spot on the edge, where I wrote, "To Johnny, love always, Tabitha M Sullivan xoxo."

Johnny looked at each signature while Ruthie poured coffee. Quinn was trying really hard to keep up the happy mood by trying to make us all laugh. He told us about how mad Ruthie would get when he would sneak out the tunnel in the basement that led to the backyard so he could play with his friends past curfew.

"One night she was standing there waiting for me when I tried to sneak out... scared the ever living day lights outta me," Quinn said. We all laughed with him. "I got grounded a lot."

"What does grounded mean?" I asked. "It sounds like a horrible thing."

"It's when you can't go outside and play with your friends or watch TV, and sometimes if you were really bad, you had to go to bed after dinner, too – with no dessert!" Quinn said, shaking his head as if that was the worst part of being grounded. "One time I got grounded because I took all of the snacks and juice boxes down to the tunnel. My friends and I were going to pretend our boat was stuck on an island," Quinn said with a giggle.

"Yes, an island filled with snacks and juice!" Ruthie laughed.

"What's in the tunnel?" I asked.

"It's just an old, long thing like a cave, except it's cozy instead of scary," Quinn said. "I used to play hide and seek with the little ones back in the day. One time my friends and I put an old beanbag, some posters and blankets down there. We even hid some snacks and some sodas down there in an old box we called the 'treasure chest'. We called our hangout the 'Cool Cave.'" Quinn smiled and shook his head at the memory. "Wow, we had a blast down there. I'll show you sometime soon, Tabitha."

Johnny put a napkin to her eyes.

"Margaret, are you all right?" Ruthie asked. She placed her arm around Johnny's shoulders.

Johnny put her head down in her arms and began to sob.

"She's just a child! I don't know how much more I can take. I'm getting too old for this!" she said through her tears.

It was hard to see Johnny cry. She was the tough one. Ruthie had tears in her eyes, and Quinn got up and put his arms around both women, vowing to find Tori. I was getting really mad at Tori again. She could at least have called. I went over and over everything we'd said in our conversation.

Then I got stuck on one thing. Tori had said, "I'm closer than you think."

Ruthie's house wasn't near anything except other houses... the school was a few blocks away and... That was it. I kept repeating what she said. *I'm closer than you think.* Where are you, Tori?

Then it came to me.

"Quinn?" I asked, breaking the silence. "Is the basement door locked on the outside of the house?"

"Yes, sweetie. It needs a key to unlock it, so don't worry. That door is thick and has a dead bolt, so no one can ever get up here from outside," he said.

I thought about this for a few minutes. Then: "Ruthie, how far away is Tori's new foster home?"

Ruthie shrugged. "A few blocks at best, sweetheart. Why do you ask?"

I looked up at Quinn. "Do you think Tori would remember the 'Cool Cave'?"

Quinn looked at me and nodded slowly. "Yeah... I'm sure she does. She spent a lot of time down there when she was little."

I tilted my head. "Do you think Tori remembers *everything* about the 'Cool Cave'?"

This time his eyes widened when he looked at me. He jumped up and ran over to the wall to the key rack.

There were two empty hooks.

He spun around. "Ruthie, have you unlocked that basement door recently?"

Ruthie reached for Johnny's hand and just shook her head no. Quinn grabbed my head and kissed the top of it. He ran to the basement door, opened it, and flew down the stairs. Ruthie clutched Johnny's hand and mine and lowered her head and closed her eyes. I closed mine too, and we sat there in silence.

After awhile, we heard Quinn's footsteps coming up the basement stairs. We all stared at the doorway, hoping. But he came around the corner alone.

"Oh... I..." Ruthie said.

Johnny looked gray and weak, like a human balloon that had been deflated.

Then Quinn smiled.

"Do we have room at the table for another plate?"

And Tori stepped through the doorway, her hand snug in Quinn's.

Ruthie put her hands to her face and ran to Tori. Johnny stood, but never moved. Ruthie hugged Tori so tight I don't think Tori could breathe. Tori looked over at Johnny, who was still standing at the end of the table, now with tears were running down her face. Tori stepped out of Ruthie's hug and walked toward Johnny.

"Johnny, I'm really sorry. I know you were worried. I love you so much and I would never hurt you on purpose," Tori said. She spun back to the rest of us. "I am so sorry to everyone. I know I should have done things differently."

She turned back to Johnny, but Johnny refused to look up as tears continued to leak down her face.

"Johnny, please say something," Tori pleaded. "I'm so sorry that I worried you."

Johnny wiped the tears from her face and finally looked up at Tori.

"Child, I have never been so happy to see anyone in my entire life. You might as well be my own daughter for how much I love you and worry about you. You were close to death only a few weeks ago..." Johnny took a quivering breath and then stamped her foot. "You always call, do you know that? You've run away five times now, and each time before this, you always call within the hour. This time was five days, Tori!" Johnny's voice broke and she started sobbing. Tori stood, fidgeting with her hands at her sides. Johnny looked up and put her hands on Tori's face.

"Tori, I thought you were dead this time. I was wondering how in God's name I would survive hearing that news. I tortured myself wondering what I could have done differently, what I did wrong... I can't remember the last time I slept. I have been to every hospital, homeless shelter and other unmentionable places. And the whole time, you have been only a few feet away? You only had to walk up those stairs to relieve the worry and pain you were putting us through?" Johnny paused and let out a long sigh. "I'm not a young woman anymore, and I thank God you're back and safe. I love you, child, like you will never understand, and I've never been happier in my life than I am this very second to see your face, but I can't allow you to do this to me anymore."

She reached in her pocket and placed a bottle of medicine on the table. She walked past Tori, who stood in place with her back to us, and walked out of the room. Quinn turned and followed her.

"Margaret," we heard him call. "Just wait."

We heard the door close and then the only sound was Tori's soft crying. Ruthie walked up behind Tori and wrapped her arms tightly around the girl while she wept. We heard the low rumble of Quinn's voice in the driveway, and then a car started and drove away.

I gave Tori and Ruthie privacy and went to sit in the living room. I was so relieved that Tori was back. Hopefully it meant that everyone would look and feel better again. Except Johnny, who seemed worse than before. I heard the front door open, and Quinn walked into the living room.

"Is Johnny coming back in? Is she all right?" I asked.

"She's fine. I offered to drive her home, but she insisted she just needed some rest. I'll stop by to check on her in a little while just to be safe. She took this whole thing really hard. She's relieved that Tori's back and she's safe, that's for sure, and we can all thank you for that, you little detective." Quinn messed up my hair with his huge hand, and that made me giggle.

"What made you put all that together?" he asked. "It never even occurred to me. I feel kind of silly about that, to be honest with you."

"When Tori came to see me at school, she said 'I'm closer than you think,' remember?"

"Yes, I remember you telling us that," he said.

"When you're a kid you think like a kid," I said. "I know that if it was me I might have done the same thing: A cool cave with blankets and the ability to come up and snack after everyone was asleep. It was pretty smart actually. Plus she was here in the only place I think that feels like home."

"Well, I'm really impressed and awfully proud of you," he said.

"Thanks," I said, feeling my cheeks getting warm from the compliment.

While I had one-on-one time with Quinn, I decided to ask him about the old woman at the hospital.

"Well, Tabitha, she seems to think she knew your mom way back when you were a baby," he said.

"Maggie?"

"No, your real mother. You know, I need to tell you that you're dealing with the news about Maggie really well. I have been meaning to ask you, do you remember what the 'M' in your name stands for, by any chance?"

I looked at Quinn and decided if I couldn't trust him, I couldn't trust anyone.

"If I tell you, will you promise to help me with something?" I asked.

"Of course! I'd do anything for you, sweetie. You know that. What's wrong?"

"Nothing's wrong... it's just that Maggie didn't name me Tabitha. My mom said that she didn't have the right to name me and that I could choose one when I was older."

I explained why I chose my name, and Quinn watched me, smiling.

"You never stop surprising me, sweetie," he said. "I love the name Tabitha. It's a very nice choice. But what about the 'M'? What does that stand for? 'M' after Maggie?"

"No. This is where I need your help," I said.

I explained what the elf had said about me needing a mulligan, but that I didn't know if a mulligan was a thing, a person, or something you wished for on a wish flower or with a coin in the fountain.

"Quinn, it's a second chance... a do over. It's magic and I need to find one. Whatever it is, can you help me?"

Quinn was looking at me with his head slightly tilted. I could almost see his mind working as I looked in his eyes.

"I'll tell you what, I will do my best to find one for you, but keep this between you and me, all right?" he said.

"Thank you, Quinn! Thank you so much!" I stood up and hugged him tightly.

He pulled me back so we were eye to eye again and said, "Tabitha, you never have to be afraid or nervous to talk about anything. I need you to know that, okay, goofball?"

"Okay!" I smiled. "Quinn, that old woman... is she crazy?"

"No, I don't think she is, Tabitha. But she said a few things that might help us put everything together. Kind of connect the dots like in your coloring books, but it's connecting the dots with who your family is and how Maggie fit into your life.

Hopefully you're finally going to get your answers, sweetie, isn't that exciting?"

"I guess. I'm just happy here with all you guys. I'm not sure I want it to all change again," I said.

"Even if you have a real family out there that can't wait to meet you?" he asked.

"I'm not going to get excited yet, Quinn. I don't want to be disappointed if nothing comes of it, you know?" I said.

"I gotcha, kiddo," Quinn said and winked at me. "Now, do you want some dessert?"

I shook my head. "I think I'm going to get ready for bed and let Tori have time to talk to you guys."

I gave him a hug and said goodnight. "Tell Ruthie goodnight for me too, okay?"

I went upstairs and soaked up to my neck in bubbles. I was crawling into bed when I heard a knock on my door.

It was Tori.

"Can we talk?" she asked.

We were sitting on the edge of my bed, and even though Tori's bruises were fading, her eyes were swollen from crying.

"Shamus and Ruthie told me how you were the one that figured it out. Ruthie tried to make a joke downstairs about me staying, as long as I promised to sleep in a bed... it was pretty funny," Tori said. "They said I needed to okay it with you first. Tabitha, would it be all right with you if I stayed here with you and Ruthie?"

"Of course, Tori," I said, and I meant it.

I hugged my knees to my chest. Tori wiggled her toes in the carpet and looked up at me.

"You seem a little quiet," she said. "Are you mad at me?"

"Mad?" I asked in a low questioning voice. "Did you see Johnny? I've been watching everyone get more worried every day because you didn't call or come home." My voice started to get louder. "Or should I say come upstairs? I just don't understand why you couldn't just talk to them when you've known them your whole life. It was hard watching them suffer like that. I'm sorry to say all that Tori, but I just don't understand. I am happy that you're safe. I really am, and so is everyone else, but I just don't get why you let it go on for so long."

Tori turned to face me. "Tabitha, I really am sorry. I was just messed up, and every time I thought about coming up, I decided I needed one more day. It turned into a lot of days, I guess." She shrugged and frowned, kicking her feet against the carpet. "I would never hurt Johnny or Ruthie on purpose. They're the only family I've ever really had."

"I know... and I know you love them," I said. "I just don't get it, that's all."

"I just don't know how to explain it so anyone understands it, so all I can do is say 'sorry' and hope that everyone forgives me," Tori said. She clenched her hands together in her lap.

I reached out and put my hand on hers. "Tori, everyone does forgive you. They love you so much. Did you see the look on everyone's face when Quinn brought you around the corner?"

She looked up and smiled at me. "Thanks, Tabitha."

She jumped to her feet. "Would you feel like coming back downstairs with me? So Ruthie knows we're both okay?"

"Yeah! I'll be down in a second," I said.

Tori stopped halfway to the door and turned. "Did you really scrub the toilet with my toothbrush?"

"Did you really lick mine?" I asked.

We both smirked. Tori rolled her eyes and left.

When I got downstairs, Ruthie had left. Quinn said Kendal was coming over to watch us for a little while. He looked white and pasty, like the old woman at the hospital.

"Are you all right, Quinn? And where did Ruthie go?" I asked.

"I'm fine sweetie," he said. "Ruthie had to go help a friend, but she'll be back before you know it."

But he didn't look fine. He sat down and glanced at his phone, then popped up and paced back and forth. When he turned and saw us looking at him, he sat again.

"You girls thirsty?" he asked.

Before we could answer, he'd poured two glasses of milk. He was setting the milk on the table when the doorbell rang. He jumped, and some of the milk splashed over onto his hands. He ran to the door with a towel in his hands.

Kendal was at the door and immediately gave Quinn an extra long hug. As much as I thought I wanted Quinn and Kendal to be boyfriend and girlfriend, it was different when I saw it with my own eyes. I had this urge to jump between them and tell Kendal that I was Quinn's special girl. But before I could, Quinn brought her over to introduce her to Tori.

"Holy crap, Quinn! Nice job! She's gorgeous."

Kendal and Quinn both laughed.

"Yes, and this is Tori, the shy one of the house." He winked and Tori stuck her tongue out at him.

Kendal gave me a hug and then she and Quinn walked into the living room. Tori and I looked at each other. "What's the matter with everyone tonight?" I asked.

Tori shrugged. "Let's find out."

She tiptoed toward the living room.

"Tori!" I whispered. "What are you doing?"

"Shh!" she said. "I'm going to listen."

But before she could go any farther, she saw the canvas that Johnny had left behind. Quinn came walking back into the dining room with Kendal in hand.

"What's this?" Tori said.

When he explained, Tori looked very sad.

"You can sign it, Tori. I just did tonight," I said and handed her the pen.

"She's quitting." Tori said. "This is what they pass around in school for all the kids to sign when a teacher leaves or quits. That's what's she doing, isn't it Shamus? All because of what I put her through."

"No, Tori. I mean... yes. She is retiring from her job as a social worker, but no, not because of you, I swear." He placed his hand over his heart. "She's been talking to Ruthie for almost a year about retiring. That's what gave Ruthie so much time to get all of them to sign it," he said. "But she's not leaving until you both are where you belong, with a good family."

Tori glared at him. She was trying to look tough, but there were tears in her eyes.

"I swear, Tori," Quinn said, putting his arm around her. "It has nothing to do with you. Her doctor has been urging her to slow down. The stress has been hard on her heart. And I've heard her and Ruthie making plans to travel together when she retires."

My head snapped up. I felt like someone had slapped my face. Ruthie was going to stop, too. I wasn't going to grow up here no matter how hard I tried, and that thought crushed me. Tori looked like she was going to explode with emotions. It was something neither of us wanted to hear.

Quinn checked his phone. "I have to get going, but either Ruthie or I will be back soon, all right? It's bedtime, so why don't you both get ready and then maybe Kendal can tuck you in."

Quinn kissed each of us on the head and left.

Tori and I didn't feel much like talking, and we went to our separate rooms after saying goodnight to each other. Kendal tucked me into bed and hugged me goodnight. I tried to inhale as much of her scent as I could, and it lulled me to sleep.

CHAPTER TWENTY

The three of us stood back while Tori talked to Johnny.

"Johnny, I'm so sorry. I love you with all my heart. I'm going to change, and you'll be so proud of me, okay? Just watch and see – you won't even recognize the old Tori."

She dropped to the cold ground and placed the roses on Johnny's grave.

Johnny was gone.

No matter how many times I said it in my head, it just didn't seem real.

It was a heart attack. It happened that night after she left Ruthie's. The last time I'd seen her was at the dining room table, sitting next to Ruthie. And now I was looking at her grave in the cemetery where they'd buried her.

Today was Christmas, and Ruthie said that Jesus was busy today, his birthday, welcoming Johnny to her new home in heaven.

It was too much to accept. It was as if we were walking in thick mud and couldn't get out of it. We were crying and Quinn went to pick Tori up to get her out of the cold, but Ruthie asked him to let her be, that she needed to do this. I buried my face in Ruthie's chest and cried until I couldn't catch my breath. Quinn put his arms around both of us. My heart was breaking for everyone. I could only imagine the torment everyone else was feeling. I had only known her for a little while and I loved her, while everyone else had known Johnny for most of their lives. Ruthie had been her best friend since childhood. Quinn had known her since he was a little boy, and Tori might as well been Johnny's own daughter. It was going to be so hard, but convincing Tori that Johnny's death wasn't her fault would be the hardest.

Ruthie walked up to her and laid a hand on her shoulders. "We will be in the car, sweetheart. Take your time. We will leave only when you're ready."

She's broken, I thought. If we didn't stop her, she would shatter.

"I asked my mom to help," I told Ruthie, and she smiled, holding my hand a little tighter on the way to the car.

Quinn stayed outside the car for a while and when he finally opened the door, his eyes were swollen. I wished my mom had so many people to love her and be sad when she died, but she'd only had me, and that made me even sadder.

When we returned home, Kendal was waiting for us with lasagna hot from the oven and a huge salad. Ruthie gave her a long hug. Ruthie told us she would return shortly and went upstairs to her room. Quinn sat at the table and drank a cup of coffee with Kendal. Tori had already walked straight to her room the moment we'd arrived home.

I went to check on her, hoping I could help her somehow. When I passed Ruthie's room, I could hear her sniffling. I knew she was letting out the hurt she was feeling after trying so hard to stay strong for everyone else.

Tori was lying face down in her pillow. I placed my hand gently on her back to let her know I was there.

"I killed her, Tabitha. I killed Johnny, and I never really got to tell her how sorry I was. She was so disappointed in me," she said as she sobbed into her pillow.

"Tori, you did tell her you were sorry and that you loved her. I heard you myself," I said. I rubbed her back to soothe her. "And you didn't kill her. She had a bad heart, remember?

Tori, remember Johnny telling you how much she loved you?"

Tori slowly turned around. "Yeah, she did say that, huh?" She sniffled.

"Yes, she did. She loved you, Tori, and you said that you'll change and make her proud of you, and you need to believe that. I know my mom sits on a cloud and watches over me. I try to show her something to make her proud of me every day."

"Is that what that cloud around your neck means?" Tori asked.

"Yep, and I touch it every time I feel sad. It reminds me she is watching me from heaven," I said.

"She was so mad and hurt by what I did, Tabitha. How am I supposed to make that right? It's too late! She's gone!" Tori buried her face in her pillow again.

"You change, Tori. You do exactly what you said you would do. Little by little, keep your word to her like you said. That's all you have to do, and that will make her smile."

"She's right," Ruthie said from the doorway. "Margaret took care of hundreds of children over many, many years, but I never saw her love a child the way she loved you, Tori."

Tori was looking at Ruthie now, absorbing every word she said. Ruthie walked over and sat between us on the bed.

"Sweetheart, I'll tell you something that might help you understand the love she had for you. She was going to adopt you years ago, but before she could, she learned that her heart was seriously damaged. She couldn't bear the thought of dying young and leaving you without a mother again. Tori, she passed away knowing you were safe, and I know that was a great gift for her to bring to heaven. I think she may have gone to the hospital earlier, but she refused to let go until she knew you were home safe," Ruthie said.

"I didn't kill her, Ruthie? Swear to God it wasn't my fault?" Tori cried.

Ruthie pulled Tori close. "I promise you that you had nothing to do with Margaret leaving us. She was sick for many years, and she knew it. Having you blame yourself and feel guilty would not make the Johnny I knew very happy, now would it?"

"No Ruthie, Johnny wouldn't be happy at all," Tori said. "She would be really mad."

"She would, wouldn't she? She had a nasty little temper, that woman did," Ruthie said half giggling which made both Tori and I giggle with her. "Now, how about we go downstairs and eat the lovely meal that Kendal so generously prepared for us?"

When we walked into the kitchen, Kendal was sitting having coffee in Johnny's chair. Tori froze.

"What are you doing?" Tori yelled.

Kendal jumped, startled, as Tori walked quickly toward her.

"Get out of her chair!" Tori yelled. She grabbed the cup from Kendal's hand and smashed it in the sink. "That's Johnny's chair! Get out of it! That's her place!"

Kendal leapt out of the chair with wide eyes. Quinn crossed the kitchen in two strides and wrapped Tori tight in his arms. Tori shook and whimpered, but she didn't fight him.

"Johnny is gone, sweetie," Quinn whispered. "She's in heaven now, and everything's going to be all right."

I went to Kendal and hugged her, trying to assure her she'd done nothing wrong. Quinn picked Tori up and brought her into the living room where he slowly rocked her while she cried. Ruthie poured Kendal another cup of coffee and directed her to Ruthie's usual chair. Ruthie kissed the top of Kendal's head and placed her hands on her shoulders to ease her shaking. Ruthie then turned Johnny's chair toward the window.

"There are more than enough chairs for us without that one," she said and wiped a tear from her eye.

A few cups of coffee later, Quinn returned to the kitchen alone.

"Where's Tori?" I asked.

"She fell asleep on the couch."

He knelt next to Kendal and asked her if she was all right. She nodded, and Quinn gave her a long hug. We decided to let

Tori sleep and sat down to dinner. We were a few bites in when Tori stumbled into the kitchen, still half asleep.

"Something smells really good," she said.

"I made lasagna," Kendal said. "Would you like a plate?"

Tori looked up at the sound of Kendal's voice. Her eyes misted over. "I'm sorry for what I did to you. I didn't mean to..."

Kendal put her arms around Tori and rubbed her back gently. "Shhh... no worries. No worries at all."

"Kendal?" Tori said.

"Yes, sweetie?" Kendal said.

"You smell really freaking good." Tori said, and we all broke into laughter, even Tori.

As I was getting ready for bed, Tori knocked on my door.

"Would you feel like sitting up and talking maybe for a while?" she asked.

"Sure! How about I come into your room so if I get sleepy, I'll already be on a bed?" I said.

When I sat on the bed across from Tori I could tell by her swollen eyes she had been crying again.

"When I was in the hospital and found out about my mom, I felt like my heart was always going to feel broken, that I was going to feel that way forever," I said. "But Athia told me that time and happy thoughts would help me heal."

Tori scrunched up her nose and sniffled. So I continued. "She was right. It still hurts now and then. It hurts a lot, but all I have to do is imagine my mom with her feet dangling from a cloud watching over me, and I feel good again."

"I hope you're right." Tori wiped her face. "Tabitha... I was thinking that I never said I was sorry about your mom... that she went to heaven."

"I forgive you, Tori. It's all behind us now," I said.

She gave me a half smile.

"What did you want to talk about?" I asked.

"How did you get hurt?" Tori asked.

A question that I wasn't expecting.

"You don't have to tell if you don't want to, honest."

"I'll tell you if you tell me," I said tilting my head to one side and raising my eyebrows slightly. She thought about it for a while, so long that I started to get a little sleepy.

"All right," Tori said. "Deal."

I told her everything from my mom getting sick, the crazy guy beating us up, and everything that had happened until I arrived in her room. She just stared at me with the sad eyes I had gotten my entire life.

"Tabitha, I had no idea. How do you deal with all that? I mean that's a whole lot of bad shit. How do you walk around so happy and you're never mad or angry?" she asked.

"Tori, I wanted to die and be with my mom. I was broken, believe me, but Athia helped me to get out of my dark place, and seeing Dr. Katherine has really helped me in so many ways."

Tori was quiet.

"How about you?" I asked.

Tori fidgeted with the blanket and scrunched up her mouth.

"C'mon!" I said. "We had a deal!"

"I can't, Tabitha! I can't tell you what happened to me," Tori burst out. "I want to, but it makes me sick to my stomach, and angry, and all sorts of shit goes through my head. I'm sorry. I didn't mean to lie to you... I thought I could, but I can't."

"Tori, it's fine. I don't care if you tell me, really. We can talk about anything you want or nothing at all. You don't have to tell me what happened to you," I told her.

Tori took a long breath.

"Tabitha, after the way I treated you and everything, why don't you hate me?" she asked.

"I was never taught hate, Tori. My mom would ignore mean people, and she would tell me that they weren't worth an ounce of her time. She told me that time was precious," I said. I thought for a moment. "I learned that the hard way. If I'd known she wouldn't be here with me, I would have tried harder to get to know her."

Tori squinted in confusion. "What do you mean you would

try to get to know her?"

"My mom was a very, very quiet person, and I can't remember one personal thing she ever told me about herself. I would have tried harder if I had known she would be taken from me so soon."

The next morning I woke still in Tori's room. I could smell breakfast cooking. Tori and I looked at each other and bounded down the stairs.

"Good morning, my little ones! How did you sleep?" Ruthie asked.

"We actually shared my room last night, Ruthie. I asked Tabitha if she felt like hanging out and we did," Tori said winking at me with sleepy eyes.

"How nice! That sounds like fun," she said. "Maybe you two can get to know each other better."

Ruthie placed breakfast on the table. "Are you both ready for school to start again? The doctor has given you the okay to return to school, Tori!"

I looked at Tori, wondering if I should mention the things I had heard about her at school.

I decided to tell her. "Tori, before you go to school, I need you know what other kids are saying about you."

Ruthie stopped eating, but Tori continued like she wasn't the slightest bit interested.

"It's pretty bad," I said. But that still didn't get her attention.

"What is it, Tabitha?" Ruthie asked. "What are they saying?"

"It's nothing, Ruthie. Just some silly stuff is all," Tori said.

"No, it's not, Tori. It's really nasty stuff," I said.

Tori rolled her eyes. "Tabitha I know everything they're saying, so it's fine, all right?"

"No. No! It's not fine." I slammed my cup. "Some of the things make it sound like all foster kids are crazy people that kill our parents in their sleep! I have to go there too, Tori! It has to be fixed!"

Ruthie dropped her fork. "Excuse me, Tabitha what did

you just say?"

"Listen. It's not a big deal. I know what everyone is saying because I'm the one that made up those stories," Tori said.

The kitchen went silent. Ruthie and I stared at Tori, waiting for an explanation. Except none came. She continued to eat.

"Victory Galloway, I want an explanation and I want it this very instant," Ruthie said in an even tone that was even scarier than yelling.

Tori glared hard at me, and I was afraid the old Tori was back.

"When I was at that other school two years ago, the one over on Miles Avenue... you know the one I'm talking about, Ruthie?" Tori asked.

"Yes, I know that school. Go on," Ruthie said with her eyes glued on Tori.

"There was a group of really mean girls that liked to pick on me about being in a foster home. I was crying in the bathroom one day when another girl two grades ahead of me told me that she had gone through all that once because they found out her dad was in prison. She changed things by spreading really scary lies about herself. How her father was a really dangerous man and taught her everything he knew, and that made the mean girls fear her and not pick on her. She helped me write on some bathroom stall doors, and she said she would help spread the rumors about me."

Tori smiled and snapped her fingers. "And just like that, I wasn't bullied anymore. Instead, I was feared. The only problem was that by the time I went to a new school, the rumors were already there waiting for me. I couldn't start over, and I couldn't get away from my own words." Tori threw her hands in the air.

"I'm utterly shocked at what I'm hearing. You figure out a way to change this on your own or I will. Do I make myself clear?" Ruthie asked. "I refuse to have a child bullied for being in the foster system or for any other reason for that matter. I simply won't have it." She slapped the table, making Tori and I both jump.

"Yes, ma'am," Tori said. "I'll figure it out."

"I can help Tori. I can help you change everybody's minds," I said.

"Great, Tabitha. I would love to hear how," Tori said, rolling her eyes.

"Why don't you just try to be Tori? If they get to talk to you and you show them the real Tori, they will forget about those stupid rumors," I said. "I'll help because I won't let them think that just because I'm a foster kid, I'm evil. It's not like we chose not to have a family."

Tori looked at me, but this time her eyes weren't angry.

"Except for one thing," she said. "I don't remember the real Tori."

"Well, I'm getting to know her, and she's pretty cool," I said, making Tori smile.

"By the way," I said. "I've been wondering something. Why did Ruthie call you 'Victory'?"

Tori and Ruthie exchanged a smile.

"Tori is a nickname, sweetheart," Ruthie said.

Tori nodded. "When I was born my dad said I was his greatest victory. He said he'd never cried in his whole life, but on that day, his tears came down like rain. So my whole name is Victory Rain Galloway."

My mouth was open and my eyes were the size of quarters. "Tori that's the most beautiful name in the world, and you have a story about your dad naming you? That makes it extra, extra special."

Tori blushed and Ruthie agreed as she poured herself a second cup of coffee. It would have been the perfect time to tell them how I got mine, but I decided to wait just a little longer. I wanted to ask her so many more questions about her father, her family, and how she became a foster kid, but if Tori wanted you to know something about her, she would tell you herself.

CHAPTER TWENTY-ONE

As we were coming downstairs from making our beds and doing our morning chores, the snow began to fall and there was the sound of ice hitting the window.

"Well, it looks like it's going to be a cold, icky day," Ruthie said. "What a perfect time for a beach party."

We both looked at Ruthie.

"Did you hit your head when we were upstairs?" Tori asked.

Ruthie smirked. "No, I did not hit my head! Now, go upstairs and get two t-shirts out of the bottom drawer of the dresser in Tabitha's room. Put them on and start a bubble bath. I'll be right up."

Ruthie also gave us both two big floppy hats. I had never been to the beach before, and neither had Tori, so we were both excited for our first beach party. When Ruthie came upstairs, she had two big plastic glasses filled with a bright red juice, and each had a tiny umbrella twirling in it. On the edge of each glass there was a piece of pineapple and a cherry stuck together on a long toothpick.

"There," she said. "Now that's a beach party drink."

We both got in the bubble bath with our beach drinks, and Ruthie handed us each a pair of sunglasses. She held up a camera and Tori and I gave her huge smiles for the picture. She snapped a few more pictures of us posing and giggling each time.

We asked Ruthie to tell us what it was like at the beach, what it looked like, how it felt, and the people there. As we sat there in the bubbles, sipping our fancy drinks, we closed our eyes and listened to every word she said. We could smell the sea air and feel the waves crashing against our feet as they dug deeper into the warm, white sand while the sun warmed our faces. By the time the bubbles had disappeared, the drinks were gone, and the water was turning cool, we had been to the beach and back without ever leaving the tub.

After the beach party, Tori and I laid out our clothes and backpacks for school the next day. Ruthie read of a list of school supplies for Tori to make sure she added them to her bag and gave each of us lunch money.

When bedtime came around, Tori asked me if I wanted to sleep in her room again. I grabbed my stuff and crawled into my new bed.

"Are you nervous about tomorrow?" I asked.

"No, not really. I've had to start a lot of different schools, and I've been to Hobbes before, and it was one of my favorite schools," she said.

I realized that if I ever left Ruthie's, I would have to go to a new school, too.

"Has anyone, you know, besides Johnny, ever wanted to adopt you, Tori?"

She nodded. "I've been close to adoption before, but something always seems to happen right before the papers are signed."

"Wasn't it kind of scary?" I asked.

Tori must have seen the look on my face. "Tabitha you shouldn't be afraid. There's a ton of really cool people and families out there that are just waiting for a kid to take care of, so don't worry about that."

I just stared at her. "So you *want* to get adopted?"

Tori laughed. "Oh! No. I don't want to be adopted at all. I

need to keep this up for eight more years so I can stay here at Ruthie's. Whether she wants to admit it or not that woman isn't retiring or going anywhere. I love it here, and it's the closest thing to home that I've ever had." She paused and crooked an eyebrow. "It's hard sometimes though because Ruthie won't put up with my shit for a second."

I couldn't help laughing, which made her laugh too.

Without warning Tori said, "You know I never met my mother. She never wanted a kid and she left me and my dad three days after I was born."

Tori stared down at her bedspread. I held my breath, not wanting to interrupt her, hoping she would continue. She didn't disappoint.

"We never saw or heard from her again, or at least I didn't," Tori said. "I don't remember her at all. My dad was the best, from what I can remember, or maybe I've just made him up in my head! Anyway, this one day we were walking... he had my little bag with my things, and he was talking, but I don't remember what he was saying. I remember he kept wiping his eyes and his voice was low. Usually it was loud and happy."

Tori's story made me think of the walks my mom and I would take to the fountain every day. I shivered and hugged my knees. Tori didn't seem to notice. She was lost in her story.

"We walked to church, and he sat me on his lap on one of the long benches. He said 'I love you' a lot and hugged and kissed me a bunch. Then he sang me a song, which made me sleepy. When I woke, I had my bag and a note pinned to my clothes with a priest sitting next to me, but no dad. I never saw my dad again. The priest called the police, who called Johnny and... that's, that," she said.

"I'm sorry Tori... that's awful that they... that he... well, I'm sorry," was I could think of to say.

Tori shrugged. "Between you and me, I think he'll come back one day. He left me a letter. I found it one day when I was in the car with Johnny. She had to get out, so while I was waiting for her, I noticed a bunch of files between the seats. I peeked through them and one had my name on it. When I opened it I saw a bunch of papers and an envelope with my name on it and a note that I could receive it when I was 18. I thought that was bullshit – it was a letter from my dad and it was mine." Tori frowned and her voice sounded angry. "They had no right to keep it from me! So I took it."

I couldn't help myself. I blurted out, "What did it say? You took the letter?"

Tori stared at me for a second or two. I bit my lip. I shouldn't have said anything. Now she was going to clam up. But to my surprise, she continued. She trusted me!

"He said he and my mom were really young when they had me and had no idea how to take care of a baby. They weren't married, and my mom liked to drink and party a lot, and she wouldn't come home for days. Eventually she didn't come home at all. He heard she ran away with some guy to a place called California, but he wasn't sure. All he knew was she wasn't coming back to us. My dad had to go back to Ireland because some kind of papers ran out on him and he had to leave. He didn't have anyone there to help take care of me, and he wanted me to have the American dream. So he was going to leave me here so I could be a success and have a happy life. He wrote that he loved me a million times and he would come back someday."

"Did Johnny ever find out you took the letter?" I asked.

Tori nodded. "I told her."

My eyes went wide. "You did?! What did she say?"

She told me that my dad signed a paper that said he didn't want any parental rights, which meant he didn't want to be my dad anymore." Tori tossed her head. "But I don't believe that. Someday I always think he'll ring that doorbell and want me back," she said.

"I'm so sorry Tori," I said. "But thank you for sharing that with me."

She shrugged and went silent. I didn't want the conversation to be over yet. I searched my head for something else to talk about.

"Tori do you really think it's possible to stay here with

Ruthie? I asked her once and she said she was too old now to raise kids that she can only do it for a little while at a time? Now with Johnny gone, she might quit even sooner," I said.

I wanted to stay with Ruthie so badly, but I didn't want to get excited about something that wasn't true.

"Tabitha, I have another secret. Ruthie doesn't know it, but I am granted three wishes a year. You know, because I'm Irish, and we're magical, and all that shit," she said.

"Tori, you cuss an awful lot," I said.

"Shit, I'm sorry."

I raised my eyebrows and we both giggled.

"Anyways, I have taken my wishes and used most of them on Ruthie to get her to slowly change her mind about having a kid grow up here again," she whispered. "Now that you're here, it will be two kids, which will be easier because we'll take care of each other and Ruthie won't have to do anything except cook."

I didn't know a thing about the Irish or their three spells, but Tori seemed very serious about all of it.

"What does it mean? You know, to be Irish?" I asked.

"It means that my parents were from a country called Ireland," she said. "What are you?"

"I'm part spinach," I said lifting my head a little higher.

She looked and me and fell over laughing.

"What? What's so funny?" I asked.

"You're part spinach, huh?" Tori asked trying to keep a straight face. If a potato or a piece of celery rings the doorbell, I'll assume it's your family coming to get you!"

"Tori, what do you mean? What's wrong with you?" I was getting frustrated with her laughing at me.

"Tabitha, spinach is a vegetable that taste like grass that's been rubbed in the dirt. It's nasty. What you are is Spanish. You need to get that straight before someone else asks you!"

Spanish, I thought. No kidding!

"You know what?" Tori asked. "We should really stick together. I think if we do, we could be very powerful, you know like Batman and Robin!"

"Who?" I asked.

"Ummm... only the most powerful duo on Earth! Tori said. "They fight crime and get the bad guys, all while living in this cool cave and wear awesomely weird clothes and masks! Not to mention they drive this amazing car called the 'bat mobile.'"

Well that sounded weird and creepy.

"I don't want to look for bad guys... and wear weird clothes? I've had to wear enough of them. Masks scare me, and we don't know how to drive! I don't even know how to ride a bike," I said.

Tori stared at me. She finally blinked and shook her head. "Listen Tabitha, I don't mean we have to be exactly like them. I mean we can be a team, you and me. Like, be inseparable. Wouldn't that be cool? We can take care of each other, in case no else can?"

I thought for a moment and decided that it was the best plan I had heard. Tori asked if I wanted to make it an official pact. To do that, we had to stand up and meet in the middle of the room. We each spat into one of our hands said, "The cats on the roof, but you can't let him in, 'cause all he's gonna do is play the fiddle again." Then we spun to the left three times, to the right five times, and then we put the hands that we spit in together, and I had to promise to never let the fiddle playing cat in. After that we were best friends forever.

I noticed a beautiful heart that Tori wore on very long chain around her neck that must have come out of her pajamas while we were spinning.

"Tori where did you get that? It's beautiful!" I pointed to her heart.

"Umm... I got this from the Irish wish fairies," she said.

She opened it and inside was a picture of a blonde man with eyes exactly like Tori's.

"It's my dad," she said.

"Who gave it to you?" I asked.

She crawled back under her blankets. "Every time I use one of my wishes for someone else, the wish fairies reward me with a special gift," Tori said.

"Do you see them? What do they look like? Did you feel them put that on you?" I asked.

"You can't look at a wish fairy, Tabs. If you do, you get screwed out of all your wishes. When we feel them around us, we don't look at them – not even a peek, or poof!" she said, making magical motions with her hands.

"How do you know if you still have all your wishes?" I asked.

Tori looked towards the ceiling and shook her head slowly. "My dad must have seen one. I remember him writing that in the letter. He said some little dotted bastard took away his wishes," she said.

"Oh my God! That's awful! I'm so sorry, Tori!" I said.

"Don't worry about it," she said and started throwing her pillow into the air and catching it. "The Irish are very strong people. We can take a lot and dish a lot," she said with a smirk.

"A lot of what?" I asked.

"Malarkey, Tabitha. We give and take a lot of malarkey."

Before I had a chance to ask, she jumped out of bed and put her finger over my mouth, scaring the breath right out of me.

"Shhhh! You can never say that word unless you're Irish," she said. "If you do, your ears... your cute, tiny little ears... well, they will fall right off your head and hit the floor! Do you understand what I'm telling you?"

She kept her finger pressed against my lips and had a concerned look on her face. I nodded my head, not completely sure what I was agreeing to, yet so grateful to Tori for preventing me from losing my ears.

Then her face relaxed. She sat back and smiled. "Hey, thanks for talking tonight."

I smiled. "It's nice having a friend."

We turned off the lights and a comfortable silence draped over us.

In the middle of the night, I awoke to yelling and crying.

"GET ME OUT OF HERE!"

I sat up and looked over at Tori.

"HELP ME!"

It was coming from her. She was writhing in her bed, and her arms were covering her face.

"PLEASE GET HER OFF!" she cried. "TANYA, WHERE'S TANYA?"

Ruthie rushed in before I could get out of bed and held Tori, gently trying to bring her out of her nightmare. Tori kept insisting that someone was on her, that someone needed to find Tanya. Ruthie slowly eased her awake. She opened her eyes and saw that she was safe at Ruthie's and that everything was going to be all right.

I watched Ruthie rock Tori as she cried. I found myself wanting to wish on every coin thrown in a fountain and every wish flower ever grown, for Tori and I to be able to stay here, safe with Ruthie. I had to find that mulligan, and I had to find it soon.

CHAPTER TWENTY-TWO

When I met Tori at recess the next day, she was leaning against the chain link fence that surrounded the school, acting as if she were the coolest person on earth. The funny thing was that she could pull it off easily, and I was beginning to believe her. Several girls said hello to her as they walked by.

"Having a good day?" I asked.

She shrugged. "It's okay, I guess. Same faces, same work, different school."

"What about those girls that said hello to you just now?"

"They would follow each other off a bridge if the others decided to jump," she said. "And anyway, I'm never at any school very long and will most likely have to leave here soon too, so why bother, ya know?"

"What about all the stuff we talked about at dinner with Ruthie? We might leave tomorrow or we might be here until the end of the year. Let's try to make the best of it and make friends. If you stop the rumors here, they can't follow you again," I said.

She rolled her eyes. "Okay, okay. I will! Calm yourself already."

After school, I waited for Tori and we walked to our first after school meeting for foster kids.

"So, how did the rest of the day go?" I asked.

I had to shove one of girl's head in the toilet and punch another girl," Tori said nonchalantly.

I looked at her with horrified eyes and she busted out laughing.

"I'm kidding! It was fine. I actually made a few friends."

I sighed a breath of relief. "And maybe we'll make a few more at this meeting."

Tori groaned. "I doubt it. This is gonna be so freaking boring, you know that?"

When we got to the gym, there were cookies and milk set out on a table and ten chairs in a circle. There were already five girls sitting down eating cookies and talking to each other.

"I had no idea there were this many foster kids at our school," I said. "That's amazing!"

"Yeah, Tabs. I thought you and I were the only ones in the whole world," Tori said. "Unless they're faking it for the free cookies."

I shot her a dirty look. "Be nice, Tori. And my name is Tabitha."

Tori reached for some cookies and shrugged her shoulders. "Whatever."

Tori didn't want to sit near the other girls, so she plopped on the opposite side of the circle. I sat next to her, but I was worried we'd look stuck up. Tori's plan failed as more girls came in and filled in the other chairs.

The grown up leading the meeting introduced herself as Ms. Gage, but said we could call her Ms. G. She was older and kind of manly with very short black hair, and she might have the beginning of a mustache, but she seemed very nice.

"The boys are having their meeting in another room because it's easier to talk freely when it is just us girls," Ms. G said looking at all of us.

I was already shocked at the amount of kids that were in this room, so I was surprised that there were more in another meeting.

"I would like to welcome each of you from here at Hobbes

and the surrounding schools. This is a place to share our thoughts, feelings, and experiences no matter what stage in the system you are in." Ms. G spoke in a deep, loud voice.

"Would anyone like to start our conversation today? All right then... Riley! You were just placed in your new home a few weeks ago," Ms. G said as she thumbed through some papers she had placed on a clipboard. "Would you like to share your experiences so far?"

Riley stood up and told everyone how happy she was. How her new family made her feel terrific and how they were talking about maybe getting a puppy so she felt even more at home. Everyone clapped for her, including me. She seemed really content, and it made me feel less nervous.

Some kids were in transition homes like Ruthie's and some had just started living with a foster family, wondering if they would be chosen for permanent adoption. You could see the faces of the ones that were new to the system. They looked scared and paid deep attention to what the other kids were saying. A few talked about how things were good, but that it was hard to feel at home yet.

"Things take time, and you have to take each day as it comes," Ms. G said. "You have to remember that your foster families are also going through a change as well, so remember to be patient."

One girl named Avery Ryan seemed extra sad. She had big brown eyes and brown curly hair and was tiny like me. She said that she missed her parents so bad that she still cried a few times a day. She explained that her parents died in a fire a few months ago. She felt guilty that she hadn't been home that night, and that she had been at a friend's house for a sleepover. She was in a transition home at the moment, and they were very nice to her, but they were old and busy with the four other kids that lived there too. She said that she felt so alone and missed her parents and her long talks with her mom.

I couldn't help but think about Quinn and how he felt the same way about being with his friend when his family was killed. Tori paid extra attention to Avery, which was strange for

Tori. She would normally say she "didn't give a rat's ass" about people she didn't know.

Ms. G told her not to give up, that each day that goes by is a new day, and things would get better. Other girls were supportive of Avery as well, telling her that it would be okay, and if she needed to talk during school, that they would be around and would be there for her. It made me want to cry, seeing so much support coming from other kids.

Two other girls announce excitedly that they were getting adopted. Ms. G gave them each a badge and a balloon. It was fantastic to see how happy they were. I might have a real parent out there, but if it ended up that I didn't, this meeting made me calmer inside.

Kendal joined us all for dinner that night, and I couldn't stop talking about how great our new class was and how I couldn't wait until the next one. Tori seemed bored, so I tried to quiet down about it a little.

"Your hair is growing in really nice, Tabitha. Are you planning on growing it out or keeping it short?" Kendal asked.

"I hadn't really thought about it," I said.

"I think it's great just the way it is! You look just like how I picture the Tooth Fairy," Quinn said.

"My goodness! You really do," Kendal said, staring at me with smile. "I never saw it until just now. It's amazing how I always pictured her looking like that, too."

"What's a... who is the Tooth...?" Tori started to ask, then stopped.

"Haven't you ever had the Tooth Fairy visit?" I asked. "I just did for the first time ever."

I told her all about it, and I was almost as excited as Quinn was when he had first described her to me in the hospital.

"Yeah, sure I have...lots of times, Tabitha..." Tori said.

I could tell by the squishy face she made that she was fibbing.

"When you lost a tooth, did you put it under your pillow at bedtime, so during the night the Tooth Fairy would come?" I asked.

Tori crossed her arms and looked the other way, but I could tell that she was listening to every word I said. So, I continued.

"Isn't it cool how she's this tiny little fairy with wings, and taps on your tooth or teeth with her magic wand and changes them to…"

"I'm not fibbing I've had it stop by tons of times!" Tori said before I could finish. "I've lost forty teeth so there. She came by forty times!"

"Wow, Tori! You must be rich!" I said, excited for her.

"Why would I be rich?" she asked.

"Tori, what does the Tooth Fairy leave all over your teeth?"

She hesitated and quickly said, "Spit! There's spit all over the coins so they stick to the Kleenex. So there! Ha ha, I told you I've had the Tooth Fairy come!"

"Spit? You think the Tooth Fairy spits on your teeth?"

By this time everyone at the table was very interested in our conversation.

"Well, maybe we had tooth fairies from different neighborhoods. Did you ever think of that?" Tori asked. "Mine spit, and as I can see by your reaction, yours did not!"

"There's only one Tooth Fairy, Tori! Not a bunch from different neighborhoods," I said. "She taps on your tooth or teeth to change them to coins, and she leaves pretty sparkly fairy dust that falls off her wand."

Tori's mouth dropped open. "Coins…? Fairy dust?" She stared at me with one eyebrow pointing straight up.

"Oh yeah! Coins!" she added quickly. "Yes, I am quite wealthy, Tabitha. You're very lucky to have such a rich best friend!" She turned to Ruthie. "Ruthie, does a winged chick come by, sneak in your room, and put fairy dust under your pillow while you sleep?" Tori asked. "And why haven't I heard about her until now?"

"Maybe she just couldn't find you among all the children that were at this house, or maybe she got confused when you moved to other homes," Ruthie said.

Tori shoved her plate back. She was *not* happy. "Well, lucky for her I don't even like the thought of a creepy little mini-winged chick. I would get her with bug spray!"

Quinn choked on his coffee and Kendal laughed out loud.

"You would kill the Tooth Fairy, Tori?" I said, my eyes wide in disbelief.

"Yep! Spray till she dropped. Then I would shake her magic little wand until all the coins were out of it, and then I would nail her wings to the wall to show any other fairies what I would do to them if they ever showed up in my room again."

Kendal got up from her chair. She was laughing so hard she was making squeaking noises. Quinn and Ruthie had tears rolling down their faces. But I wasn't happy at all about the thought of Tori killing the Tooth Fairy, not at all. Ruthie noticed that I wasn't laughing.

"It's okay, Tabitha. Tori wouldn't really hurt the Tooth Fairy, isn't that right, Tori?" she said.

Tori looked over at me, and her face softened. "Naw, I'd capture her in a jar and bring her to you. How's that?"

After dinner, Quinn and Kendal left, and Ruthie took us into the living room and sat us on the couch facing the wall of pictures. Ruthie kissed the top of both our heads and said she had something to show us. She left and came back with her hands behind her back.

"Are you ready?" she asked.

We nodded and watched as she held out a framed picture of Tori and me from the beach party tub day. We were smiling, laughing, and having a blast.

"Is it okay to put this one on the wall, or would you rather have separate pictures of yourselves put up?" Ruthie asked.

Tori and I looked at each other and blurted at the same time, "Together."

Ruthie turned to face the wall. "Okay... where should we put you?"

"Next to Shamus!" Tori said.

Ruthie smiled. "I have the perfect spot."

She moved a few pictures around and there we were side-by-side with Quinn's picture.

We stood and admired our photo on the wall, taking its place among all the others.

Ruthie went back to the couch and lifted up a chair cushion. "I have one more thing to show you both."

She handed us each a beautifully wrapped package the size of a book. We unwrapped our very own photo albums filled with the beach party pictures. We were so happy and excited to have the beginning of our friendship's life in pictures, with extra pages left for us to fill with future memories. We both threw our arms around Ruthie and gave her a long hug.

"Okay, girls. Time for bed," she said.

As we ran up the stairs, I looked back and saw Ruthie dabbing her eyes.

CHAPTER TWENTY-THREE

After my bath, I went to our room, where Tori was already lying in bed, throwing her pillow in the air and catching it.

"Tabitha, what do you think heaven is like?" she asked.

"I see it lined with white Christmas trees with white lights, and it smells like flowers. You can sit on a fluffy cloud whenever you want and look down and watch anyone you want from above," I said.

"I think it's a bunch of tables filled with candy and cupcakes that you can eat and eat and never throw up," she said. She caught her pillow and tossed again.

"That's it? Just a ton of candy and cupcakes? What do you think it looks like?" I asked.

"I don't know... I'd go right for the cupcakes without looking around."

She didn't say anything else, but kept tossing her pillow. I kissed my fingers and placed them on my mom's picture. The only sound was the "whoosh" of the pillow in the air and the "plop" of it into her hands. Whoosh, plop. Whoosh, plop. I knew there was something on her mind. I yawned and stretched extra big and extra long. Maybe that would provoke her to talk. It didn't.

"Well, goodnight, Tori."

"How come you haven't asked me about my nightmare?"

There it was.

"Tori, I figured if you wanted to talk about it, you would be the one to bring it up. I've had a ton of them, so I know how awful they can be," I said.

She caught her pillow and turned to face me.

"Before I came here, I was at school, the one on Miles... the one I was talking to Ruthie about, remember? I was with a really cool family and they were going to adopt me.

"They had an older kid of their own, a daughter who was 18 named Tanya. She was awesome and had the coolest car. It was bright red and totally badass. Johnny told me I wasn't allowed to ride in the car with her for any reason, no matter what. I told Johnny that Tanya was going to be my older sister soon, and I should be able to do things with her. Well, Johnny put her foot down and said I wasn't adopted yet, and until I was, she could still tell me what I could or could not do. Driving with Tanya in her new car was a huge no."

Tori looked down at her hands. "So one day Tanya pulled up right in front of school with another girl in the back seat. Tanya was tan from a trip to Florida, and with her long brown hair and sunglasses, she looked like a model. She looked up at me and said, 'Come on! We're going to the mall, little sister!'

"I had never been called anyone's sister, and it made me feel like a million bucks. I told her that Johnny said I wasn't allowed to. All the kids were watching me, standing next to the beautiful older girls and the cool car.

"'I'm your big sister, and I say you can, so are we shopping or not?' she said. I couldn't help myself, the thrill of being called little sister, all the other kids envious of me being with the older popular girls. I opened the door and slid onto the cool leather seats.

"We joked around and the older girls talked about something called 'the prom,' and what boys were hot and which ones were fugly. We were having a great time. The other girl's phone started to ding. She looked at it and told Tanya she just had to read this text from a boy. She handed Tanya the phone. They kept passing the phone back and forth.

"I saw the stop sign, but Tanya didn't. I yelled for her to stop. It was too late. A van hit us, and the last thing I remember was the car rolling. When I woke, the girl from the back seat was lying on top of me. She was crushing me. I could barely breathe. I couldn't see Tanya, and everything was upside down and covered with glass and blood. There was blood in my eyes, and my ears were ringing. I heard sirens and people yelling, but that's all I remember before I woke again in the hospital."

She stopped talking and tossed the pillow back and forth between her hands. I wiped tears from my eyes.

"Tori that must have been the scariest thing in the world, I'm so glad you're all right," I said.

"They all died, Tabitha. Tanya was thrown from the car. Both her friend and the guy driving the van, they died, too. I waited for her parents to come see me in the hospital, but they never did. I guess if I were them, I wouldn't want to see a foster kid who survived when their real kid was dead. They probably felt screwed. I thought they cared about me though, I really did. I waited every day for them to come see me, and then Johnny told me the adoption was off."

Tori's face was dry. She pursed her lips and knotted her eyebrows.

"I never got to go to her funeral or say goodbye. I was in the hospital too long. I miss her, Tabitha. I miss her every single day and wonder what it would have been like if she hadn't touched that phone. Maybe if I had grabbed it, none of that would have happened," she said.

"Tori..." My throat felt choked up. It was hard to speak. "I... I don't know what to say."

Tori shrugged. "There's nothing to say, Tabitha. It happened. There's nothing that can ever change it." She stared at the floor and shook her head. Finally, she said, "Well, we better get some sleep."

She rolled over and turned off the light. In the dark, I heard her sniffling.

"I love you, Tori," I whispered.

"Love you too, Tabitha," she whispered back.

The next morning I woke to Tori muffling cuss words. "Holy shit, hot damn!" Her eyes were huge and she held a clump of green tissue paper.

"Tabitha! Are you awake?" Tori whispered.

"Yes...What? It's kind of hard not to be, Tori. What are doing?" I asked, wiping the ick from my tired eyes.

"Look what was under my pillow! It's heavy! What do you think it is?" she asked.

"Open it and find out," I said.

She slowly unwrapped the tissue paper to find a small note attached.

She held the note in both hands. "It's a message."

She came over and sat on the edge of my bed. I sat up and looked over her shoulder as she read the note:

> *Dear Victory,*
>
> *I'm sorry I haven't been able to find you all the times you lost your teeth. I was flying by the window last night when I heard you had lost several teeth... I hope these will help you to believe in me. I promise to be there for any more teeth you may lose in the future.*
>
> *Sincerely,*
> *The Tooth Fairy*

Tori looked at the note, then at the tissue paper.

"Do you think that's true? Did she really fly by the window and hear us?" she asked.

"There's only one way to be sure, Tori," I said. "You need to open the tissue paper."

She unwrapped it and found seven silver coins, all with a touch of fairy dust. Tori held the coins nestled in the tissue paper as if they might disappear any second.

"Tori, she did come! Look at all her fairy dust all over them!" I said.

"This is the most awesome thing ever. I can't wait to show Ruthie!" Tori said.

She gathered up her coins and we ran downstairs to the kitchen.

"Look, Ruthie! The Tooth Fairy found me and she gave me coins! She even left me a note!" she told Ruthie.

"What a very lucky girl you are, Tori! That's wonderful!" Ruthie clapped her hands in excitement. It was rare to see excitement on Tori's face, so that morning the Tooth Fairy made magic in more ways than one.

While Tori was putting her coins, still in the tissue paper back upstairs, I went to Ruthie and thanked her for getting in touch with the Tooth Fairy for Tori.

"It was just a lucky night that she was in the neighborhood," Ruthie said.

"Lucky was right!" I said.

After school, Tori had her first appointment with Dr. Katherine. She refused to see the doctor that had been treating her in the past, calling him a 'quack.'

"He's a huge jerk, and I told him that. He treated me like I was a freaking baby," Tori said. "I'm not dealing with him anymore, no way, no how."

"Well, you're going to love Dr. Katherine. She really listens to you like you're a grown up," I said.

After Tori went into Dr. Katherine's office, Ruthie and I went to the cafeteria to wait. Ruthie played with her napkin and kept glancing around the room. She smiled at me, but her smile was off.

"Ruthie, are you all right?" I asked, suddenly very frightened. "You seem like you're worried about something. You're not sick, are you?"

"No, Tabitha, I'm just fine. Why don't you take your homework out and get a head start on it while we wait for Tori."

And that was that.

Tori left her appointment in a really good mood.

"She really did listen and treated me like I was grown up.

She got me to talk about things that I never thought I would, and it was easy!" Tori said.

In the car on the way home Tori asked Ruthie if she believed in witches.

"No, Tori. I don't believe in witches," Ruthie said, looking back at us in the rear view mirror.

"You believe in the Tooth Fairy, but witches are a no, huh?" Tori said.

"Why do you ask?" Ruthie said.

"Well, that doctor... she's a witch" Tori said. "There's no doubt about it. She got me to talk about stuff without me even knowing I was talking about it. Plus her eyes are strange. Tori looked over at me and winked. "She looks like she ate a kid and now that kid is staring back from behind her. It's freaking weird," she said.

"Ruthie, she must be able to open her mouth crazy wide... like an alligator... to eat a kid whole like that, right?"

Ruthie was laughing so hard that she was practically begging her to stop. I was pretty sure that Ruthie didn't know Tori was saying all these things just so Ruthie would do one of her really loud belly laughs.

"Well, Ruthie, when you come to pick me up and she tells you I left, but you notice that these wild blue eyes I got here are staring back at you from hers, you have to promise to give her that Heimlich maneuver thing people do to make other people spit stuff out that they're choking on, and get me out of her!" Tori said, practically rolling in her seat belt covering her mouth so Ruthie couldn't hear her laughing. And there it was – Ruthie's loud, uncontrollable belly laugh. Tori had succeeded, and we pulled over until Ruthie got herself together again.

When we were setting the table for dinner, Tori brought up Dr. Katherine again.

"Ruthie, do they really think that no matter how many hours we sit and talk to a doctor or anyone else, that we'll forget everything that's happened to us? I know we will both take our memories and carry them with us until we're old and dead. There is no way around it. We can only hope that the future will have so much good in it that it will take over the bad."

Ruthie stood with her arms folded, listening to every word Tori said.

"Tori, I have to agree," she said. "Dr. Katherine doesn't have magic powers or spells that she can place on you so that you forget everything. That's not her job. But she can teach you how to deal with what has happened so you can make sense of it and hopefully put it away, instead of allowing it to be an uninvited guest in your life every day."

Tori nodded. "That makes a lot of sense. Thanks, Ruthie."

Ruthie smiled and put her hand on Tori's cheek. "I'll be right back. Would you children finish setting the table?" And she went upstairs.

Tori looked at me, "What the hell is going on with Ruthie?"

"I don't know," I said. "I asked her while we were waiting for you if she was sick. She said she was fine."

We both thought about it.

"Maybe she's missing Johnny. They had coffee every day and dinner a few times a week. Maybe she is having a hard time today," I said.

"I hope that's what it is, Tabitha," Tori said. "I couldn't stand it if...well, you know," she said.

"Yeah, Tori, I know. Me neither."

When Ruthie came back downstairs, we sat down for dinner.

Ruthie fluffed her napkin and spread it on her lap. She cleared her throat. "Girls, I need to let you know that your new social worker will be meeting you here Saturday afternoon. I heard that she's a lovely young woman, and if it helps any, Margaret trained her and taught her everything she knows."

The food stuck in my throat. I looked at Tori and could tell she felt the same way. Just then, Quinn walked in.

"Hey goofballs!" He looked at each of us and then Ruthie. "What's with the long faces?"

"They're replacing Johnny already, like anyone could take her place," Tori said. She played with the food on her plate.

"They are NOT replacing Johnny," Quinn said. He put his hands on his hips. "This new social worker trained with Johnny, and now she is keeping her promise to her. So empty your heads of that nonsense right now."

"You're absolutely right Shamus," Ruthie said. She seemed to feel a little better. Tori watched Ruthie make Quinn a plate and asked, "So what else is going on? That's not all you wanted to say, is it?"

"No sweetheart it isn't." Ruthie looked as if she might cry right in front of us, but regained her strength and moved her shoulders back. "Tori, Saturday is an even bigger day for you. You'll move into your new foster home!"

We stared at her. She swallowed and forced a smile.

"A young couple has asked to foster you, and they are decorating a new room for you as we speak," she said. "They live right up the road, and you will still be attending Hobbes. That means you and Tabitha can still have sleepovers on weekends. Isn't that wonderful?"

She seemed like she was forcing her voice to sound excited. "You'll be going to live with them on Saturday as well. It's turning out to be quite the busy day."

Tori looked at Ruthie. "So that's what's been bothering you all day? You can't do that to yourself! You're going to make yourself sick, and then where will we eat?"

She was trying to make Ruthie laugh, and Ruthie gave her a weak chuckle.

"I'm sure they are great people, and you're right, at least Tabitha and I can go to school together and have sleepovers. So, no worries, all right? Stop looking so sad! It makes me nervous."

Quinn stared at his plate, and I wanted to throw up. They were taking Tori away, and she didn't even care. Maybe I wasn't that important to her after all. I pushed my chair back and started toward the stairs. Quinn stopped me before I hit the landing.

"Tell me what's going on in that head of yours, sweetie," he said.

I plopped onto the stairs. "She doesn't seem to care at all!" I threw my hands in the air. "We planned on never being apart, and now that plan isn't going to work out. Quinn, it scares me all the way through my whole body. How can they separate us? We're Batman and Robin," I said. "Best friends forever."

Quinn nodded and was silent before he looked at me again. "Don't you want Tori to have a family and start a new life?"

"No, Quinn, I don't! I want her to stay in this life... in my life... in this house. That's what I want. We're a family! Why can't it stay like this?" I said.

"That's not how all this works, sweetie, but everything will be fine. I swear." And he put his hand over his heart.

I wanted to believe him. I wanted to believe him so badly. "But Quinn, what if I have a family out there, and they want to take me far away? What do I do then?"

"You cross that bridge when you get to it," he said.

I put my face in my hands. "There are no bridges around here."

Quinn patted the back of my head. "No, Tabitha. That means not to worry about things when you don't have to."

I looked up at him. "Quinn, have you found anything about the mulligans yet? I need some really, really bad."

"Now it's more than one?" he asked.

"If I had one, I could change something. If I had a bunch, I could change everything," I said.

"What do you mean you could change everything?"

"I could bring my mom back, Tori's parents, and her almost-sister that died in the accident and her friend. We could bring back your family and Johnny," I said.

Quinn shook his head. His eyes were so sad. "Sweetheart, no. No, you couldn't. You can't bring people back from heaven. You just can't, even with a million mulligans. Things are the way they are, and we all have to deal with them."

My heart broke. I'd been depending on that mulligan for so long. I burst into tears. "Then what good are they? If you can't make people come back, they're no better than a coin in the fountain or a wish flower!"

"They are second chances... a new home... or family you didn't know you had. Sounds like a pretty good thing to me, don't you think?" he asked.

I shook my head. "Maybe. But I'm still not happy, Quinn. This whole think stinks and I hate it," I cried.

"I know, sweetie," Quinn put his arm around my shoulder and we rocked back and forth on the stairs until my tears slowed.

"You want to come back to dinner?" he asked.

I shook my head. I ran upstairs to my old room, threw myself onto my bed, and buried my face in the pillow.

I must have fallen asleep because I woke up to Tori's voice.

"What are you doing in here? Why aren't you in our room?"

I sat up. Tori stood in the doorway with her arms folded.

"Our room?" I said. "So it's okay for you to leave me, but I can't leave you, is that it?" I said.

"What are you talking about, fruitcake? I'm not going anywhere!" Tori said with a laugh. "I'll leave here Saturday morning and be back for lunch!" She smiled so wide she was almost laughing. "When I said friends forever, I meant it. The new fosters are probably nice people, but my home is here. Whether Ruthie accepts that yet or not, this is our home."

"What if they're perfect for you? What if Ruthie can't handle kids long term like she said? What if the next call is for me, and it's a new family, or maybe my real mom or dad, and they take me far away? How are we going to stay together, Tori?" I asked.

"One ticket for Tabitha to 'What-if-Ville,' the last stop to Crazy Town," Tori said in a deep, manly voice. "Listen, you have to believe in things. We're going to stay together. My dad wrote in his letter that if you don't have something to believe in, you don't have much of a reason to wake in the morning."

Something about the way Tori talked, she could make you believe anything. I had no doubt that when she left Saturday, she would be back for lunch. My stomach felt sour and my legs felt like they were made of spaghetti, but as long as Tori said it,

I believed it.

"Now are you coming back in our room on your own, or am I gonna have to put you over my shoulder?"

I smiled and jumped off the bed.

Back in our room again, Tori asked me what Quinn and I were talking about on the stairs. I told Tori everything I knew about mulligans. Tori just stared at the ceiling. She held her pillow without tossing it.

"Mulligans are second chances, huh?" she said.

"Yeah, that's what the elf said."

"Fantastic! This mulligan thing could be the answer," she said.

"To what?" I asked.

"Just wait. In the next few days you'll understand and I'll show you a mulligan," she said.

"For real, Tori?" I asked.

"For real."

And up went the pillow.

CHAPTER TWENTY-FOUR

On Saturday we were sitting at the breakfast table, Ruthie, Quinn, and Kendal. It felt like a goodbye and good luck breakfast. Everyone seemed sad except Tori, who was calm as could be.

When the doorbell rang, Ruthie welcomed our new social worker into our home. We'd promised to be nice to her, at least I did. I was pretty sure Tori's fingers were crossed.

"Everyone," Ruthie said, "I would like you to meet Miss Winnie Owens."

Tori looked at the tiny blonde woman. "You've got to be kidding me. Winnie? What did ya do with Tigger and Rabbit? Leave them in the car?"

The social worker smiled, not bothered by Tori's attitude. "My full name is Winnifred, Miss Galloway."

"You're killing me! Winnifred? Seriously?" Tori said.

"Tori, watch your manners," Ruthie said quietly.

But Winnie was smiling.

"Well now, I was hoping you would come up with something a little more original than that, Vicky," she said.

"Yep," I thought. "Johnny definitely trained her."

She looked at me and held her hand out. "You must be Tabitha?"

"No, no, that's not Tabitha. That's Ruthie," Tori said.

"This is Tabitha," and she grabbed Ruthie's hand. "She needs a home, but no one wants to take her, and we just can't figure out why. She's an excellent cook, and if it weren't for her potty mouth she would be absolutely perfect," Tori said in a distraught voice, pretending to be upset.

Ruthie grabbed Tori and hugged her tight.

Winnie looked at me. "I will be back later to visit with you, okay?" she said.

I nodded. Tears welled up in my eyes as Tori gave everyone hugs and told them she would see them soon. They spilled over when she got to me.

Tori whispered in my ear, "Don't let them serve lunch until I get back," and winked at me.

Quinn offered to carry her suitcase, but she picked it up by herself.

"Come on, Pooh! Can I call you Pooh? Or perhaps you prefer Freddy? Freddy... I like it! What do ya think?" Tori asked on her way out the door.

"I think you look like a Vicky," Winnie said. "I used to know a young girl named Vicky. She was a doll! You know what? She actually collected dolls, too!"

We listened to Winnie go on and on about dolls all the way to the car. Tori's face was priceless, as if she had just eaten a lemon whole.

It was 9 a.m., and lunch was always at 12:30 p.m. Three and a half hours to hold my breath. I can do this, I thought. Ruthie wiped a tear from her eyes, and Kendal was upset as well. Quinn stared at me, grinning.

"What might our little Tori have up her sleeve?" he asked.

I felt my face grow hot. "What? I don't know what you mean!"

"Really? Would you like to put your hand over your heart and tell me that again?"

Kendal and Ruthie were watching me now.

"Tori seemed very relaxed about leaving, don't you think? No potty mouth, dirty looks, or arguments. Just her usual sarcasm," Quinn said. "That's not like Tori at all, don't you agree, Tabitha?"

"Well, you know how people handle things in different ways, right?" I said. I desperately did not want to break Tori's trust in me.

"You seem to be handling it pretty well too," Quinn continued. "Tears only lasted a few seconds, and you have looked at the clock at least five times since she left... so what's our little Tori up to, Tabitha?"

With all eyes on me, I stood firm and said, "I, Tabitha M. Sullivan, choose to plead my fifth amendment."

Quinn started smiling again. I mean, really smiling.

"Nicely played Tori, you little shyster," he said. "How long did it take you to memorize that statement after she taught it to you?"

"Not long," I said and clapped my hands over my mouth. It had only taken a few minutes to screw up.

"Well, Ruthie, if you don't mind I would love to see how this plays out today." Quinn looked at Kendal.

She giggled and said, "I'm all in!"

Ruthie suggested I take a bubble bath and get ready for the day while she made some fresh cookies. I went upstairs and soaked in the tub for a long time, letting the bubbles take away my butterflies. I took my time cleaning the bedroom and making the bed. I was sluggish picking out my clothes for the day as well. I think I just wanted the clock to race by because I would do anything not to lie, and I really doubted that I could, even if I tried, without throwing up.

I lay down in my bed and listened to the voices downstairs. Winnie was there now, and her high-pitched voice traveled up the stairs like the scent of Ruthie's cookies, but not as enjoyable. Then I saw Quinn standing in the doorway.

"How come you're up here all by yourself, goofball?" he asked.

"I'm just thinking," I said.

"Do you need to talk about anything?" he said.

I sighed. "It seems weird to have a stranger here instead of

Johnny, and to hear her weird voice. It just makes it hurt a little that's all," I said.

"I'll tell you a secret. Ruthie isn't doing too well having anyone except Margaret in her home, either. Maybe having you down there might help," he said.

I sat up and took a deep breath. "I'll be down in a minute."

Quinn nodded and left. The clock on my dresser read 11:17.

Only one hour and thirteen minutes to go.

We were eating cookies and talking with Winnie when we heard a car pull up. I looked at the clock.

It was 12:20.

"What in the world is going on?" Winnie said. I hadn't noticed how short she was until she stood on her tiptoes to see over Ruthie's kitchen window. "It's Victory... She's with Mr. and Mrs. Hynes and... they're hugging and smiling."

She turned back to the table with a frown. The rest of us were smiling. Tori was back, just like she said she would be. The doorbell rang and in walked Tori with a young couple.

"Hi everybody!" Tori said as if she were supposed to be there. "I want you to meet two wonderful people. This is Chris, and his wife Lori, and they're awesome!"

Chris was tall with broad shoulders and blonde hair. Lori was tiny and blonde as well, like the beautiful ballerinas that danced in the jewelry boxes in the store. Everyone shook hands and Ruthie offered them cookies and coffee, but they politely said no, asking Winnie if she had some time to talk with them. They hugged Tori and kissed her cheeks, telling her what an amazing child she was and how proud of her we all should be. Tori watched, waved, and smiled at them as they followed Winnie into the living room.

We all stared at Tori, but no one said a word. Tori got a glass from the cupboard, grabbed some milk and a cookie, and leaned against the counter. When the Hynes left they hugged Tori again and thanked her. When the door closed, we all sat back to watch the show between Tori and Winnie.

"Victory Rain Galloway! What exactly do you think you are

doing?" Winnie said.

"Freddy Pooh! Didn't you listen to what they said?" Tori asked.

"Yes, I listened," she said with her lips beginning to pucker slightly. "They loved you. They thought you were charming and lovely. You loved them too, but decided that you weren't the perfect match for them. You decided that you were going to set them up with a better kid that really needed a home badly... a girl named..." and she looked at the paper in her hand, "Avery Ryan? They not only want to foster her, but to start adoption proceedings as soon as possible."

"See, Freddy Pooh! Isn't that fantastic news! I got a kid adopted by two amazing people that will make her incredibly happy. You might think about retiring. I'm pretty good at this don't ya think? Maybe we should start splitting that paycheck of yours there," Tori said.

"My name is Winnie Pooh... I mean Freddy Wind..." and she stopped and began to fan herself.

Ruthie got up and took a glass out of the cupboard. By this point the table was about to explode with laughter.

"Ruthie, I didn't miss lunch did I?" Tori asked.

"No," Ruthie said. Her back was to the sink, and her shoulders were shaking. "I was just about to start it."

"I just don't understand. Those people were perfect for you!" Winnie said. Her voice grew higher pitched when she was frustrated. And now it was almost high enough to hurt your ears. "You need a home. You deserve to be happy."

Ruthie came back to the table with pursed lips and smiling eyes. She set the ice water down in front of Winnie.

"No, Freddy Pooh, I don't. I have a home, and I'm about to have lunch in it as soon as I get washed up. It's not your fault because you don't know me. I've never been happier." And with that, she walked upstairs.

Winnie walked into the hallway and grabbed Tori's suitcase that she'd left by the door. She held it up and looked at it funny. Just as she set it on the counter, it popped open. Winnie's eyes opened wide and she placed her hand on her throat. That did it for everyone. Quinn almost fell off his seat. Ruthie was laughing so hard she was making squeaking noises, and even Kendal covered her face, but her shoulders were shaking uncontrollably. I laughed so hard I almost wet my pants.

The suitcase was completely empty.

She'd never even bothered to pack.

At bedtime Tori and I stayed awake and talked.

"Why did you pick Avery?" I asked.

"She needed a family really bad, and they were amazing people. Their house was awesome and their backyard was like a park with a pool, swing set, slide and a pond with really huge goldfish in it," she said.

"Tori, I don't understand. If these people were so great and perfect, why would you give them away to someone else? What if something changes and we end up being split up anyways? You gave away a perfect home," I said.

"Well, I thought about that. I considered it all, and decided that I would stick with my first plan, and that's what I did. I don't regret it at all. Avery is like a wounded bird, she's so sad and fragile. She feels like she should have died with her parents and she's feeling guilty because she was somewhere else when the fire happened. The Hynes are perfect for her, and she's going to love them, just wait until the next meeting. I'm going to give mine away every time I get a call that a foster family wants me. Tabitha, I'll give them mulligans, one by one, until Miss Winnifred Owens just gives up on me, and Ruthie realizes I'm not going anywhere."

My mouth dropped open. The mean, nasty Tori that I had first met had a heart as big as the whole world. She wasn't looking for a mulligan like I was trying to. She just decided she didn't need to see them with her own eyes or hold them in her hands. Instead, she was giving them away like other things you can't see or hold, like love, kindness, hopes, and dreams.

"It's the perfect plan, Tori, and I can't wait to see a mulligan work," I told her.

"You'll see soon," Tori said in a sleepy voice. Shortly after she was sound asleep.

Never in a million years would I have thought that she cared so much about other people. She was truly a surprising puzzle.

CHAPTER TWENTY-FIVE

At the next meeting there were a few more girls than last time. Ms. G introduced them and asked, "Would anyone like to start out the meeting?"

One of the new girls spoke and told us she had been with her foster family for quite a while. She just wasn't sure about the meetings but would give them a try. She was hopeful that she would soon be adopted.

We all clapped for her, and then Ms. G asked another new girl if she would like to speak. She had the blackest hair I had ever seen. It was long, past her shoulders, and had bright pink and purple streaks in it. Instead of standing like everyone else did, she leaned forward in her chair and introduced herself as Sloan Reynolds. She had been in the system from the beginning.

"I could never be completely adopted because my mother would never allow it. I never even knew her that well. Mommy dearest hasn't seen me in two years, and now she's not allowed to see me at all. I have no idea who my biological father is and neither did my mom. I'm not a pity case. My social worker said I had to come to this meeting or I wouldn't be here. I've been in many foster homes, and they didn't do anything wrong."

She waved her hands as she said it. Her words relaxed a lot

of newbies, including me. "But I don't care to be honest with you. I know you all want homes with a little white picket fence, but I don't need one. I'm eleven years old and I've gotten this far. I don't need anyone trying to blow butterflies up my ass about how great my life could be."

I watched Tori while Sloan spoke. Her face was a blank slate, but her eyes were stuck on Sloan. I knew my Tori, and her wheels were spinning.

Then it was Avery's turn. She stood and smiled from ear to ear.

"I met a wonderful couple who not only wanted to foster me, but filed for permanent adoption! I have no idea how they found me, but in my heart I feel like my mom and dad sent them to me," she said.

Her eyes welled with tears and fell down her cheeks. Everyone clapped for an extra-long time and surrounded her with Avery. It was a moment when your heart felt like it was going to burst. Ms. G brought her over a badge and balloon and gave her a huge hug as well.

Tori looked down at me and said, "That, Tabs, is a mulligan."

While we were waiting to get picked up, most of the other girls went to get another helping of cookies, but Tori headed straight for Sloan. I followed, just in case Tori was up to no good.

"You think you're a real badass, don't you Sloan?" Tori said in a low, quiet voice.

"Who the hell are you supposed to be, my conscience? How about this, when you get home later, why you don't look in the mirror and preach to yourself, you arrogant bitch," Sloan said.

Tori shrugged off the insults. "I just had a question for your badass self. What do you want?"

Sloan smirked and rolled her eyes. "I want you go lick an electric socket and get the fuck out of my face. Is that clear enough?"

Tori continued in a calm voice like she hadn't even heard

what Sloan had said. "I mean, do you really want to be shuffled around for the next seven years from home to home? Do you want to use the fact that your mother was a screw up for everything that sucks in your life? Poor you! Lend me a Kleenex so I can catch my tears."

"What business is it of yours how the hell I run my life when you can't even get a decent haircut?" Sloan said and pointed to Tori's head.

Tori started to walk towards her and I grabbed her arm.

"I see you have your little yard gnome here to keep you in line." She pointed to me this time.

Tori shook off my hand. "You have the power over your own life even though it doesn't seem like it," Tori said. "Wouldn't it be nice to have people around you that you can actually talk to and depend on? Wouldn't that be freaking cool instead of pretending you like the way your life is right now? It's lonely isn't it?"

Sloan didn't say anything and actually looked like she was listening to Tori for a second.

"You want to let your walls down, but if you do, that means you're weak, that you broke your own rules about being happy. Think about that because you never know what may be coming your way. You might have to make a decision pretty quick, so make sure you make the right one."

Tori walked away, and I walked behind her, relieved that Sloan hadn't taken a swing at her, and in awe of what Tori had just said. It was as if she had been talking in the mirror to her old self. I turned back and to see Sloan watching Tori. Her face was blank, just like Tori's.

A few weeks later, a second couple returned Tori in the same way the Hynes had. Winnie met them at Ruthie's house shortly after. It was easy to see that she was using every ounce of patience she had to deal with Tori. This couple couldn't compliment Tori enough and hugged her several times before they left, thanking her the same way the couple before had.

Winnie took a deep breath. "Who is Sloan Reynolds?"

"I don't know why you're mad," Tori said. "Another kid, a

badass kid, might get adopted. You have no idea what a miracle it will be if that goes through."

Winnie gathered her things to leave. "What about you, Victory? Why do you want to be left behind?" She shook her head as she headed for the door. "This isn't the promise I made, not at all."

Tori sat down. Everyone was quieter than usual, and I was getting nervous. They didn't seem to understand what a great thing she was doing.

"Tori?" Quinn asked. "Why don't you want a home? What's next?"

"Well, we need to keep our fingers crossed for this girl Sloan. She goes to the meetings. She's mad at the world, and she's 11 years old and a complete pain in the...Well you know, and she needs to know that things can be good and that it's not wrong to be happy. She kind of reminds me of the old me. That's why I think this couple is perfect for her. I just hope Sloan sees it, too," Tori replied.

"No." Quinn said. "I meant what's next for *you*? Are you just going to keep giving away these great foster families to other kids? Winnie made a promise to take care of you, and you're making it awfully hard, Tori."

Tori looked at me as if to ask permission to tell him and I nodded.

"Mulligans, Quinn. I'm giving away mulligans, and they're working. These kids are all happy and have permanent families, so what am I doing that's so wrong? Johnny would be proud of me! I'm helping her more than that Winnie woman ever could," Tori replied.

Ruthie stared into her coffee. Quinn studied Tori's face before speaking again.

"You're not doing anything wrong sweetheart, but what about *your* mulligan? Don't you want a permanent family?" he asked.

Tori leaned forward and grabbed his pinky finger, which made Tori's hand look tiny. She looked right at him.

"What do you think I have, Shamus? I've got Ruthie in my

life, Tabs, you, and Kendal. I always feel Johnny with me. I count five mulligans right there. A permanent family? Not on paper, no, but in my heart I do. It makes me feel good to see these people and other kids so happy together and knowing it was Tabitha's mulligans that did it. No matter where I end up, I'll be okay, but *this,*" she pointed to the ground, "This will *always* be my permanent family. This is where I learned what it was like to love and be loved, it's where I turned hate and anger into happiness and laughter, Shamus. You guys are my mulligans."

Quinn and Tori never lost eye contact with each other. I had never heard Tori talk so softly and so seriously. She looked angelic with her hair growing out and her soft blonde curls tipping over into her face. Ruthie never looked up from her coffee.

Suddenly Quinn broke away from Tori's eyes, picked up his phone and said, "Hello? Yeah, of course. I'll be right there."

He stood up, gave us all a kiss on the head, and was gone.

Strange thing was, I never heard his phone ring.

At the next meeting, Sloan stood up.

"After a long talk with a friend, I decided that I wasn't truly happy with my life the way it was going. I realized that even though the state has a lot to do with what happens to me for a while, I still have power over how I live my life."

She explained that a couple she had never met, not only filed for fostering, but for permanent adoption. Before anyone could start clapping she put her hand up to stop them.

"I'd never met these people and said I wasn't interested and would leave before they got there."

Tori suddenly looked at the floor.

"They asked to just have lunch with me, and I agreed. They were different. They didn't try hard to impress me or make me like them; they were just themselves. It made it easy for me to be myself, a person I hadn't seen in a long time. I laughed a lot. It was easy with them."

Sloan's eyes fluttered and she cleared her throat. Tori's head was up now and she was on the edge of her seat.

"After lunch they dropped me off at my foster house. They will be picking me up tomorrow, and I will eventually be adopted by an amazing couple that I almost ran away from."

Everyone clapped, and Ms. G gave a badge and balloon to Sloan, who was smiling for the first time since we'd met her.

Sloan walked over to Tori. "Thank you. I don't know how, but I know you had something to do with this, and I will always be grateful to you, Tori."

They smiled at each other nodded. After Sloan walked away, Tori turned to me, a glitter in her eyes.

"I freaking love mulligans, Tabs. I just freaking love them."

CHAPTER TWENTY-SIX

The next day Quinn stopped in with Kendal. He peered into the living room with a funny look on his face.

"Why is Tori in there reading the dictionary? Doesn't she know you have a million books around here that would be more interesting?" he asked Ruthie.

Before anyone else could answer Tori yelled in from the living room that it was a magic book.

"Excuse me?" he said.

Ruthie, Kendal, and I followed Quinn into the living room.

"Guys," Tori said, looking up from the heavy book. "Every book in the whole world was squeezed into this one book, and my dad asked me to read it, so that's what I'm doing. It's magic, you know, the Irish kind."

We stared at her and then looked at each other.

"I'll be damned. I never thought about it that way. It is indeed a magic book." Quinn smiled. "That's the coolest thing I've heard in a long time."

Ruthie smiled and shook her head, "That's a new one, and I thought I had heard them all."

Kendal just stared at her with wide eyes as if she'd invented peanut butter.

"Tori, you feel like meeting in the kitchen for a second?"

Quinn asked.

"Am I in trouble? I have alibis," she replied.

"No, you're safe," Quinn said. "At least for today."

She scowled and stuck out her tongue. He winked back. We all laughed and piled around the kitchen table.

"Tabitha, as you know we had to get all the information we needed from Mrs. LaPage in order to go forward, and that's exactly what we did. Mrs. LaPage said she would love to spend some time with you, if you're willing to," Quinn said.

"Did you get any answers from her, Quinn? Good answers that can help explain stuff?" I asked.

"We did," Quinn said. "She has been an unbelievable help, and we are all very grateful to her. We are waiting for one more piece of the puzzle, and we will have all your answers. But, some are good, and are some are bad, sweetie. If you decide you want to know the answers to your questions, you need be prepared for the answers you may receive. It could get pretty rough. I want you to know that right now. Do you understand what I'm saying?"

"Yes, Quinn," I said.

I had never really thought that it was a choice to know the answers. Could I really be all right, leaving all the unanswered questions behind? It took me five seconds to make up my mind.

"When does she want to meet?" I asked.

"How about after school tomorrow?" Quinn said.

"Sure," I said. "Under one condition: We meet here, if that's okay with you, Ruthie?"

"Of course, Tabitha." Ruthie nodded. "We will all make ourselves scarce."

"No, I want everyone to be here with me, Ruthie. You guys are my family, and I want whatever she has to say to be said to all of us. Also, I want you here in case it does get real bad or if I miss anything or get confused. Do you think she would mind that, Quinn?" I asked.

"I don't think so, but I will ask to make sure and let Ruthie know in the morning," he said.

"Thanks, Quinn!" I said and gave him a huge hug.

"Shamus! You're absolutely sure this woman has her facts spot on and there's no malarkey she might fill Tabitha's head with?" Ruthie asked.

"NO, RUTHIE!" I screamed and covered my eyes. I couldn't believe that Ruthie said those words.

Ruthie tried to pry my hands away from my eyes, but I refused. I just couldn't take seeing Ruthie's ears on the floor.

"Tabitha, what in the name of Jesus is wrong with you?" she asked.

"Your ears! You said the word!" I said.

"What word, child?"

Then I realized she could hear me, so I cautiously looked up at her.

"Why are her ears still there, Tori?" I asked.

"Where were my ears supposed to go?" Ruthie asked, beyond confused.

"What in the world is going on?" Kendal asked.

Tori was laughing so hard she couldn't catch her breath. "I told Tabitha that if she ever said the word 'malarkey' out loud and she wasn't Irish..." She was laughing too hard to finish, so I finished for her.

"She said if you weren't Irish and said that word, your ears would fall right off your head. Why does Ruthie still have her ears, Tori?" I demanded.

Everyone was looking at me as if I had said that word, and then they looked at Tori, who was trying her best to get herself together, while still catching tears that were still running down her face. Now everyone was laughing but me.

"It was just a joke, Tabs! Don't be mad. Come on! You have to admit it was funny," Tori said.

I wasn't sure if it was or not, but I did know I felt silly.

Quinn stood. "Hey, Tabitha. I need to talk to you in the living room."

We sat down on the couch. Quinn sighed and looked at his hands.

"Tabitha I have to tell you something. I can't have a stranger tell you tomorrow... it just wouldn't be fair to you. Your real mom..." He looked at me with the saddest eyes. "Your real mom, who loved you so very, very, very much, died when you were only a toddler. She had something go wrong in her head and it took her to heaven very quickly."

"I don't have a mom out there looking for me or waiting for me?" I said. "You mean I'll never know what happened or if she missed me or wondered where I was?"

"Tabitha, you were never missing. She never planned on leaving you. She had something called an 'aneurism.' It's sort of like Johnny's heart attack, except it was in her brain. It happened in seconds, but sweetie she never, ever planned on leaving you. Your mom loved you with all her heart, and even though Maggie had her problems, she loved you just as much right until she went to heaven to be with your real mommy. Now they are both looking down from heaven and protecting you," he said.

"What was her name?" I asked.

"Her name was Julia, and you know what? She had an angel's kiss too. The angels wanted you to know that your mom loved you so much that she asked the angels to give you one too, so you always have something of hers with you always," he said.

That made me smile. "Julia. That's such a pretty name. Maybe when I grow up, I'll ask the angels to give my baby a kiss too, and if it's a girl, I'll name her Julia," I replied.

Quinn picked me up and hugged me tight for a long time without saying anything.

"It's okay, Quinn. I can't really miss someone I never knew. I've already cried for the only mom I ever had," I said.

"You might have a father out there," he said. "We have a pretty good lead on that answer, but have to wait until we're sure. We don't want to make any mistakes when it comes to making sure someone is related to you for sure, now would we?" he asked.

"No, Quinn, that would be a very big mess up. The last

thing I want is any more confusion."

A father! I never thought about having a father.

"Tori was so close to her dad and loved him so much. Do you think that could happen for me?" I asked.

"Sweetie, I think anything is possible." Quinn put his arm around me and we started to walk back to the kitchen when Quinn ask me to forgive Tori and not to make her put her hand on her heart because he was pretty sure that the only reason she fibbed to me was to make me laugh, which was something that Tori did best. I agreed and we both laughed.

Once we were back in the kitchen, I told everyone about my real mom and that there was still a chance that I had a father somewhere. Tori looked especially sad.

The next day school seemed to last forever. I counted the minutes until Mrs. LaPage came to our home. This could be the day I had so many of my questions answered. Maybe she would know if my mom ever named me. I was excited and wanted to run and hide at the same time.

Tori was excited. "It is crazy shit that some fancy old lady you ran into at the hospital completely by accident could have all the answers to your questions! I would be so excited to know what Maggie and your mom were like when you were a baby. I would be crapping my pants – I'm not kidding! I'm so excited! Why aren't you excited?" Tori said.

"I am! I really am!" I replied.

"You could have fooled me! You look like someone threatened to put you face first into a bucket of fire ants," she said.

"I guess I'm just being cautious. She might not have good news," I said.

The excitement drained from her face. "Tabs, you've been praying for answers good or bad for as long as I've known you. So start being happy that your prayers are being answered one way or another," and she walked away.

I wondered why she was so mad. Then I realized that Tori had a lot of questions that I'm sure she would love to have answers to. Why her mom never came back, if her dad was ever coming back, and why Tanya's parents didn't come to see her. Now that I could be having all mine all answered, I must have seemed selfish in her eyes. Suddenly, I felt very guilty.

Back at home in our room, I apologized.

"It's not that. I don't think you're selfish. I would love the chance to get some answers to a lot of crap that I know I never will, but that's just the way shit happens sometimes. That's how life works... you should already know that. You need to turn it around and say to yourself, 'I hope it's great, but if it's not, I'll deal with it,' ya know what I mean?"

Just then the doorbell rang. We went silent and watched each other, listening. First we heard Quinn's voice, and then, the voice of Mrs. LaPage.

"Well?" Tori said. "What are you waiting for?"

I grabbed Tori's hand, and we made our way downstairs.

Mrs. LaPage stood there, talking with Ruthie, and they both smiled and laughed as if they were old friends.

"Hello Mrs. LaPage," I said. "It's nice to see you again."

Tori held out her hand and introduced herself.

"Well, it's my pleasure to see you both, my dears! Thank you for agreeing to spend some time with me this evening. Everyone, please call me Olivia."

Ruthie led us all to the dining room table, which had tiny plates overflowing with fancy cookies and little cakes the size of your finger. After Ruthie served tea and coffee, we settled into our seats for whatever Olivia had to say.

"Tabitha, I never dreamed I would ever see you again, and it means more than I can say to have you sitting across from me right now."

I studied her as she spoke.

"You're very pretty," I said without thinking.

She was, too. She was old, but classy and elegant. Olivia smiled at me with teeth as white as sugar cubes and thanked me for such a lovely compliment.

"You're quite a beauty yourself, as are you, Miss Galloway."

Tori smiled and shyly said thank you. Everyone relaxed

under her warmth and she began her story with a voice that was nothing short of silk.

"One day when I was out front weeding my small front yard, a beautiful young blonde woman approached me with a bag of groceries in her arms. She asked if I needed any help and introduced herself as Maggie Sullivan."

I felt like my heart was going to explode, but I kept my posture straight like Ruthie had taught me, and when I thought I might tear up, I concentrated on the wallpaper behind Olivia's head until I was sure that I had stopped them. Olivia seemed to sense what I was doing and paused before continuing.

"That day we became fast friends as if we were meant to be in each other's lives. We spent time with each other every afternoon after that. Maggie confided in me that she'd had a drug problem in the past, but had just recently finished a bout in a rehab center because quitting drugs was something she wanted more than anything."

Olivia read the shock on my face, "Yes, child. She tried with all her might to beat those drugs. Maggie was afraid I would judge her, but I hugged her and told her I was proud of her for taking the step to quit. She was the happiest, most eager young woman I had ever met, dreaming of being a teacher one day. Afraid that her use of drugs would ruin her chances, but I told her to never give up or let anything stand in her way. I surprised her with a few college textbooks on teaching to help her confidence and begin her journey into the teaching world. She was overjoyed with them," Olivia said, smiling at the memory. "I asked her about her parents, and if they supported her choice to be a teacher, but she said they never wanted anything to do with her after they found out about the drugs, even after she went to rehab and was clean. They wouldn't even answer her calls. She was their only child. She never told me their names or where they were from, though. Maggie kept some things tightly to herself.

"I walked into her apartment one day, and it was sad... just a sad, little place. There was no real color or decent furniture.

As I stood around looking at the dismal place, I had an idea. I told her we were going for a ride, and we stopped at my storage unit where I had enough furniture to decorate a small village, left over from the much larger house I had lived in with my husband before his passing. I hired a small delivery service to bring over certain pieces to Maggie's address the following day. Then we were off to the paint store for bright, happy paint. We rolled up our sleeves and we got to work. In no time at all, that entire sad apartment was a beautiful, happy place that was a joy to live in."

My mouth was open so wide my throat was dry. "A beautiful, happy place? A joy to live in?"

"Yes, it was child. Are you doing okay? I can stop if you are upset," she said.

"I'm all right," I said, and I could feel Tori's hand grab mine and give it a little squeeze.

"Maggie's new surroundings seemed to make her brighter and happier, just as I thought they would. Then one night we had the worst storm in ages, maybe to this day, in fact. It thundered so loud you could feel it roar in your chest and make its way down to your toes. The wind bent trees and sent planters and lawn ornaments flying through the air as if they were paper planes. Then the skies opened and the rain fell. I swear Noah's Ark could have set sail that night! I was lying in bed when I heard a car pull up and wondered who in the world would be crazy enough to be out in that weather. I looked out the window and saw a shadow running up the stairs towards Maggie's apartment. Maggie's door opened, and the figure disappeared into her apartment.

"The next morning the sun was shining as if the storm had never happened. I walked up to Maggie's to make sure she was all right and I was greeted by another beautiful young woman, tiny as a mouse she was, dark brown hair, hazel eyes. When I shook her hand I noticed the most extraordinary birthmark on her hand. Do you know who that was?" Olivia asked me. "That was your momma, Julia. You have her same angel's kiss, child.

I could feel all eyes on me, but I didn't take mine off Olivia's.

"Julia was holding this teeny, tiny, little baby in her arms all wrapped up in a fluffy pink blanket. Maggie introduced Julia as her cousin. I asked what your name was, and Julia told me she hadn't named you yet. Julia and Maggie had been very close when they were growing up. Maggie was a little older and moved away first, following those drugs. Julia went away to college, met a boy, and fell in love. Julia explained that she and her boyfriend fought about what direction they wanted their lives to go in. They couldn't mend their differences, so they broke up shortly after graduating from college and moved on with their own lives. A few months later your momma realized she was going to have a baby. You were growing in her belly," she said, pointing and smiling at me.

That made me smile for the first time since she'd started talking.

"She thought about contacting your daddy but decided that after everything they had talked and fought about, she didn't want to disturb the life that your daddy had started for himself. Maggie didn't agree, but said she would support any decision that her cousin made, and told her she could stay there with her forever and a day if she wanted too. That's what they planned, and they were doing great. Maggie already had a job at call center at night, and Julia got a job as an accountant during the day. She was amazing with numbers, that Julia was," Olivia said.

"I'm really good with numbers," I said.

"Another trait you got from your momma," Olivia said making me smile once again. "Maggie would watch you during the day, then I would watch you until your momma got home, and then she would watch you all night. We had the perfect schedule. We all loved you so much, child. One special day when Maggie had a day off, we were all sitting in my living room sipping some hot chocolate when you took your first steps. We were all speechless with our eyes wide, and I thought your momma was going to burst with pride. That's the day she decided she was going to tell your daddy about you. She decided that it wasn't fair to keep any more wonderful things about you from him. She told us what an amazing man he was, and how silly and ashamed she felt to have kept you from him for as long as she already had.

"Maggie and I were almost as excited as she was. It was a Saturday night, and she planned on leaving the next morning and driving to wherever he was and introducing him to his baby girl."

Olivia's voice grew quiet and she started to look sad and distant. "We decided to celebrate, and I wanted to take us all out to dinner. But first, you needed a bath and some diapers. Maggie offered to bathe you. She loved putting you in the tub. She got such joy watching you try to eat the bubbles! That left Julia to make a run to the store for diapers... That's when it happened... "

Olivia's voice drifted off and she stared at the table. We were all silent with her. Then she shook her head, smiled, and looked back up at me.

"You know, if Maggie hadn't offered to put you in the tub, your momma would have been holding you when she, well... You both would have died that day. You would have drowned, sweetheart, and I know your momma is looking down and holding hands with Maggie, grateful that they traded places that day."

Ruthie made the sign of the cross on her chest, and Quinn rubbed his hands through his hair several times.

"Holy shit," Tori said under her breath and under Ruthie's radar.

But there was more. Olivia reached across the table and gently grabbed my hand.

"When we found out about your momma, we nearly broke into pieces. We loved her so much, and knowing you would have to grow up without her was hard enough, but she'd never told either one of us who your daddy was, so we couldn't contact him either. Julia had no family to call, and Maggie's family didn't want anything to do with Julia either. We buried your momma, just the three of us, in the beautiful cemetery up on Bernard Street overlooking Piper's Ridge. When I found out about Maggie, I took the liberty to make sure she was buried next to Julia, with family," she said.

"Thank you. That was a wonderful thing to do," I said, in awe of her generosity.

"Well, it was something I had to do," Olivia said, and squeezed my hand. "After that, Maggie started to shut down. Julia was the only real family Maggie had. Julia had made her feel special and had shown her warmth, laughter, and acceptance. She let her know she was worth something. With Julia gone, I was worried Maggie was going to slip back into her old ways. I told her your momma depended on her to keep you safe, and she had to keep it together for you. Maggie went back to work, and I watched you until she came home. Everything seemed to be getting back to normal.

"I started noticing Maggie was taking her duty to Julia to an extreme. She was protective of you, but it began to go far beyond that. She quit her job because she was afraid someone might steal you while you were asleep in your crib. She wouldn't let you out of her sight. I told Maggie that she needed to breathe and to let you breathe as well, to allow you to interact with other children. That nursery school was a wonderful option for you.

"Maggie would hear none of it. She had stocked up on teaching books and decided to teach you herself. She said that if teachers knew that you weren't hers, they would take you away from her, and she owed it to Julia not to let that happen. Maggie was convinced that she would lose you because of her past, and no matter what, I couldn't convince her otherwise.

"A few days later, we were at my house, just finishing the lunch I had made for us, and Maggie began gathering your toys to go home. I asked her when she was going to give you a name. She told me she had to wait for Julia to come back so she could name her baby herself. Until then she would call you 'my love' because until Julia showed up, that's what Maggie would give you: all her love."

I tried so hard to keep the tears from falling. "That's who she was always waiting for," I whispered.

"What was that you said, Tabitha?" Olivia asked.

"Maggie was always waiting for a special visitor," I repeated, a little louder this time.

Olivia nodded. "She would walk around the neighborhood every day, as though she were searching for Julia. At the same time, she was afraid that if Julia returned, she would have to give you up. One winter day, I finally decided that Maggie needed help, and so did you, Tabitha. You deserved to be taken care of by someone who wasn't in the midst of a nervous breakdown. I made up my mind to place the call. That way, Maggie would be taken care of, and I would take care of you until she could return healthy.

"I decided to go outside and salt my walk from the ice that had built up overnight. I didn't want you to fall when I moved you over to my house. However, I'm the one that slipped and fell. I knocked my head on the ice and passed out. I never saw Maggie again.

"I woke up in the hospital, and I asked my family to check on my neighbor. When my son returned, he said the woman who had answered the door said she had never heard of anyone named Maggie and knew nothing about any child. My family said they would stop by Maggie's a few more times, but they said when they did no one was home and their notes went unanswered. I called child protective services and explained that Maggie was a good person and loved you with all her heart, but that she just needed some help with the loss of her cousin. Well, they gave me the run around, and after several conversations they said they would take care of it, and I foolishly believed them."

Olivia frowned and shook her head. "I moved a few towns over to be with my family for several years and watched my grandchildren grow. They always reminded me of you, and I knew I had to come back here, even if only a little while, to find my own answers. I found a neighbor who knew a little about Maggie, a woman named Mrs. Finley.

"Mrs. Finley told me how Maggie painted her apartment walls that ugly sad color again, probably thinking that she didn't deserve nice things. She always thought she must have done something wrong to have made Julia leave that night. She must have started using again because she sold the furniture, the stove, refrigerator... just about everything.

"Maggie had told her that I wasn't really injured, and that she thought her parents got to you and they wanted to take away Julia's baby. They thought that Julia would be coming back soon and would be upset if you were missing. Mrs. Finley had no idea that Julia had passed away and thought Maggie was just a little eccentric. Mrs. Finley offered her telephone to Maggie so that she could call me herself, and even asked her if she could bring her to me, but Maggie thought it was a trick and would no longer talk to Mrs. Finley either. Eventually Maggie disappeared.

"I shouldn't have waited so long to come back. I should have been here to prevent all this," Olivia said, looking as if she were about to cry. "I went to the apartment the minute I got back in town, but it was empty."

Tears raced down my face. I finally understood Maggie Sullivan and the horrible pain and guilt she'd carried with her.

Olivia's eyes welled. "My poor Maggie! Dear sweet Julia!" She closed her eyes and tears dripped down her cheeks. "They deserved so much better than that...so much better, and so did you, my sweet child." She grabbed my hand.

Ruthie put her hand on Olivia's shoulder, trying her best to comfort the old woman. Quinn scooped me into his lap. Tori crawled up beside me, her hand never letting go of mine.

"Olivia, can I ask you one more thing?" I said.

"Of course! Ask me anything, child." She took out a square of fabric and dabbed her eyes.

"Do you know when my birthday is?"

"You don't know, sweetheart?" Olivia asked.

"No, my mom, well... I mean, Maggie, said we had to wait for a special guest before we could celebrate my birthday. Now I know she was waiting for my mom," I said.

"You were born on June 16, sweetheart."

My heart raced. I never thought I would ever know, and now the answer came so quickly it stunned me.

CHAPTER TWENTY-SEVEN

After Olivia left, we talked about everything she had said. I promised Ruthie with my hand over my heart that I was really all right with everything. I was better in a way. I finally understood Maggie, and every time I looked at my angel's kiss, I would think of my mom.

Quinn reached behind his chair and gave me a huge box wrapped in pretty paper.

"What's this for? It can't be my birthday already, is it?" I asked.

"No goofball! Just open it. It's from all of us," he said.

"Not me," Tori said. "I didn't know anything about it, and they didn't seem to find it important to include me, for some reason."

Tori had her arms folded in front of her and her left eyebrow was curled up. She was not happy.

I unwrapped the box and found a black shirt with a pink heart on the front, a pink skirt, black leggings, and a new pair of fancy shoes that looked just like the kind ballerinas wore.

"This is awesome!" I said. "Wow! Thanks everyone! But seriously, what is this all about?"

Quinn stood up. "We thought that you would like a new outfit when you meet your father tomorrow."

I couldn't swallow.

"Holy shit! For real?" Tori popped up like a Jack-in-the-box.

"Tori! Language, please," Ruthie warned with a smile on her face. "Yes, Tabitha will be meeting her father tomorrow."

Quinn nodded. "All the tests came back, and there is no doubt whatsoever that he is your father."

"Tabs, you have a dad!" Tori jumped up and pulled me out of my seat.

"I have a dad. I have a dad?"

I repeated it over and over while Tori and I spun around the room, stopping long enough at each chair to hug the person in it. After we settled down, Quinn explained that we would go to the courthouse tomorrow morning where my father would be waiting for me.

"Ruthie and Winnie will be there with you, and I'll stop by here as soon as I get off of work," he said.

I froze. "You're not going to be there, Quinn?"

"I will be with you to celebrate before you even notice I'm missing." He put his hand over his heart, which calmed me instantly.

Ruthie added that afterwards she was taking all of us to a fancy lunch to celebrate.

"Can I bring my dad?" I asked.

She laughed. "Yes, silly child! Of course you can bring your father!"

That night, Tori and I couldn't stop talking. Would my dad be short or tall? Skinny or fat? I wondered if he would hug me or shake my hand because we really didn't know each other.

"He's gonna pick you up and swing you around. I bet he cries," Tori said.

"What if he thinks I'm ugly and doesn't want me?" I asked.

"Are you serious, Tabs? Then you simply kick him in the nuts!"

We laughed so hard that Tori said she was going to pee the bed.

The next morning, Quinn and Kendal were there for breakfast. I was excited, happy, and so nervous that I was afraid I was going to throw up all over everyone. Ruthie brought out a huge box wrapped in fancy paper just like mine last night, but this time it was for Tori.

"What's this for?"

"Well, Tori, just open it!" Quinn said.

The box had a black skirt, green leopard print shirt, black leggings, and a pair of black boots that went over Tori's ankles, and when you rolled down the front of the boot, the same pattern on the shirt was on the inside. It was Tori in a box.

"This is cool as hell!" she said. "But why do I get a new outfit?"

"Tori, you're meeting your new parent today as well," Ruthie said.

"New parent? You mean new fosters, Ruthie. We all know by now how this turns out, so do you want the clothes back?" Tori asked.

"Tori," Ruthie said as softly as she could. "You are not being fostered. You have been adopted. You're a very lucky girl. Your new mother has a daughter about your age. You'll stay at the same school, and they don't have any problem with sleepovers wherever Tabitha's father lives. Tori, you have a mother. Isn't that amazing?"

Tori just stared at the box.

"So this is my going away gift then, huh?" Tori said.

"No, Tori, this is a happy day," Ruthie said, "You're getting a mother, and Tabitha is getting a father. There shouldn't be any sadness, only joy," she said, clapping her hands.

"Yeah. Sure, Ruthie," Tori said in a defeated voice, "You don't want kids anymore anyways. I'm gonna go change. Should I pack, or will I be able to come back before they take me away?" she asked.

"You can come back right after our lunch today, sweetheart. She's in no hurry and wants you to take your time to adjust." Ruthie said.

Tori looked like she was going to burst into tears.

"Go on, girls! Go get changed so we're not late!" Ruthie pushed the box into Tori's arms and ushered us toward the stairs.

"It's going to be a great day!" Quinn called after us.

"Yeah, for Tabitha," Tori muttered.

All of a sudden, I wasn't sure what to feel. With my best friend so upset, it felt wrong to be so happy.

On the way to the courthouse Tori and I held hands and wiped tears from our eyes. Tori was worried that my dad might be an asshole, and I was worried that Tori gave all the great families away to all the other kids.

"The good thing is we both look freaking awesome," Tori said.

As we entered the courthouse, our shoes echoed so loud that we sounded like one hundred people walking instead of four. The floor was shiny and looked like swirls of hard sand. There were pictures hanging from the walls that were taller than Quinn. Winnie met us at the front door. We found a bench and there we sat, Ruthie, Tori, Winnie, and I. Kendal had given us huge hugs at the house. She said she had a bridal party coming in to her salon, so she would be unable to join us. Tori and I were pretty bummed and just sat there quietly while Winnie yapped in her high-pitched voice. Suddenly Tori looked up at Winnie with a strange look on her face as if Winnie was a human riddle and Tori had finally figured out the answer. Tori started laughing really hard.

"Are you all right, Tori?" Ruthie asked with a concerned look on her face.

"I'm fine, Ruthie," Tori said, and she pointed to Winnie. "Johnny made you take care of us to screw with me, didn't she? She had this planned because she knew she was gonna die, huh? Your annoying, high-pitched, constant chatter? I used to drive her crazy with the same thing... and all your talk about dolls? Johnny knew how much they creeped me out. I changed everyone's name, and it drove her bananas. So she picks someone by the name Winnie who insists on calling me Vicky?"

Tori shook her head and laughed.

"Tori, you're being awfully rude. Now apologize this very minute!" Ruthie said.

But to our surprise, Winnie started laughing and said, "My goodness you are a smart one! Just like Margaret said you were!" in a voice that was no longer high pitched.

Ruthie and I watched, shocked, but Tori smiled from ear to ear.

"Tori," Winnie said, "She planned and instructed me to do exactly that, and I was to keep it up until the day you were adopted."

Tori spun and laughed. "I knew it!" Tori said. "There's no way she would let me off easy!"

Winnie turned to Ruthie and me and shook our hands. She told us it had been an honor to have met us and eased Ruthie's worries by telling us that she was indeed an experienced social worker, not fresh in the field after all.

She turned back to Tori. "Margaret said you would be a handful. You're everything she said and more. You're brilliant, and I haven't laughed this much in ages. You are truly comic relief. Thank you Tori," and she hugged her tightly. "My job and my promise here is complete. Good luck to both of you and God bless."

She stood and started walking down the hall toward the entrance.

"Wait!" Tori called after her. "Is Winnie your real name?"

"No! It's actually Victoria. My friends call me Vicky."

She winked and left us all smiling, as if Johnny had been in the room with us that very second.

"How did you know, Tori?" Ruthie asked.

"I could feel Johnny today, Ruthie, really strong like she's been standing right next to me. I remembered her saying a long time ago, 'Tori when I go to heaven someday, I'm going to have so much fun with you, and you won't be able to sass me back,' and she laughed a really evil laugh, and it was really funny. Then for some reason while I was looking at Winnie, I remembered what Johnny said, and it just hit me. I did know she would never let herself leave me without messing with me and getting the last laugh that I was sure of."

A woman came out and asked for Victory Rain Galloway. She introduced herself as Mallory Hay. Ruthie nodded at Tori.

"Go on, dear," she said.

Tori stood, and I stood with her and hugged her hard.

"Good luck. I hope they're awesome," I said.

Tori clung to me. When I pulled back, her cheeks were wet with tears.

"Come with me," she whispered.

"I... um..." I looked back at Ruthie for permission.

Tori sniffled and wiped her face. She grabbed my hand.

"I'm not going in there without my best friend," she declared.

Mallory Hay raised an eyebrow to Ruthie. "We don't usually..."

"Let her go," Ruthie said firmly.

Mallory nodded. "Okay, girls. Let's go."

Tori gripped my hand and I walked with her as we followed the stranger to meet the strangers that had adopted her. Inside the courtroom, I had to sit in the back. Tori sat up front in a black chair so big her feet couldn't reach the ground. A woman wearing a black robe sat at a high desk, so high that it seemed like she was sitting on a mountain. She introduced herself as Judge Kauffman and said she would oversee the adoption of one minor child, Victoria Rain Galloway.

"Is that you?" she asked Tori, looking over her glasses.

"Yes, I'm her," Tori said.

"Congratulations, Miss Galloway," the judge said. "Congratulations to you as well," she said to the other black chair.

The other chair was turned sideways, so neither of us could see who was sitting in it.

"Thank you very much, your honor."

But we both knew that voice. Tori spun her chair and looked at me, her eyes wide. I almost fell off the bench.

The judge handed a piece of paper to the person in the

chair, wished them both the best, and left. Tori slid out of her chair on shaky legs.

"Why...what... what are you doing here?" Tori asked.

"Well, that doesn't seem to be a great way to welcome your new mom... if you'll have me, that is. Aren't you going to hug me?"

Tori started to walk and than ran straight into Kendal's arms.

"My new mom? You're my new mom? Forever?"

Kendal and Tori held each other, and for a moment, all I could hear in the courtroom was the sound of tears and sniffles. I stayed in the back of the room, wiping tears off my face.

Tori looked up at Kendal. "But why?"

"Because I love you, Tori, and you deserve a mom and a mulligan of your own," Kendal said.

"Oh my God. Oh my God. You're really my mom? You adopted me? You're my mom no matter what? And no one can change this for any reason?" Tori asked.

"No, they can't, and yes, sweetheart, you're all mine," Kendal said.

Tori wrapped her arms around Kendal's waist and whispered, "Thank you, thank you, thank you."

Kendal kissed the top of her new daughter's head.

"Well, are you ready to introduce your new mom to Ruthie?" Kendal asked.

"She doesn't know?" Tori said, a smile spreading across her face.

Kendal winked and shook her head.

"Then what are we waiting for?" Tori said, and grabbed Kendal by the hand.

As they came down the aisle, I stood and hugged both of them. I was so happy for Tori, and a little jealous that she already knew her new mom so well, and it was Kendall, who was amazing! We walked out into the hallway where Ruthie was still sitting on the bench. She had a paper cup of coffee steaming in her hands.

"Kendal! I'm so glad you could be here!" Ruthie said when she saw her. Her forehead crinkled. "But I thought you had a busy day."

That's when she noticed. "Tori..." Her voice had a hint of alarm. "Where is your new mother? Please don't tell me you found a way to get rid of her, too!"

"I can introduce to you, if you'd like," Tori said, playing it cool as a cucumber. "Ruthie, I would like you to meet my new mom, Miss Kendal Jameson."

Ruthie looked as if she had been struck by lightning, her coffee dropping from her hands and splattering to the floor. She stood up slowly and walked up to Kendal, grabbing both her hands.

"Kendal, is this true? You've adopted our Tori?" she asked.

"Yes, Ruthie. I hope you approve."

Ruthie put her hands to Kendal's face and began to cry, reaching her arm out to Tori. She stood, holding them both.

"God bless you, you amazing woman," she said to Kendal. "You are a gift from heaven and for our Tori."

Ruthie eased back onto the bench. "God bless this day," she said.

Kendal knelt in front of Ruthie, and Ruthie looked into Kendal's eyes. They hugged until they were both crying.

"Tori, get your mother a Kleenex," Ruthie said, and clapped and laughed at those words.

Tori spun in circles repeating, "I'm getting my mom some Kleenex! I'm getting my mom some Kleenex!"

And then Mallory was back for me.

"Do you want me to come with you, too?" Tori asked.

She was already nestled against Kendal's side. I couldn't bear to ask her to leave her mom so soon, so I shook my head. Tori popped up and gave me a hug and then I marched down the hall with Mallory. She left me in a small room to wait.

I waited. Maybe he wasn't going to come for me after all.

Finally the door opened and my shoulders relaxed. It was Quinn. He'd found me.

"I didn't want to meet a stranger without you," I said.

"I know. I'm sorry, sweetie," he replied.

"Quinn, I'm really scared. I'm not sure I can do this. I don't know if I can meet a stranger and think of him as my dad. I feel like I'm going to throw up and I'm hungry at the same time. Can we just go home, Quinn? I don't want to do this anymore!" I said in a rush.

"Tabitha, you need a father. I hear he's a real good guy, and he can't wait to meet you. You don't want to leave him here alone without meeting his daughter, do you?" Quinn asked.

"No, I guess not. I'm just scared and nervous and all that stuff, Quinn," I said.

"Sweetie, your father wanted me to explain a few things to you so that you had more time to celebrate your reunion then to talk about details. He wanted you to know that he loved your mother very much and that he wrote her every day for months with no response. He never knew he had a daughter. When he found out, he was happier than he had ever been, so he didn't want you to think that he didn't care about you. He can't wait to start the rest of his life with his daughter."

Just then the door opened and woman walked in.

"Are you Tabitha M. Sullivan?" she asked.

I nodded.

"Right this way," she said.

I gave Quinn a huge hug, not wanting to let go. I followed the woman to another room.

"Your father will be in momentarily," she said and left.

To keep from throwing up, I tried to think about Tori and how she was doing, but it didn't help. Why wasn't my father already in here? Did he chicken out? It was going to be so embarrassing to tell everyone that he didn't show up.

Then the door opened.

I slowly looked up.

But it was just Quinn. My heart sunk.

"He's not coming, is he? Did he change his mind?" I asked, not wanting to hear the answer. My chest was tight and tears started to blur my vision.

Quinn scooped me up and said, "No, baby girl, I'm here."

I wiped my eyes and looked at Quinn.

"What did you say?"

He had tears in his eyes when he said, "I didn't change my mind. I'm here. I'm your dad, Tabitha. I knew the minute I saw your angel's kiss, but I just had to make sure that I was your daddy. I'm the father your mom was coming to tell about you," he said.

"Quinn," I said as I reached up with both hands and grabbed each side of his face. "You're telling me that you're my father? My real father? You looked for me when I was lost, you found me in the tent, and you were my protector and friend. You're Ruthie's son, and you're my father? My daddy?"

I couldn't believe what I was hearing.

"I'm still your protector, I'm still your friend, but most importantly, my greatest role is now being your daddy," he said.

"Quinn, I can't believe this! I must be dreaming, and I'm going to wake up any minute," I said.

"Hey, maybe now we can think about calling me something other than Quinn, huh?" he said with a smile.

"I can call you daddy!" I said with excitement

"Yes, baby girl, you can."

I put my face in my daddy's neck and cried, letting the happiness and joy pour out.

"Shall we let the others know?" he asked.

Yes, daddy, I want to go tell them. Hey daddy, guess what?" I said.

"What, my beautiful daughter?" he asked. His tears traced trails down his cheeks.

"I love you," I said.

"I love you more," he replied, hugging me tight.

"Will you ever get sick of me calling you daddy?" I asked.

"Not if I live to be a thousand years old."

As we came around the corner we could see everyone huddled around the bench.

"Tabs, where is your dad? What happened?" Tori asked with a worried face. "Was he an asshole... sorry, Ruthie... jerk?

Quinn, what happened? Did you have to arrest him?"

All eyes were on us and I said, "No, he's here."

Ruthie smiled.

"Everyone, I would like to introduce to you to my real father."

Everyone was looking around as if I had lost my mind.

"Mr. Shamus Matthew McCormack Quinn."

Tori's face was priceless, and Kendal and Ruthie smiled from ear to ear.

Tori stared and said, "Are you serious? Shamus is your real father? Holy shit!"

Ruthie didn't even scold her.

"Yep, he was the father that Julia never had a chance to tell about me. He knew the day he saw my angel's kiss," I said.

"Mom?" Quinn said to Ruthie. "Are you all right?"

She cupped my face in her hands. "There were so many times I wanted to grab you in my arms and tell you, but like Shamus said, we couldn't until we were absolutely positive. I told your Johnny. I wanted her to know, and I'm so glad I did before... Well, I didn't want her to be left out, and she was overjoyed." Ruthie folded me in a hug and reached over to kiss her son.

"We have one more surprise today," Quinn said. He nodded to Kendal.

Kendal handed a piece of paper to Tori. "Tori, would you mind reading this out loud?"

"This is what the judge lady gave you?" Tori asked.

Kendal nodded and put her arm around Tori's shoulder, pointing to what she wanted her to read. Ruthie and I huddled around Tori so we could see it as she read:

This document finalizes the sole adoption of one
Victoria Rain Galloway
to
Mr. Shamus Matthew McCormick Quinn *and* **Mrs. Kendal Faith Quinn**

Tori looked up slowly, as confused as the rest of us. Ruthie stood there with her mouth dropped open and eyes as wide as I had ever seen them. Kendal walked over to me and Quinn walked over to Tori.

Kendal bent down and said, "Tabitha M. Quinn, would you accept me as your new mom?"

I stared at her, trying to figure out what was happening. Quinn bent and asked Tori if he could be a dad to her. She stared at him, confused as I was.

"How can you be my mom, Kendal? You're Tori's mom," I said.

"I married your dad, Tabitha," she replied.

"How can you be my dad, Shamus, when you're Tabitha's dad?" Tori asked.

"I married your mom, Tori."

The fog lifted off all our brains and we finally got what was happening.

"You guys got married?" I asked.

"We were going to wait, but Kendal is the love of my life, and we couldn't imagine starting a new family together without starting out as Mr. and Mrs. Shamus Quinn," our dad said. He looked over to Ruthie. "Mom, don't worry! We're planning a church wedding as soon as were all settled."

"We're all a family! A real family!" Tori jumped into our dad's arms and hugged him until he started to turn red.

I looked at Kendal and said, "I've been jealous of your future kid because they were going to be so lucky. I never thought it would be me," and put my arms around her and cried, knowing that at that moment the world was absolutely perfect and our dreams without a doubt could come true.

Then, Tori and I froze and screamed at the same time, "We're sisters!"

We started spinning and grabbed Quinn and Kendal to join us. We were a family, a real family that no one could take apart. Quinn and Kendal took the rings they had been hiding in their pockets and placed them back on each other's fingers.

Ruthie reached for our parents' hands and with tears rolling down her face, looked to the sky and said, "Thank God for blessing them and making them a family on this glorious day."

Tori and I wrapped our arms around Ruthie and I said, "We were always going to have you in our lives, Grandma."

"That's right, Grandma! I knew it the whole time," Tori said, and we hugged her tighter.

Quinn and Kendal wrapped their arms around the three of us. We sniffled and cried as one family. I smiled and closed my eyes.

"Hey Tabitha!"

I opened my eyes to see Tori smiling at me on the other side of the group hug.

"You know what this is?" she said. "This is the ultimate mulligan!"

THE END

ABOUT THE AUTHOR

J.S. Edwards is married with two grown daughters and three grandchildren. She and her husband, along with her personal assistant, a 3.5 lb. Morkie named Zoey, share their time between New York and Florida. *Mulligan* is her debut novel.